Ma pointed at the tapestry. "Those predictions are going to keep coming true."

I said, "And everyone in Vengekeep is going to look to us to keep them safe. What are we going to do?"

Da pulled himself up to his full height and stuck out his chin defiantly. "What we do is what Grimjinxes have done for generations when faced with insurmountable odds. A time-honored family tradition for con artists."

We all nodded.

"Run."

THE VENGEKEEP PROPHECIES

BRIAN FARREY

illustrated by
BRETT HELQUIST

HARPER
An Imprint of HarperCollins*Publishers*

The Vengekeep Prophecies
 For information address HarperCollins Children's Books, a division of HarperCollins Publishers, 195 Broadway, New York, NY 10007.
www.harpercollinschildrens.com

Library of Congress Cataloging-in-Publication Data

Farrey, Brian.

The Vengekeep prophecies / Brian Farrey. — 1st ed.

p. cm.

Summary: "A magical tapestry prophesies doom for the town of Vengekeep, and to everyone's surprise twelve-year-old Jaxter Grimjinx and his family of con artists appear to be the town's saviors"— Provided by publisher.

ISBN 978-0-06-204929-2

[1. Swindlers and swindling—Fiction. 2. Prophecies—Fiction. 3. Magic—Fiction. 4. Monsters—Fiction. 5. Fantasy.] I. Title.

PZ7.F24614Ven 2012 2012025282

[Fic]—dc23 CIP

AC

Typography by Megan Stitt

14 15 16 17 CG/OPM 10 9 8 7 6 5 4

First paperback edition, 2013

For my Ma and Da,
who encouraged me to pursue what I loved

· CONTENTS ·

PART ONE:
THE CON

· CONTENTS ·

PART TWO:
⋆ THE QUEST ⋆

· CONTENTS ·

PART THREE:
THE PROPHECY

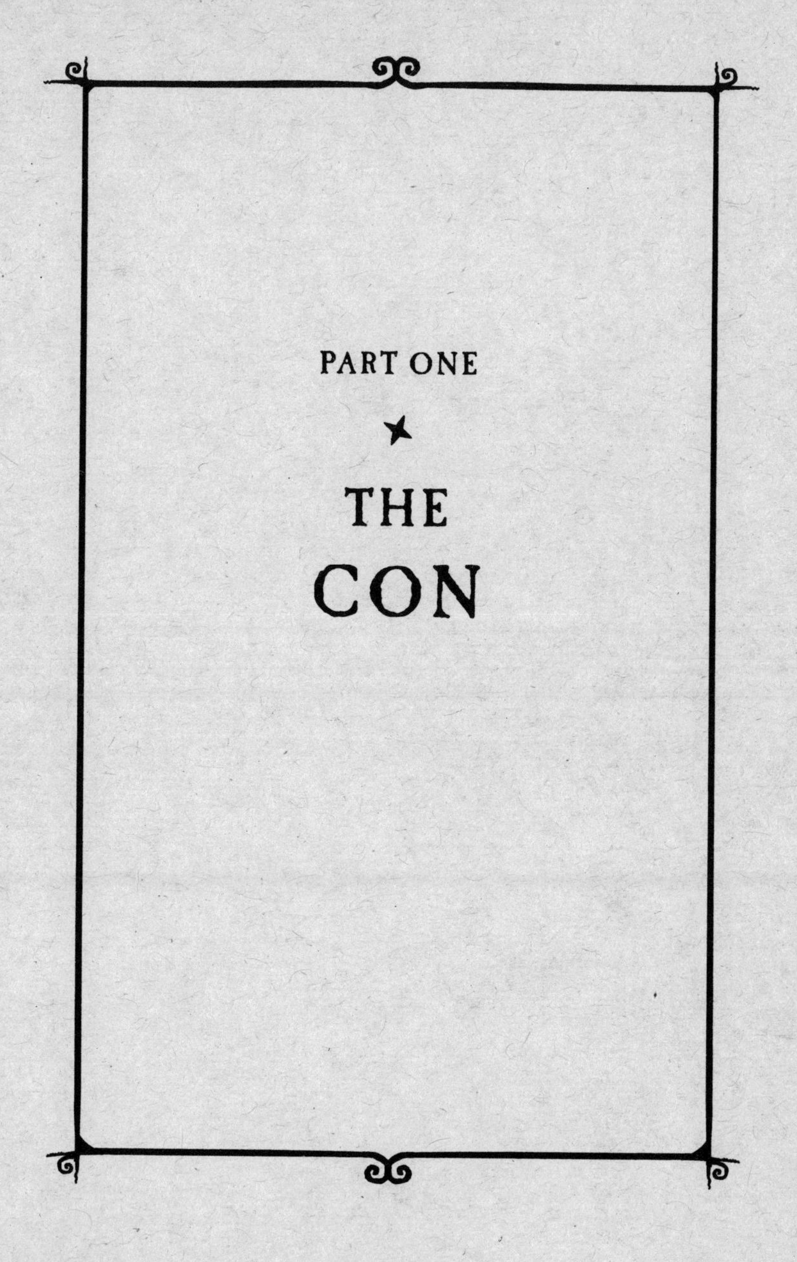

PART ONE

THE CON

1

The Festival and the Fire

"The best truth is one you make yourself."

—The Lymmaris Creed

Even weeks later, I heard rumors that *I* had ruined the Festival of the Twins. Which was complete rubbish. I was nowhere near the Festival grounds at the time.

I was too busy escaping from a house fire. That I'd caused. Accidentally.

All in all, the weeklong Festival that opened every new year had gotten off to a fantastic start. Four days and nights filled to bursting with merriment, all paling in comparison to the fifth, most jubilant evening of the whole Festival: the night of the Unveiling.

The entire population of Vengekeep had turned out in Hogar Square to celebrate. Garlands and colored lanterns with magical green-blue flames decorated the tall, gray mordenstone walls surrounding the town-state. Everywhere you looked, people were lining up to compete in singemeat-pie-eating contests or to drink their weight in ashwine before the Unveiling ceremony at sundown.

Everyone but me and my family. We had a job to do.

Da and I were the last to arrive at the festivities. If the entire Grimjinx clan had shown up at once, it would have been far too conspicuous. Might have brought the entire Festival to an instant halt, with women clutching their purses and men tightening their money belts. So instead, we spaced out our arrivals to avoid panic. Then we bled into the crowd to *make sure* everyone knew we were there.

The Lymmaris Creed, the code by which every thief in the Five Provinces lived, stated, "Let the eyes of another be your ironclad alibi, as your own tongue may only offer rust." If people could say they'd seen us at the Festival, it would be harder for the stateguard to prove we were involved in anything illegal that might have happened at the same time. Because, after all, how could we be in two places at once?

After thievery, being in two places at once was a Grimjinx specialty.

"Look sharp, Son," Da whispered with a smile as we strolled into the square. I followed his gaze and saw Aronas, captain of the stateguard, marching toward us with a frown I think he reserved just for our family. We saw it at least once a week.

"Grimjinx," Aronas said, sneering from Da to me. "I don't want any trouble tonight."

Da gave an obedient nod. "You'll get no trouble from us here at the Festival, Captain. Right, Jaxter?"

I snapped to attention. "Absolutely, Da. No trouble at the Festival."

Outside the Festival? Well, that was another story.

We tried to step around him, but the captain moved to block us. He seemed angry. I think it was because, in all the years we'd lived in Vengekeep, he'd never once been able to have us convicted of any crimes. And it wasn't for lack of trying.

"I don't trust you," Aronas said.

Da smiled meekly and shrugged. *"Enk vessara, enk talmin."*

Aronas snarled. "What's that supposed to mean?"

"Nothing," Da said innocently. "Bit of par-Goblin wisdom."

The par-Goblins' thievery skills were legendary. Thieves everywhere had adopted their dying language as their own. It gave thieves a special way to communicate without being caught in anything they shouldn't be doing.

Enk vessara, enk talmin, roughly translated, means: "You can't convict what you can't confirm." It had unofficially become our family motto. A reminder that the only thing harder than pulling off a good bit of thievery was ensuring no one could prove a thing.

Aronas peered down at my waist. "What are those?"

Twelve forest green pouches, each cinched tight with a drawstring, dangled from my belt. I leaned in and peered at Aronas over the top of my silver-framed glasses and hit him with my sauciest stare. "Are you a mite jealous, Captain? I can see why. They're very handy for carrying this and that around. My mother made these for me. I bet if you asked her nicely, she'd make you a set too."

Aronas ground his teeth and gave us each another stony look before turning back and storming through the crowd. Da tossed him a smile and a nod as he left. Then Da leaned to me and said quietly, "You know what to do."

Da made his way to the hammer toss competition while I moved closer to the stage in the center of the square. As the sun set in the distance, the stateguard were busy lighting dozens of torches. From atop the stage, Castellan Jorn—the town-state's chief magistrate—barked orders. A rotund man with fleshy pancakes for cheeks, Jorn had been Castellan of Vengekeep since before I was born, a position that answered only to the High Laird of the Five Provinces himself. He loved his power almost as much as he loved his wealth. With a bit of luck, I'd be relieving him of a bit of the latter tonight.

Next to Jorn stood a tall, thin man in burgundy and black robes, designating him a mage. Tradition stated that Vengekeep's town-state mage presided over the Unveiling with the Castellan. Sadly, Lotha, our mage, had passed away recently. His apprentice, a young man named Talian, was currently off in Tarana Province taking the Trials that would allow him to serve as the new town-state mage. In the meantime, the Palatinate—the order of mages who worked for the High Laird to govern and police the use of magic—had sent a member of their Lordcourt to assist Jorn. I gave the mage a wave. He offered a puzzled grimace in return.

As Jorn yelled at his workers, he froze when he saw me grinning up from the edge of the stage. I curtsied. He scowled and turned away, taking his frustration out on an unlucky stateguard standing nearby. I felt bad for the soldier Jorn was yelling at. But it wasn't my fault that Jorn, like Aronas, couldn't prove the Grimjinx clan responsible for any of the burglaries, swindles, or thefts that had plagued Vengekeep for years. Oh, he *knew* we'd committed every last one but . . .

Enk vessara, enk talmin.

My job was done: Jorn knew we were here. I looked around until I spotted Ma at her assigned station near the drinking well. She was playing with the ebony braid that spilled down over the front of her shoulder, smiling a patient smile while listening to the widow Bellatin ramble on about who knew what. Ma glanced at me only briefly. I touched my finger to my temple and she casually did the same.

Turning, I spotted Nanni near the food area. My silver-haired grandmother hunched over a boiling kettle, where she sold bread bowls filled with singemeat stew to the Festival-goers. When she looked my way, we both touched our temples and went about our business.

I felt a tug at my sleeve. Looking down, I found the bright eyes and gap-toothed smile of my ten-year-old sister, Aubrin. She winked, tossing back the thick red hair she'd inherited from Da. I winked too. She pulled her apron pocket open, revealing a treasure trove of fob watches, purses, and bracelets. Crowds of shoulder-to-shoulder people like this were the very lifeblood of pickpockets. Just two years younger than me, Aubrin was proving to be the best pickpocket in our family.

"Bangers, Jinxface!" I said approvingly. She'd been trained well: only target people with copper or silver braiding on their clothes. They were the ones who could afford to lose a watch or coin purse.

Aubrin giggled at my nickname for her, touched her

temple, then darted into the crowd to see what else she could score. I looked up in time to see Da and Ma making their way to the entrance of Prender Alley, which separated the bakery from the funeral parlor. Ducking between people, I joined them.

Ma licked her palm and ran it over my head to smooth out the wild cowlicks. "Are you excited, Jaxter?" she asked, beaming with pride.

I nodded, fearing that if I said anything, I'd throw up and betray how terrified I actually was. I'd assisted Da on dozens of burglaries, but tonight . . . tonight, I was going solo. Oh, Da would be there if I got in a pinch, but the hard work was all on me.

"Citizens of Vengekeep!" Jorn's growly voice rang out over the din of the Festival. The Castellan spoke into a mammoth cone atop a stand on the stage. "The Unveiling ceremony will begin in one half hour." Cheers went up from all around.

"That's our cue," Da said, kissing Ma playfully on the cheek. "Do tell us if anything interesting happens."

Ma grinned a grin that told me she knew more than she

was letting on. "Oh, you'll be the *first* to know."

Ma melted back into the crowd as Da and I ducked into the alley. We wove through the deserted side streets of Vengekeep, sticking to the shadows to avoid the occasional stateguard on patrol. As the noise of the Festival became a distant buzz, we emerged into the plaza outside the townstate hall. Across the way stood the Castellan's house, a beautiful two-story mansion where no expense had been spared to let anyone who looked at it know that an important man lived there.

We nipped around to the back, which faced the fortified wall on Vengekeep's east side. Night had fully set in, cloaking us in darkness. Taking a deep breath, I knelt at the back door and squinted at the lock, barely visible in the light from both moons above.

"I really want to light a candle," I muttered, fumbling with my belt.

Da shook his head. "Too risky. You know that."

Yes, I knew that. Didn't stop me from wanting to light a candle.

I pulled a small leather pouch from the underside of my

belt and opened it to reveal a shiny set of lockpicks, a gift from Ma and Da a few months ago on my twelfth birthday. I carefully selected three pins, but when I went to insert them into the lock, Da stopped me.

"Ah," he said with a smile, "what are we forgetting? What do we know about Jorn?"

Where most parents taught their children the alphabet at a young age, some of my earliest memories were of Ma and Da teaching me to observe people. From weeks of watching Jorn in preparation for tonight, I could deduce how far he'd go to protect himself from being robbed. It was one thieving skill I excelled at.

I closed my eyes and summoned all I knew about him. Well, Jorn was a blowhard. He was self-important. He was moderately wealthy. And he was deeply suspicious. Which made him an excellent candidate to have . . .

I touched the copper trim of the lock. It vibrated slightly, just enough to tickle my fingertip.

"Magically sealed," I announced.

"Well, then, we picked the right man for this job, didn't we?" Da nudged me with his elbow.

Smiling, I pulled a tattered leather book, the size of my palm, from where I kept it tucked in my belt. The weathered letters on the cover said *The Kolohendriseenax Formulary.* I thumbed to the first of many dog-eared pages and squinted to read the text in the scant moonlight.

"Right," I said. Following the *Formulary*'s instructions, I opened two of the pouches on my belt. From the first, I pulled two pinches of amberberry pollen, which I cupped into the palm of my left hand. From the other pouch, I took a small vial filled with oskaflower honey, which I added drop by drop to the pollen. I mixed the ingredients together with my finger until they became a thick, blue paste, which I quickly spread on the outside of the lock. Using my picks, I pressed some paste into the lock and waited. When I touched it again, the lock was still. I smiled.

"Bangers!" Da whispered.

With the magical seal neutralized, I slipped my pins into the lock and went to work on the tumblers inside. My hands shook the entire time. Someone who didn't know me would have assumed I was nervous. But the truth behind my trembling was something far more ominous. A thief's worst nightmare.

The Grimjinx clan was one of the oldest thieving families in the Five Provinces, if not *the* oldest. Two of the revered Seven master thieves who wrote the Lymmaris Creed were my ancestors. My great-great grandfather plundered the onyx sepulchre of Mithos. My father and mother were, respectively, the greatest living burglar and forger. Generations of cunning, guile, and agility should have distilled into me, making me the perfect thief.

Instead, I was a complete klutz.

This, a simple Class 1 Armbruster house lock, would have taken Da less than five seconds to trip. Me, I was still fumbling with it ten minutes later. But Da never once got impatient. He stood aside to make sure I had as much moonlight as possible.

"Zoc!" I muttered as the picks slipped from my fingers for the fourth time.

Da tsked. "Don't let your ma hear you use that kind of language. Concentrate. Try again."

I retrieved my picks and maneuvered them inside the barrel of the lock. When the door finally clicked to let me know I'd succeeded, Da clapped me on the back.

"Excellent, Son," he said. "We can, er, work on your timing later. After you."

We entered and stood for several moments to get our bearings. The silhouettes of the furniture seemed almost indistinguishable from the rest of the darkness. We made our way down a narrow hall to the staircase at the center of the house.

"We need to be especially careful," Da said, eyes darting everywhere. "Jorn can afford enchanted protections, more powerful than the spell on the back door. Be on the lookout for yellstops or any other traps."

I nodded. My right hand hovered close to the *Formulary,* ready for trouble.

"Okay, what next?" Da asked. This was my burglary. I'd been planning it for weeks, watching Jorn and trying to deduce where he might hide his valuables.

"For this," I said slowly, "we start in his bedroom. He'd want to keep it close by at all times."

"My thoughts exactly," Da said. "Lead the way."

We trod carefully up the stairs until we located Jorn's bedroom at the end of another long hall. Inside, we found a huge four-poster bed with thick, silk curtains on all sides, an antique writing desk, and a bureau that nearly reached the ceiling.

"Next?" Da asked, smiling to show his complete faith in me.

My mind raced. There was probably a safe behind the painting on the far wall. But that was most likely for cash. No, what we were looking for would be closer to Jorn. . . .

I knelt at the bedside and thrust my arm between the mattresses, feeling around until my fingers found something cool and hard. I pulled out a long, thin box made of dark wood. Da's eyes lit up.

"That must be it," he said as we moved to the moonlight near the window.

I went to work on the box's lock and, again, it took several minutes when it should have taken mere seconds. But finally, the lid popped open, revealing a bronze, jewel-encrusted flute within. Jorn had been bragging for months to anyone who'd listen about how he'd purchased the flute that had once belonged to the great musician-sculptor Anara Hamwith. Worth thousands of silvernibs, he boasted. And as my second cousin twice removed, Vellinda Grimjinx, always said, "Boasters reap a harvest of loss."

In other words, loudmouths deserve to have their pretty flutes stolen.

Da retrieved a cloth hidden under his shirt. From inside, he pulled another flute and held the two up to the scant moonlight. Absolutely identical in every way. Ma's skills as a forger were second to none. This one was especially impressive. She'd made it based solely on sketches in old books. But she'd gotten every detail perfect. It would fool Jorn long enough for us to sell the real flute far from town.

Outside, we heard a distant cry and applause. "That'll be the Unveiling ceremony starting," Da noted with a sniff. "Which means we have a bit of time." He tucked the real flute under his shirt while I placed the box—now containing the fake—between the mattresses.

"Might as well see what else we can get away with while we're here," he said with a wink. "Find yourself a souvenir of your first solo heist. Oh, your ma and Nanni will be so proud. You check around here, I'll nip across to the library for a look-see."

It was family tradition to take a souvenir from extraspecial heists. Something small and memorable. As it was my first burglary, I wanted something great.

I poked through Jorn's bureau, under his bed, and in his closet, but nothing really grabbed my attention. I was about to give up when I spotted the small, silver stamp on his bedside table, the one he used to seal his letters.

Now *that* was a souvenir. Not the stamp itself but with a few drops of wax, I could make an impression of Jorn's crest from the stamp. Like an autographed memento of my first mark.

I grabbed the candle next to the stamp. While Da insisted on never using light during a burglary, I figured it wouldn't hurt this once, seeing as the entire town was several blocks away at the Festival and I needed the wax.

I pulled a small tinderbox from inside my boot and went to strike the flint. But as I brushed my hands together, the flint and stone flew from my clumsy fingers, shooting a single spark that leaped onto the curtains of Jorn's bed. The very old, antique, and highly flammable curtains.

I fell back as, in a flash, the entire canopy erupted in

flame. I froze, watching the fire rise higher and higher until it had ignited the ceiling. Waves of fire roiled down the walls, inching toward me.

"Da!" I called out. And realized my mistake too late.

The bedroom door shimmered with golden light for a moment before slamming shut. I reached out, twisting the knob, but the magical yellstop seal—designed to trigger with any loud noise—held tight. No doubt, every door in the house was now sealed.

"Jaxter!" I heard Da's muffled cry from beyond the door. "I'm trapped in the library."

By now, black smoke had forced me to my knees as the heat of the approaching wall of fire blistered the paint on the door. Gasping for air, I dug through my pouches for the amberberry pollen and oskaflower honey. Tears filled my eyes as I raced to mix the ingredients that would neutralize the magical lock. *If* it would neutralize something as powerful as a yellstop charm. I'd never tried before.

Once I had a tiny ball of paste, I rubbed it on the lock and prayed. With a yank, I was able to pull the door open and stumble out, just as the flaming ceiling collapsed in the bedroom. Smoke quickly filled the hall as the fire started to burn through the walls. Crawling to the library door, where I could hear Da pounding, I smeared what was left of the paste from the palm of my hand on the door lock and released Da. His eyes widened as he spotted the fire.

"Come on!" he cried, slinging my arm over his shoulder and helping me down the stairs. In the distance, I heard bells. Someone had alerted the fire brigade.

By the time we got downstairs, the fire had spread to the ground floor. We yanked at the front door, but the yellstop charm held it tight.

"Jaxter . . ." Da began, but I shook my head.

"I used the last of the honey." Without my blue paste, there was no way to counter the yellstop charm.

Looking around, Da spotted a brass coat rack. We picked it up and started battering at the front door. Once . . . twice . . . On the third heave, the door flew off its hinges and we fell out into the street, crawling as fast as we could across the cobblestones, away from the flaming house.

Only to find the entire population of Vengekeep in the street just outside, with Castellan Jorn at the head of the pack, shaking so furiously he couldn't speak. Instead, he pointed a trembling finger at me and Da. Captain Aronas and two of the stateguard stepped forward and pulled us to our feet.

"What do you have to say for yourself?" Aronas asked, binding my hands behind my back.

"Um . . ." I said sheepishly, "*Enk vessara, enk talmin?*"

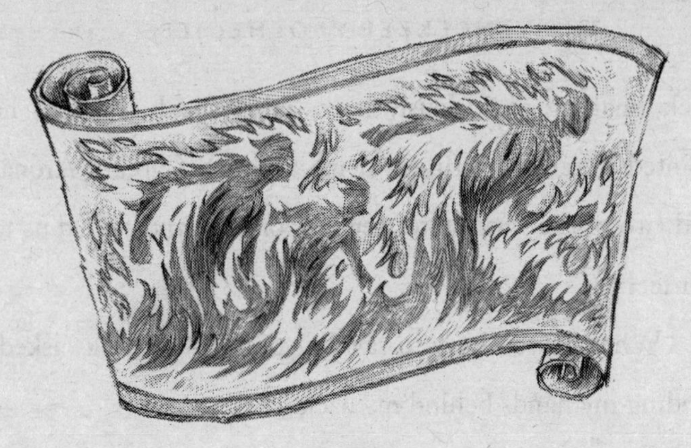

2

The Tapestry

"A stranger is just a mark you haven't bilked yet."

—Ancient par-Goblin proverb

Da and I spent the night in the Grimjinx summer home. Known to most as the Vengekeep gaol.

Everyone in the family had spent at least a little time there for various accusations. Usually only for as long as it took for the stateguard to realize they didn't have enough evidence to make charges stick. But, covered in ash and soot and seen leaving the Castellan's burning house by hundreds of witnesses . . . well, it seemed like the Grimjinx knack for avoiding prosecution was over.

And it was all my fault.

"I'm sorry, Da," I finally said. We'd been sitting for hours, Da quietly contemplating the ceiling and me feeling horrible the entire time.

Da waved it away. "It's my fault, Jaxter. I picked the target. I thought if we robbed anyone less than the Castellan, you'd think I didn't have total confidence in your abilities."

"I bet you didn't burn down the first house you burgled."

"True, but I never would have been able to beat a magical lock. We all have our talents, Jaxter. And that's yours. Don't you forget it."

It was my unique contribution to our heists. Da could sneak into a house, steal a painting, and be out in five minutes flat. Ma's forgery of that painting could fool people for years. Aubrin's sleight of hand skills were the best in the family. Me, my clumsiness prevented me from perfecting the skills that made the Grimjinx clan infamous. Kept me from being a true thief.

All that changed a year ago when Nanni moved in with us and gave me *The Kolohendriseenax Formulary*. It detailed twelve magic-resistant herbs and plants deemed "the essentials of nature" and how they could be used to negate low-level magic. From there, I read more and more books, each adding to my knowledge of how to beat magic through natural means. Da called it "invaluable backup support" when we did our cons. It came in handy from time to time.

A loud clang and squeak, and the steel door leading into the gaol swung open. Captain Aronas, looking happier than I'd ever seen, sauntered into the room.

"Burglary!" he said, brandishing the flute they'd found on Da when searching us. "Willful destruction of property! Arson! The best list of charges I've ever seen filed against the Grimjinxes. This time, you can't weasel your way out."

Da didn't approve. "Willful destruction *and* arson? Seems a bit redundant, don't you think? And not at all original."

Aronas leaned against the bars that separated us and shook his head. "Make all the jokes you want, Grimjinx. As we speak, Castellan Jorn is in his office, drawing up the papers of exile. When he's done, you and your little band of thieves will have an hour to pack up and remove yourselves from Vengekeep. If any Grimjinx dares enter this valley again after today, you'll spend the rest of your life in

Umbramore Tower."

"Exiled?" I asked, excitement coloring my voice. "You hear that, Da? We finally get to take that tour of the Five Provinces you always promised the family."

We linked arms and did a celebratory dance as Aronas fumed, but inside, my stomach fell. I'd gotten the family exiled. With the Grimjinx reputation, the chances of finding another town-state that would let us set up roost were slim at best.

Our celebration stopped as Aronas's lieutenant, a tall, wingless Aviard with a gray feather beard and talons for fingers, entered with a grave look in his yellow eyes. Da tugged lightly on his left ear—a family signal to pay attention—and stared knowingly as the Aviard whispered to the Captain.

"What?" Aronas spat in disbelief.

"Something the matter?" Da asked in a voice so innocent no one was buying it.

Aronas opened our cell with the key at his belt and stepped aside. "By order of the town-state council, you're summoned to the Viewing Room."

"A summons?" Da said, as he stepped out of the cell.

"Well, now, that's a far cry from an order of exile, wouldn't you say, Captain?"

We followed as Aronas, grumbling all the way, escorted us out of the gaol and into the streets of Vengekeep. I half expected to be pelted with rotten vegetables, or at least receive murderous glares. But as we walked through town, the looks we got were . . . odd. Not angry like last night, when my accidental fire brought the Festival to an unwelcome end. Now they looked at us pensively, like they were trying to figure us out. It was creepy.

Nearly five centuries old, the town-state hall was the oldest building in Vengekeep. Most days, it was packed with stern-looking officials, who did boring things like make laws and, even worse, enforce them. As we turned the corner to find the hall looming ahead, I felt a lump in my throat to see workers clearing away the pile of ash and scorched debris nearby, all that remained of the Castellan's house.

Once inside the hall, Aronas led us down a long, pillared corridor to the Viewing Room, one of the most sacred locations in the town-state. It was fairly small, with walls of speckled green marble and a thick glass skylight that provided the room's only natural light.

To one side, I saw a group of three women and a man, dressed in the blue-and-green robes that marked them as town-state council scholars. They spoke in hushed tones to one another and stopped dead when we entered. Da and I were ushered to the center of the room, but before we could ask what was happening, we heard a clamor from down the hall.

"Watch your hands!" The unmistakable shrill of my grandmother's voice echoed across the room. A moment later, the rest of our family—Ma, Nanni, and Aubrin—was escorted in by two stateguards.

Nanni was slapping at one guard's hands. "I'm seventy years old! Don't you know I'm fragile?" To demonstrate, she swung her arm up and struck the guard's helmet.

Ma swept into the room and, like Da, didn't seem nearly as perplexed as I was at this new development. She went straight to the scholars.

"Hello," she sang brightly. "Allia Grimjinx. I believe you know my husband, Ona."

Da waved. When the scholars didn't respond, Ma, Nanni, and Aubrin joined me and Da. Ma kissed us both.

"Summons?" Da asked quietly.

"Imagine my shock," Ma said, sounding anything but shocked.

"I'll try."

Aubrin and I shared a squint. We knew our parents. What were they up to?

Castellan Jorn entered next, hunched over, cane in hand, in the same splendid azure and black robes of a provincial magistrate that he'd worn last night. It looked like he'd slept in them. Which, of course, he had, seeing as I'd torched his house and everything he owned. They were probably all the clothes he had in the world right now. My ears burning, I gazed at the floor.

Jorn appeared exhausted. In gaol, I'd heard the guards talking. Because of the Festival, there were no vacancies at the inns. Jorn had been forced to spend the night in the guest room of the widow Bellatin, who most likely kept the Castellan up all night with stories about her long-dead husband. Our night in gaol was looking better and better.

If Jorn could have killed us with a look, the one on his face would have done the job twenty times over. He peeled his gaze away from us long enough to consult with the scholars in a raspy whisper. He was clearly angry, and from their body language, the scholars were doing their best to convince him of something.

Finally, Jorn snorted, turned, and hobbled over to us, his face a mask of contempt.

"I was nearly rid of you," he snarled. "I had the order of exile drafted and ready to sign. So close . . ."

He pivoted on one foot to face the room's centerpiece—indeed, the very reason for the room's existence. A large tapestry, as tall as Ma and three times as wide, woven with threads of varying brown shades, hung from a shiny copper frame, suspended from the ceiling by thick cables. Jorn regarded the tapestry for a moment, then spoke over his shoulder to Da and me.

"It's a shame you missed the Unveiling last night. I'm sure you'll agree the Twins had a very interesting message for us this year."

He motioned with his cane to the tapestry. I looked to

where he was pointing, but Ma and Da, doing their best to appear deeply interested in what the Castellan had to say, never took their eyes off the portly man.

Everyone in Vengekeep knew the story of the Twins. Powerful seers who lived almost five hundred years ago, the Twins had visions of Vengekeep's future that they wove into a series of tapestries. They wove a tapestry a day on enchanted looms, each tapestry representing a forthcoming year. And because the Palatinate believed it was dangerous to know the future too far in advance, the tapestries were sealed in glass tubes, marked with the corresponding year, and locked away in the catacombs beneath the town-state hall.

Every new year, the town-state threw a massive festival in honor of the Twins. At the end of the weeklong celebration, the Castellan and our town-state mage would unlock that year's tapestry, unveil it to the city, and then hang it in the Viewing Room for all to see. Scholars would spend hours interpreting it and then prescribe a course of action to the Castellan.

When I was eight, the tapestry warned of a drought,

allowing the town-state council to create water reservoirs. In the nearly five hundred years that Vengekeep had been relying on the tapestries for guidance, they'd often predicted as much good as they did bad and most of the bad they predicted was avoided. And none of it was ever terribly bad.

Until now.

I studied this year's tapestry. It was a familiar mix of pictograms and sparsely worded passages. And while I was no scholar, even I could tell that Vengekeep's future looked bleak. Crudely rendered dead animals suggested some sort of livestock plague. Stick figure people were covered in flames. Squiggles that looked suspiciously like monstrous vessapedes burst from the fountain near Hogar Square. Most disturbing, a flock of winged skeletal creatures dominated most of the tapestry. They looked like nothing I'd ever seen: massive, clawed, and fanged. In the pictogram, they seemed to be tearing the town clock tower to shreds. Other disasters—heavy rains, earthquakes—were mentioned in brief sentences around the ornately decorated borders. In the center of it all sat four additional stick figures, standing at all points of a four-pointed star.

“What do you think of that?” Jorn demanded, tapping the tapestry with his cane.

“I think we were safer back in gaol,” I said, wide-eyed. I thought I heard Nanni snicker.

Ma stared intently at the weaving, taking it all in. “What could it mean, Castellan?”

Jorn approached the tapestry and pointed to the words directly underneath the four stick people near the star that read, “The star-marked family alone shall be the salvation of Vengekeep.”

As the words sank in, a chill tickled my toes. I stared so hard at the passage that I'd missed Jorn sidling up beside me. He yanked at my vest and shirt, exposing my right shoulder. There, small and red, was a four-point star—the Grimjinx family birthmark I shared with Da, Nanni, and Aubrin. Everyone in town knew about it.

One of the scholars—a woman with salt-and-pepper hair—stepped forward. “The four of us are in agreement. The tapestry portends a disastrous year for our town-state. A year where the Twins indicate *your* presence is vital to Vengekeep's survival.”

"I wanted to be rid of you once and for all," Jorn said, his face so near I could smell scorchcake on his breath, "but I'm forced to allow you to stay."

"Stay?" Da asked, as though it was the most ludicrous suggestion ever. "I was just warming to the idea of exile. A nice traveling holiday. A chance to see the waterfalls at Azagan Cliffs . . ."

"And I hear the mesas at Splitscar Gorge are breathtaking," Ma added.

"I've always wanted to raft down the River Karre," Nanni joined in.

"Staying would be dangerous," Da said, stroking his chin. "After all, I believe there are some pending charges."

Jorn's face had grown so bloated and red with anger, I really thought he might explode. The scholars cleared their throats, which pulled him from his rage-induced stupor.

"All charges are summarily dismissed," Jorn croaked.

"Yes, that sounds very nice," Ma said, "but I think we could do with a bit of clemency as well."

"And immunity," Nanni insisted, leveling a glare at Jorn. "We don't want to incriminate ourselves."

Jorn's jaw dropped, ready to give us an earful, when the scholars again cleared their throats. Jorn's outburst died on his lips and all he said was, "Done."

Da clapped his hands together. "Excellent. We'll look forward to the paperwork spelling all that out delivered to our house sometime this week. Now I wonder, Castellan, as we Grimjinxes are responsible for saving Vengekeep, might we have just a moment alone to study the tapestry ourselves? So we can . . . contemplate how that saving might happen."

Jorn sniffed, and a grudging smile parted his lips. "Please. Take all the time you need."

He turned with the scholars, clip-clopped across the floor, and left us alone. For a moment. The door then opened and a stateguard brandishing a polearm entered to watch over us. We stood with our backs to him, studying the tapestry thoughtfully.

"By the Seven! Would you look at that?" Ma said, shaking her head in something akin to awe. "Who would have thought? The Grimjinxes, saviors of Vengekeep."

I gave a curt nod. "Absolutely bangers." Then I lowered

my voice. "Some of your best work, Ma."

Ma and Da continued looking straight ahead, pretending to observe the tapestry's intricate detail, but out of the corner of my eye I could see Ma's jaw drop in mock surprise. She, too, spoke quietly. "Why, Jaxter Grimjinx, whatever do you mean?"

I guffawed. "You should leave the outright lying to Da because you're not very good at it. I'd know your forgeries anywhere. I can see where anyone else would be fooled. But *you* wove that tapestry."

We all huddled together tightly. Da pointed, as if to show me something I hadn't noticed. I played along for the guard's benefit, leaning in to observe, as we continued to speak in hushed tones.

"So what was your first clue?" he asked.

"Neither of you was the least bit worried when we were arrested for what should have been an easy prosecution. Like you knew they wouldn't be able to touch you."

I glanced at them, and it's a good thing our backs were to the guard because they each wore a self-satisfied smirk. Ma pointed to the star in the center. "I made this right before

Nanni came to live with us. That's why there are only four people. An insurance policy your Da and I cooked up just over a year ago."

"Insurance policy?" I asked.

Da nodded. "This is the year, Jaxter. The Big Job."

The Big Job. Ever since I was little, Ma and Da had been planning the most ambitious heist of their joint careers. They talked about it all the time, but I didn't think they'd ever get to it in my lifetime. But now they were going ahead with it: a raid on Ullin Lek's vaults.

Ullin Lek was the wealthiest man in Vengekeep, and possibly the entire Province. To my parents, he represented the highest prize imaginable. The vaults beneath his house were legendary, said to be loaded with barrels filled with silvernibs, precious gems of immeasurable value, and rare works of art that rivaled the High Laird's own collection. They'd spent years following Lek, learning everything they could that would help them with the break-in. Now it seemed they were ready.

"There's no telling what we'll face once we get into the vaults," Ma said.

Da nodded. "Lek can afford much more powerful magical protections than simple yellstop charms. Our chance of getting caught is a mite higher than usual."

"So we needed a contingency plan, something that would keep the Castellan from sending us to prison . . . or worse . . . if we fail."

I got the idea. "So you wove a fake tapestry, predicting doom and gloom for Vengekeep, and swapped it out for the real one. And if you get caught, they can't touch the 'saviors of Vengekeep.'" I could hardly contain a smile. "Brilliant!"

Ma had folded her arms across her chest to keep from laughing. "Can't take all the credit. It was your da who dreamed up the Fire Men. Flying creatures were mine, though. Wanted to keep it plenty scary." She took a step back, giving the tapestry an admiring look. "You know, it didn't net us a single copperbit, but I'd have to say that this was our finest con ever."

Later, on our way out, we all joined arms and bowed respectfully to the Castellan and the scholars.

"Please know," Ma said, as seriously as she could muster, "that Vengekeep can rely on the Grimjinxes to stare down any disasters that may befall the city in the coming year."

The five of us made it only ten steps from the front door of the hall before we couldn't hold it in anymore. We laughed all the way home.

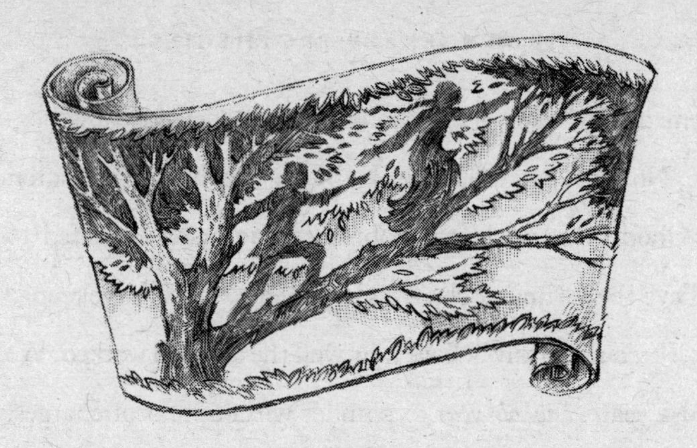

3

Apprentice Day

"There is no punishment harsh enough for the crime of stupidity."

—Baloras Grimjinx, architect of the First Aviard Nestvault Pillage

To say that the people of Vengekeep immediately embraced the idea that my family was destined to save them from unimaginable catastrophes would be like saying the Castellan didn't almost swallow his tongue when he signed the order granting us immunity from prosecution.

In other words, it would be a complete lie.

Everyone in the family was used to drawing suspicious stares wherever we went in town. Now, those stares seemed even more incredulous . . . but decidedly less hostile. No one—from Tresdin Nahr, the town-state treasurer, to Chodrin Benrick, the cobbler's snooty son—wanted to believe the Grimjinx clan was destined to save Vengekeep.

We could hardly believe how well the con had worked. We had a year. *A whole year* to plunder without fear of charges, search warrants, or grumpy magistrates. If we planned it right, the whole family could retire by the next Festival.

Retiring at age twelve. Let's see the cobbler's son try that.

As was tradition, Apprentice Day came to Vengekeep exactly two weeks after the Unveiling. Merchants and business owners set up tables around the edge of Cloudburn Park in the north of town. Anyone who'd turned twelve since the last Apprentice Day was required to go from table to table and apply for an apprenticeship at any number of mind-numbing jobs. Blacksmith. Carpenter. Seamstress. Sure, they were fine for the people doing the jobs, but when you come from a long line of thieves—where excitement is mandatory—it could lead to death by boredom.

Luckily, I'd been apprenticed to my parents since I was old enough to hold a lockpick. Officially, of course, if anyone asked, I was an apprentice at our family's phydollotry shop, a small business Ma and Da kept in the west of town. The shop was a cover. That is, it was how we gave the *appearance* of making money in a more . . . traditional way. At times, it seemed silly to maintain because everyone *knew* what we really did. But all good thieves have a strong cover and as long as my parents could claim I was their apprentice, the town-state council wouldn't bother us.

While everyone else my age stood in line, I lay out under the mokka tree at the park's center, smiling discreetly at the would-be apprentices not so far away. Aubrin was digging small holes nearby, her nimble pickpocket's fingers snatching at stickworms that she and Da could use for bait when they went fishing. Da had given me a Class 1 Armbruster lock to practice picking. He was nothing if not optimistic. So I sat, back to the tree's trunk, with the lock in my lap and my picks laid out neatly on the ground next to me.

Twok! I looked around as an acorn bounced off the top of my head. When I went back to picking the lock, another acorn followed. *Twok!* Aubrin giggled. I peered up through the thick branches and leaves of the mokka tree and caught a glimpse of bare feet dangling from near the very top.

"I don't think the mokka tree needs any apprentices this year," I called up. "You might be better off checking with Captain Aronas. He could use someone with a good throwing arm. His guards couldn't hit the perimeter wall around Vengekeep."

The leaves shook, and suddenly a girl swung into view. She hung upside down, her legs wrapped around a thick branch. Her long hair dangled like amber-colored icicles from the top of her head. She shot me a wicked grin.

"Aren't you twelve?" she asked. "I'm pretty sure you're required to go over to those tables and beg someone for a job."

"I've got a note from my ma," I said, holding up an imaginary piece of paper. "It says, 'Please excuse Jaxter from all stupidity and wastes of time.'"

The girl snorted. "Well, you're not excused from *watching* stupidity, are you? You get a much better view up here. Come on!" She patted the branch next to her.

I'm pretty sure I heard my sister guffaw at the suggestion that I climb the tree. "Pipe down, Jinxface," I said. But

I couldn't blame her. I looked up the mokka tree's trunk. We had a long, unpleasant history, this tree and I. A history that involved me vowing to get over my clumsiness by climbing to the top and the tree having other ideas. Ideas that saw me falling to the ground, still as clumsy as ever.

"Thanks," I said with a friendly wave. "I can see fine from here."

The girl folded her arms. "If I have to come down there, I'm only going to drag you up here by your collar."

I squinted up at her. Something told me she'd have no problem following through on her threat. So I handed my lockpicks to Aubrin, dug my fingers into the bark, and hoisted myself up to the first branch. No triumph. That was the farthest I'd ever gotten. I looked down at Aubrin, who gave me the thumbs-up. Swallowing, I found new footing and started clawing my way to the next higher branch, just beyond my grasp.

I teetered forward, then back, and it ended as these things do: me on my back in the dirt at the base of the tree. Aubrin sighed, having witnessed my past failures with the evil tree. Once I had air in my lungs again, I called up, "Is the offer to drag me up by my collar still on the table?"

The girl laughed. "Stay there," she said, releasing her legs and catching the next branch in a free fall. She continued this the rest of the way down until she landed at my side and offered a hand. She hauled me to my feet with a single, strong yank and I made a note never to make her angry.

I brushed dust off my rear while stealing glances at her. She was about my age, wearing large breeches and a billowing shirt that fell off her shoulders. Her smirk was more confident than cocky.

"So why are you so important that you don't have to stand in line?" she asked, nodding in the direction of the merchants and their tables.

I shrugged. "Don't need to. I'm apprenticed to my parents at the family phydollotry shop."

"Phydollotry?" she asked. "What's that?"

Truth be told, there was no such thing as "phydollotry." It was a silly name Da made up when he and Ma moved to Vengekeep years ago. If a customer walked in and asked what phydollotry was, Da would stroke his chin and say in a mysterious voice, "It's easier to experience than explain."

Then he'd immediately begin taking a series of measurements: the width of the customer's head, the distance from their armpit to their hip, the exact height of each tooth. It could take hours. If that wasn't enough to scare the person away, Da would open a large cabinet filled with the rustiest, sharpest tools you'd ever seen and carefully select the nastiest looking one, all the while eyeing the customer and grinning.

That's usually when they ran for the door.

"Doesn't matter," I said. "How are your lessons with the widow Bellatin going?"

She blinked. "What?"

Aubrin nudged me and clicked her tongue. Okay, I admit I was showing off. But the girl had hit me with an acorn. Twice. I owed her. "It's a good thing your uncle isn't short of cash," I continued. "The widow charges a heap. I wouldn't worry, though. Your uncle will wise up once you've been living with him longer."

The girl's eyes widened in a mix of anger and surprise. "You don't know me. How could you possibly know that I'm taking lessons with the widow Bellatin? Or that I'm living with my uncle! Have you been spying on me?"

She looked ready to hit me, so I grinned. "No. I . . . notice things. I'm good at it."

Well, I'm *great* at it.

She crossed her arms. "Like?"

I sighed. "Your clothes are too big. Whoever bought them guessed at your size. Wouldn't be your parents. More like a close relative; an uncle or an aunt. But an aunt wouldn't buy you something that looks like you're about to go into the Kaladark crystal mines, so it's an uncle. The material is sturdy, which tells me he knows children need strong clothes, so he's got a child. A son. Or he never would have dressed you in that. It's unlikely he would buy you clothes if you were just visiting, so that says you've just moved here."

Before she could say another word, I brushed the hair from her shoulder. "You've got a faint tan line along your neck. You've been out in the sun, wearing a high-collared dress. When you stand, you favor your right leg because your left foot is killing you. Now, what is it that requires wearing a high-collared dress under the hot sun that would make your left foot hurt? Dancing lessons with the widow Bellatin, who believes that all ladies should be able to dance properly under the most extreme conditions. She's famous for forcing her students to dance the Aviard two-step outdoors in the coldest winter and hottest summer. And since most of the Aviard two-step is performed by hopping on the left foot . . ."

She continued to glare at me for a moment or two. Then her face broke into a smile and finally she laughed. "That . . . was . . . amazing! Go on, then, what else do you know about me?"

Well, as long as she asked . . . "You're not in line to be an apprentice. All girls in Vengekeep are required to take an apprenticeship . . . unless they're training to be a lady. Between the high-collared dress and the widow's pricey lessons, it's clear your uncle makes a lot of money. That narrows his identity down to a handful of people in Vengekeep. The wealthy businessmen in town wouldn't want a daughter—or niece—to be a lady. They'd want her to continue the family business."

"So maybe," she interrupted, "like you, I already have a family apprenticeship."

"Except," I replied, "you've already admitted to studying

with the widow Bellatin, which no apprentice does. Since you're not from a business family, you must be related to someone who works for the government of Vengekeep. Which can only mean you're the niece of Masteron Strom, the Keeper of the Catacombs. He's the only widowed councilman with a son."

The girl shook her head in disbelief and extended her hand.

"Callie Strom," she introduced herself.

"Jaxter Grimjinx," I said, shaking her hand. My sister stood and cleared her throat. "And this is Aubrin."

Callie looked at me and winked. "I'm sure the young lady can speak for herself."

Aubrin and I traded glances. "Aubrin . . . doesn't say much," I said. The truth was that Aubrin hadn't said a single word in all her ten years. No one knew why. Ma and Da pretended not to mind, saying that she'd have plenty to say when the time was right. But I knew they secretly worried.

Callie bit her lip. "Oh. Sorry." Suddenly, her eyes widened. "Wait . . . Grimjinx? As in the Grimjinxes who are destined to save us all from catastrophe?"

I shrugged. "Well, I don't want to brag, but . . ."

Then her eyes narrowed and she said more softly, "And the Grimjinxes whose thievery leaves a trail of victims in their wake?"

"No, no," I corrected. "Not 'victims.' We call them 'marks.' More dignified. For someone new to town, you know a lot about us."

Callie scoffed. "Oh, please. I'm from Ankhart village, all the way in Jarron Province. The Grimjinx name is known everywhere. In fact, since you became saviors, this is the only place I've ever heard anyone use the name respectfully."

I beamed. "Thank you! You'll be a fine lady someday."

She groaned and looked away. "Don't even joke about that. Uncle wants me to be a lady so I can marry the High Laird's son."

"But the High Laird doesn't have a son," I countered. "He's not even married."

"He will one day," she said, "and Uncle insists I be ready."

"Well, what would you be if you had a choice?"

Callie turned, her face lit with excitement. "I would be something that didn't require wearing dresses or learning to play the oxina or dancing the Aviard two-step. I'd be something that made my heart race, something that kept life interesting, something like" —she stopped and looked down at the Armbruster lock I'd left on the ground—"a thief."

I actually heard this a lot. People imagined the life of a thief was carefree and easy. They loved the idea of danger and intrigue. They didn't understand it was hard work. Especially when, you know, being clumsy comes far more naturally.

She put her arm around my shoulder and pulled me in close.

"I'll make you a deal," Callie said thoughtfully. "You teach me how to pick that lock"—she jerked her thumb at the Armbruster on the ground—"and I'll teach you how to climb that tree."

I looked up its long, intimidating trunk. "Without falling?"

"Without falling."

Given that my own thieving skills weren't exactly top of the range, it didn't seem like a fair trade. But as my great-uncle Archonias Grimjinx says, "A fair trade is fair only for the fair." And besides, my family's reputation generally kept me from having many friends. This was the first time it was working for me. How could I say no?

"Deal." We shook hands and I laughed. "What will the widow think?"

Callie hunched over and spoke in an uncanny impersonation of the widow Bellatin. "A lady must possess a wide array of skills."

I chortled. "I don't think she had theft in mind."

"Well, then, we just won't tell her."

A shadow fell between us.

"Oya."

I recognized the gruff voice. Turning, I found a familiar boy leaning against the mokka tree. He was my age but nearly a head taller. His sleeveless tunic revealed well-muscled arms. His dark hair, the same shade as mokka tree bark, was so short he almost looked bald. He stared right at me, his face hard.

Aubrin scowled, but I smiled warmly. "Oya, Maloch. Long time, no see."

I offered my hand, and his face went from hard to

downright hateful.

"Callie," I said, "this is Maloch Oxter. He's a sort of . . . well, *friend* isn't the right word anymore, is it, Mal?"

"You're Keeper Strom's niece, right?" Maloch ignored me and spoke to Callie. "You wanna be careful hanging around *him*." He shot a look at me. "His whole family are just stinking cutpurses."

I flinched involuntarily. *Cutpurse* was like a curse word in our house, even worse than *zoc*. To us, cutpurses were petty thieves who preyed on anyone, including the weak and the poor. Call the Grimjinxes what you wanted, but we did none of that.

I let the slur go, swallowing to keep my smile in place. Maloch had grown a bit since we'd last seen each other. I had no doubt he could pound me into paste.

"You know, Maloch, I'd love to catch up, but—"

I tried to move around him, but he stood in my path.

"I just became Captain Aronas's apprentice. I'll be joining the stateguard. You and your family better watch yourselves."

"In case you hadn't heard," Callie said, hands on her hips, "Jaxter's family is destined to save Vengekeep. I don't think *your* name was on that tapestry."

Maloch sneered at me. "I bet you think that means you and your family can get away with whatever you want. Well, not a chance. I'll personally be watching you." Then he leaned in until I could smell sour tarok sauce on his breath. "Well, I'll be watching your family. Watching you would be a mistake. They're the thieves. Not you."

I felt my face flush as I swallowed.

"Tell me," Maloch said, eyeing me head to toe, "just what the zoc do they need you for?" He glanced down at the pouches hanging from my belt and gave a single laugh. "Oh, that's right. You play with your little plants and roots and saps. Trying to make up for the fact that you're basically an embarrassment to them. Too clumsy to be a thief . . . so what good are you?"

I actually lunged at him, chin quivering. He took a step back, fists raised for a scrape. But I didn't get very far. Aubrin snagged my belt and stopped me.

Unfazed, Maloch chuckled. "Have a good year, savior." Then he turned and lumbered away.

I stared down at my boots awkwardly. "Thanks," I said

to Aubrin, then turned to Callie. "Good thing she held me back. I would hate to have gotten blood on his fist with my face."

Callie shook her head. "He's got to be the rudest garfluk I've ever met."

"Rude?" I asked. "He'd be so disappointed. That was Maloch at his most charming."

We talked in the park until sundown. Aubrin and I walked Callie to her house and she made me promise to start her thievery lessons soon. I was less eager to get a promise from her for my tree-climbing lesson.

When Aubrin and I got home, I went straight to my room and shut the door. I took a deep breath to clear my head. The smell of the old books on the shelves that lined my bedroom walls usually comforted me. Not tonight, though. Navigating around the collection of clay pots on the floor, where I grew the twelve essential plants for my pouches, I sank down onto my bed in the corner.

I couldn't stop thinking about Maloch. We used to be

best friends. Then, two years ago, his father caught me trying to teach Maloch to pick a lock and forbade us to see each other. After that, whenever I ran into him, Maloch treated me worse and worse. Ma said not to let it get me down, that a true friend would have stuck by me no matter what.

Truth is: it still got me down.

Much of what he'd said had already been on my mind. Aubrin's pickpocketing skills branded her a chip off the Grimjinx block. I hadn't even mastered picking an Armbruster 1 lock. Every year it became clearer: I really wasn't a very good thief.

It was well after midnight before I stopped brooding, slipped into my nightclothes, and crawled into bed. I heard a knock at the door and looked up as my grandmother stepped into my room, lips clenched around a juicy blackdrupe.

"Oya," she said softly, wiping the excess juice from the corners of her mouth.

"Oya," I said, trying not to sound as pathetic as I felt.

She pulled up a chair to sit next to me.

"You've been hiding away a long time up here," she whispered. "Usually means something's on your mind. Care to tell your old nanni about it?"

I didn't know what to say so I just blurted, "Nanni, is the family ashamed of me?"

Nanni leaned forward into the moonlight, and I saw her pale eyebrows furrow. "Now, why would you think that?"

I looked away. "Something Maloch said today."

"Maloch? Are you two friends again?"

I grunted. "Friends? Hardly."

Nanni clicked her tongue. "Happens from time to time. The friends you used to rely on change without you knowing it. Same thing happened to your da. He had a friend growing up: Edilman Jaxter. You were named for him, you know."

I nodded. Ma and Da didn't talk about Edilman Jaxter much, only to remind me every so often that I was named for him.

Nanni shook her head, a warm grin spreading across her face. "They were inseparable. Your da, a skilled burglar; Edilman, a master of disguise. Oh, the cons they pulled in their day. When your ma joined up, the three of them were positively unstoppable."

"So what happened?"

Nanni's face fell. "People grow apart, Jaxter. It happened to your father and Edilman. It happened to you and Maloch. And maybe it's for the best."

She took my hand and gently pulled me from my bed. "I think I know what's *really* on your mind. Come here."

She led me out to the hall and to her bedroom, where a lantern lit the room with fuzzy orange light. She sat me down on her bed, then pulled a thick, leather-bound book from under the mattress. I knew it well, from its frayed, brown edges to the tarnished bronze letters across the front that read GRIMJINX. Our family album.

She opened the cover. A haphazard series of lines and finely scrawled names lay across the first two pages: the Grimjinx family tree. There was my great-great-great grandmother Ioni Grimjinx, who masterminded the ransacking of the par-Dwarves' underwater cities. And my too-many-greats-to-mention uncle Vaster Grimjinx, who bilked the town-state of Annora into paying him a fee to rid the town of ghosts . . . ghosts he created with some simple parlor tricks. The tree went all the way back to the first Grimjinx, Corenus, who created our clan's unfortunate-sounding surname under the theory that a family who sounded cursed would be above suspicion in any theft.

That theory lasted an entire generation. After that, all the Five Provinces knew our family was far from unlucky when it came to thievery.

As the oldest living Grimjinx, Nanni was in charge of protecting this log of our heritage. The remainder of the book's pages were filled with centuries of accounts of my ancestors' greatest cons and heists, all written in a special code known only to our family, so as not to incriminate anyone. Since I was old enough to hold the massive book on my own, I'd spent days poring over those pages, dreaming of the day my own exploits would be cataloged for future Grimjinx thieves to see.

Nowadays, though, it seemed unlikely.

"It can be quite a legacy to live up to," Nanni said, her arm around my shoulders. "Every Grimjinx had a unique talent that they worked hard to perfect. But no matter how great the heist, the one thing that eluded everyone was the ability to run a scam where magic defenses were involved. You're the first to beat that. Thanks to all those books you read, we can beat almost any magical defense. You've got smarts, Jaxter. The things you learn in books will outshine all of us someday, you mark my words."

I stared at the family tree and nodded. She walked me back to my room and I had to admit I felt better. Zoc Maloch.

I crawled back into my bed as Nanni laid a finger aside her nose. "In fact, we'll be needing you up bright and early in the morning. Plans are afoot. . . ."

I brightened. "The Lek vaults?"

She pursed her lips. "Not quite. That needs a mite more planning. Let's just say that we'll be in a better position to raid the vaults after tomorrow. You in?"

She touched her temple and I did the same. "Always."

Nanni returned to her room as I nestled into bed. I was moments away from falling asleep when I suddenly realized: she hadn't really answered my question, whether or not the family was ashamed of me. She'd danced around it. I stayed awake the rest of the night, wondering exactly what that meant.

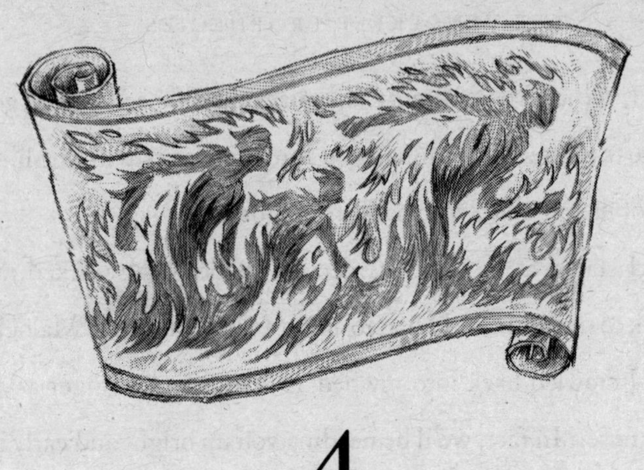

4

The Incident at Brassbell Promenade

"Think twice about the con, not the mark."

—Ancient par-Goblin proverb

Every weekend, Brassbell Promenade came to life with the town-state's biggest outdoor market. Crowds of people moved from cart to booth to get the freshest produce and best bargains. The Promenade got its name from the ancient wooden water tower located in its center. Years ago, on the hottest summer days, the Castellan would order the stateguard to climb the tower and pull the release chain. Water would come pouring out from the side of the massive wooden drum at the top of the tower and down a metal slide, showering the Promenade. The stateguard then rang the brass bell on the drum's underbelly to alert the nearby children, who would run screaming across the cobblestones to play in the downpour. Nowadays, the tower was too unstable to be climbed.

Every weekend, Nanni and Aubrin came to the Promenade to sell breadbowls filled with singemeat stew to the marketgoers. Despite our family's reputation, they never failed to bring in customers. Some people bought stew to encourage us to earn an honest living. Others most likely decided that if a Grimjinx was going to take their money, they might as well get Nanni's famous singemeat stew in exchange. At the end of each day, Nanni and Aubrin brought home a few bronzemerks . . . and tons of information on Lek, whose butcher shop was conveniently located across the Promenade from Nanni's stand.

As usual, Nanni and Aubrin arrived at the crack of dawn with the other merchants to set up shop. By midday, the market bustled with activity. It was around this time that I arrived, backpack over my shoulder, making my way through the thick crowd until I reached the base of the water tower. I leaned against one of the tower's three legs. It gave a shudder and a creak. I grimaced, hoping that my own clumsiness didn't bring the whole thing down on top of me in the middle of the operation.

From my vantage point, I could glance left and see Nanni and Aubrin, doling out their stew with smiles and humble thanks. Not far from them, I spotted Maloch and one of the stateguards, who'd no doubt been assigned to keep a discreet eye on Nanni and make sure she wasn't bilking anyone. They were doing a lousy job of being discreet.

Shaking my head, I turned to the right, where I had a perfect view of Lek's butcher shop. Lek stood behind his counter, chopping away at a side of meat with an enormous knife. His workers scrambled, filling orders from the customers who choked the entry way.

Moments later, I saw Da appear on the corner of Lek's shop. He looked over a featherless gekbeak, as if trying to decide if it had enough meat for dinner. He sent only a scant glance my way, touching his temple to signal me that he was in place.

Over at the singemeat stew table, sales had slowed.

Nanni stoked the fire beneath her kettle as Aubrin added a tub full of vegetables to the bubbling stew. I waited until Nanni looked directly at me and I touched my temple. Nanni touched hers in return and I saw her say something to Aubrin. My sister casually reached over and threw the small satchel of winkroot I'd given her onto the fire.

After a moment, I heard a low pop and suddenly great columns of thick, black smoke began to billow out from under the kettle. Nanni stepped back, her eyes widening.

"Whoo!" she screamed, like a demented gekbeak. "Whoo!" She flailed her arms and ran in place, her panicked cries drawing curious stares. Soon, everyone was noticing. The smoke had grown so heavy that it consumed Nanni's tiny stand.

Heads turned. The din of conversation became alarmed shouts. One man came at Nanni from behind, either to calm her or get her away from the encroaching smoke. But Nanni stood her ground and became more frenzied.

The merchants near Nanni came over with buckets of water, waving at the smoke to determine just where the fire was. It grew harder and harder to see Nanni or anyone on that side of the Promenade. As more people gathered, I caught a flash of red hair and knew Aubrin was weaving her way through the crowds, helping herself to whatever wasn't firmly attached.

The customers at the butcher shop had cleared out, turning their attention to the scene Nanni was making. Da feigned interest but he was really watching Lek, who'd stopped chopping meat to gawk at the fuss with an intense stare. As Lek stepped away from his shop to join the onlookers, Da made his move, disappearing behind Lek's counter.

Over the years, everyone in the family had taken turns spying on Lek. We could fill books about his every habit, every quirk. We knew he ate sanguibeast steak the first of every month. We knew his favorite color was yellow. And we knew he kept the key to his vault on a ring behind the meat counter.

Honestly, if someone that wealthy was going to make it so easy for us, he was practically begging to be robbed.

The smoke continued to envelop the crowd, and I knew that Nanni must have thrown the second satchel of winkroot onto the fire. The people closest to Nanni's stand were gagging and backing away, their curiosity turning to fear that this was something more than a boiled-over kettle. Da was running out of time. I looked back at the butcher shop and saw his fist shoot up in the air, thumb raised and wiggling. The signal for "I need you now."

Head low, I moved against the gathering throngs toward the butcher shop. I ducked behind the counter, where I found Da on his knees. He'd snagged a big, roughly hewn key that could only be used on a vault door. In his other hand, he held a large block of wax. His face had gone red as he tried pressing the key into the wax.

"It won't budge," he grunted. "I can't make the impression."

"Lemme see," I said, taking the key and holding it up to the light. No protective sigils were engraved on it. Good. My blue paste couldn't beat those. It was probably a low-level, no-clone spell. And that was beatable.

I consulted the *Formulary* and found an easy solution. Palming the key, I reached into my back hip pouch and grabbed a handful of ground roxpepper seeds. I sprinkled the dust liberally on both sides of the key and handed it back to Da.

"Try it now," I said.

This time, when he pressed the key into the wax, it sank in deep, making a perfect impression. He wiped the key clean, slid it back on the ring, and handed the wax block to me. I had to get the block to Ma, stationed just around the corner from the Promenade, where she was waiting to take the wax imprint so she could forge a perfect copy of the key later.

Separately, Da and I each crawled out from behind the counter and melted back into the crowd. The smoke had all but vanished now. Nanni was thanking everyone loudly for their help. I hid the wax block in my backpack and moved toward the water tower, aiming for the opposite corner of the Promenade.

A low rumble sounded. Everyone stopped. Vengekeep was no stranger to tremors. It had been centuries since the town had felt a full-on earthquake, but still, everyone stopped when they heard that familiar rumble and felt the pavement below their feet shift.

Just as business was about to resume, a louder roar sounded; and this time, the cobblestoned paving buckled, sending dozens of people sprawling to the ground. More than a mere tremor, the ground continued to shake. I staggered to the base of the water tower and grabbed its leg to steady myself. People around me murmured that it would pass.

It didn't. The shaking grew worse. Some of the booths began to collapse. Nanni's stand fell apart, sending breadbowls rolling everywhere. Small children cried out and I suddenly thought of Aubrin. Looking around, I picked her out near the blade merchant's stand. Her eyes were on Nanni, who wiggled her thumb. Aubrin obeyed, running as fast as she could to Nanni. Together, Nanni and Aubrin fled the Promenade.

A thunderous crack filled the air. I turned in the direction of the noise and found a lightning-shaped fissure splitting the cobblestones near Lek's shop. People gasped and staggered to get away from the opening maw. Da, just about to leave the Promenade himself, stopped to watch the crack grow.

As quickly as it had come, the rumbling and shaking stopped. Everyone in the Promenade paused. Just then, a burbling sound spat from the fissure. I caught Da's eye and we both stared at the newly formed crack, where an eerie red glow rose from below. A moment later, thick molten rock oozed up and out of the crack, moving slowly across the upheaved stones. As the lava spread, bubbles began to rise across its surface. The bubbles expanded, refusing to pop. Instead, the lava began climbing straight up into the air and branching out . . . taking form.

The first of the lava flows, inching toward a small flower stand, reared up, sprouting legs, arms, and a head. The glowing crimson goo burst into flames as the living fire creature stepped forward, igniting the flowers with a wave of its misshapen hand. I searched for Maloch and his pal from the stateguard, hoping they would take action or sound an alarm. But they had disappeared with the fleeing mob. I looked to Da, whose eyes had fixed on another finger of lava spewing from the crack, crawling toward Lek's shop, sprouting limbs as it moved.

By now, people were screaming and tearing away from the Promenade in any direction that would take them far from the approaching lava beasts. The fiery creatures shambled slowly, scorching anything in their path. I watched as a third and finally a fourth figure emerged from the growing molten pool.

We had a strong instinct for self-preservation, us Grimjinxes. No matter the con, we knew that fleeing a desperate situation was always the easiest and most sound solution. With that in mind, I planned my exit. But with a manic mob behind me and the lava creatures before me, my options were severely limited. A trickle of water from the tower overhead reminded me I had only one sensible option at this point: going up. With a quick prayer to any deity willing to help me overcome my clumsiness just once, I scrambled up the ladder to the water tower's underbelly.

I only almost fell to my death twice. A record.

Atop the high platform beneath the water drum, I could see that Nanni and Aubrin had joined Ma at a safe distance while the rest of the crowd ran past. I scanned the neighboring streets, hoping for a sign of the fire brigade or stateguard or anyone else capable of helping. Nothing.

Unsure what to do, I peered through the hazy, hot air that rose from the lava and saw Da, trapped in a corner. The fissure had cut him off from all escape routes. It was around this time that the lava creatures noticed him as well. They stopped their slow, wanton destruction and turned toward my father.

I gripped the platform's rail. "Da!" I cried, hoping he could hear me over the crowd's screams. Reaching up, I took hold of the silver chain that released the water. Unfortunately, the slide from which the water would flow was pointed in the wrong direction and wouldn't go anywhere near the lava.

I stepped forward. The decrepit tower creaked and trembled under my meager weight. Staying up there much longer wasn't a good idea. Looking down, I examined the metal struts that crisscrossed to link the tower's three thin legs. The struts themselves were rusty and each time I moved, the bolts securing them to the legs shook. I got an idea. And I hated it.

Da had backed as far as he could go into the corner. Smoke began to cloud my view of him. All I could see were the creatures advancing on my helpless father. After another quick prayer, I descended the ladder until I was next to a loose strut. Wrapping my arms and legs around it, I shimmied down to the point where it connected to the tower's leg. The leg's rotted wood barely held the bolts. Standing at the juncture of leg and strut, I started jumping.

With each stomp, the tower squeaked and shuddered. Chunks of wood dropped to the ground far below as the rusty struts whined. Gripping the tower leg, I thrust myself up as high as I could go, yelling, "Yah!"

Coming down, I heard a mighty crack. Not only had the strut come undone but the leg of the tower had snapped in two. I hugged what remained of the leg as I felt the entire structure teeter and sway. My teeth hurt as the sound of grinding metal and snapping wood filled the air. The tower groaned and finally fell forward.

I braced myself as the support beams collapsed around me, pelting my body with the tower's remains. I fell twice my height and, before I disappeared under the rubble, I saw the great wooden drum hit the cobblestones and splinter into a thousand pieces. A huge wave of water flooded the Promenade. As the water met the lava, a roaring hiss of steam perforated the air. Within seconds, the advancing lava men froze as the molten rock hardened into obsidian.

Silence. I peeked out from under the tower wreckage. Miraculously, as the tower had fallen away from me, I'd escaped any major damage. I was sore all over but, apart from a few scrapes, unharmed. The next thing I knew, Da was throwing bits of the tower aside to pull me out. Once I was free of the debris, he carried me toward the Promenade perimeter. We hugged each other for a long time. A moment later, the rest of the family emerged from where they'd been waiting, unable to get to us against the flood of departing masses. They joined in the embrace as Da and I gasped for air.

Slowly, the people of Vengekeep returned to the Promenade. They stared in horror at the shattered water tower and the slick sheet of obsidian that marred the once perfectly spaced cobblestones. People looked from us to the destruction and I'm sure the same image was in everyone's minds. I know because it's the image that my entire family was picturing.

The flaming men in the tapestry. The *bogus* tapestry that my mother made. The tapestry that shouldn't have been able to predict a daily sunrise let alone a full-fledged attack by fiery creatures from the earth.

At first, I thought I heard a whip crack. The snap was followed by another. Then another. We looked around and realized that it was applause. The people returning to the square were applauding us, the Grimjinxes . . . fulfillers of prophecy, saviors of Vengekeep.

But we couldn't enjoy it, this moment when we were being made to feel truly welcome. We could only stare blankly at one another. Finally, amid the tumult of cheers, it was Ma who whispered what was on all our minds.

"What the zoc just happened?"

5

Fateskein

"Fool me once, shame on you. Fool me twice, you die in your sleep like the dog you are."

—*Andion Grimjinx, alleged cofounder of the Shadowhands*

So, of course, they arrested us.

When it was all over, there were a hundred people in the Promenade and any one of them could have been responsible for the destruction evident everywhere. Did anyone else get so much as questioned? No. Ignoring the cheers of the crowd, which continued to hail what I had done, Aronas and his stateguards stormed on the scene, took one look at the devastation, and went right for the family of presumed felons, taking us all into custody.

It hardly seemed fair.

Crammed with the rest of us into a small, windowless cell, Nanni was the first to note that this was an occasion. "You know," she said thoughtfully, "we've each of us spent time here over the years, but this is the first time we've been incarcerated as a family." We took a moment to burn this special event into our memories.

Ironically, we hadn't done anything to deserve it this time.

Da paced restlessly down the middle of the cell, gnawing at his knuckle as he did whenever he was upset. Very little upset Da. He took most things in stride, including the threat of a lifetime prison sentence. To see him like this was rare and somewhat unsettling. Ma, by contrast, sat near the bars on a stool, the very picture of calm. Her dark blue eyes stared into space, a sign she was deep in thought.

"That didn't just happen, right?" Da muttered, his gnawed-on knuckle looking quite red and raw. "I mean, we didn't just see a completely falsified and fictitious prophecy come to life. We didn't, did we?"

"We did," Ma said softly.

"Maybe you've got a bit of seer in you, Da," I said, lying back on a haystack so Aubrin could rest her head on my lap.

"This was a fluke," Da declared. "Has to be. A complete coincidence."

"A coincidence," Ma drawled, "that imaginary creatures, never before seen in nature, sprang to life based solely on a con we played? That's some coincidence."

Da stopped pacing long enough to lean against the bars. He breathed out loudly through his nose. "By the Seven, Allia . . . you don't think it's going to happen again, do you? With . . . you know . . . the rest of the 'prophecies.'"

Ma said nothing. She reached out and took Da's hand, giving it a reassuring pat. But Da's point was well taken. I closed my eyes and tried to remember what other terrors the fake tapestry had foretold.

The gaol door opened. Castellan Jorn himself entered, followed closely by Aronas, and at Aronas's heel, Maloch. My former friend looked at me with malice. I pushed my glasses all the way up the bridge of my nose and glared right back.

"You're free to go," Jorn grumbled as Aronas unlocked the cell door.

"But we were just starting to settle in," Da protested. He pointed around the cell. "We were going to put a table there, maybe paint that wall—"

Jorn brandished a piece of parchment. "I've got scores of witnesses claiming that you lot saved the day with . . . whatever happened out there. Ullin Lek himself swears that you were"—he squinted, consulting the parchment—"'solely responsible for saving the Promenade from the lava men.' What the zok are lava men?"

Ma shrugged. "Guess you had to be there."

"In fact," I added under my breath, "I wish you *had* been there."

Da emerged from the cell to find Aronas in his path. The captain's eyes became slits. "I still say it's a trick, Castellan. Something the Grimjinxes did to make it *appear* they were the heroes. I'd bet they instigated the whole lava mess just so they could swoop in and live up to what the tapestry predicted."

I folded my arms. "I'm sorry, Captain Aronas, but wouldn't

your men be able to verify that? You did have them following us, didn't you? Can't they speak to what happened?" I shot a look at Maloch. "Or did they go running away with the rest of the crowd when all the trouble started?"

Maloch looked down as Ma's eyebrow arched. "Abandoning their posts in a crisis, Captain? Isn't dereliction of duty punishable by, and I'm no expert on the law, a year in gaol?"

Before the Captain could respond, Jorn cleared his throat, knowing that we had a point. With a grunt, Aronas and Maloch stepped aside, allowing us all to move out. As she passed Jorn, Nanni gave the Castellan a wallop.

"I'm eighty!" she hollered. "You're incarcerating an octogenarian."

Aronas rolled his eyes. "You said before you were seventy."

Not one to be called a liar, Nanni lashed out and slapped Aronas as well. "Respect your elders!" She made to whack Maloch, too, but he flinched, ducking behind his mentor.

As we left the gaol, the looks we got from people were odder than ever. News of our first official actions as the town-state's saviors had spread like wildfire. When one girl blew me a kiss, I tripped on my foot and did a face plant into the road.

Ma picked me up. "And just when did you become so nimble?" she asked. "Climbing up that water tower."

I smirked. "You saw that?"

"You couldn't hear me screaming over the crowd? 'Jaxter Grimjinx, you get down from there before you slip and break your neck!'"

We laughed, but Da stared at us with complete seriousness.

"So, none of us thinks this is a coincidence, right?" he asked. "And if none of us thinks it's a coincidence, what should we do?"

"We wait," Nanni suggested. "We wait and see what happens. It might have been an isolated incident."

Da's lips curled. "We could do that. But I was thinking about something a mite more preemptive. Something that doesn't involve waiting around for those winged creatures Allia dreamed up."

I'd forgotten about those.

"And that would be?" I asked.

Da stopped on the street corner and looked across the square at the town-state hall. "We need another look at that tapestry."

★

Lightning split the night sky as rain blanketed Vengekeep. I'd miraculously managed to stay dry during the collapse of the water tower but now, crawling along the roof of the town-state hall in the middle of the night, I was soaked to the bone.

Nearby, I could hear Da fidgeting with the lock to the skylight over the Viewing Room while Ma secured the rigging of ropes and pulleys that would lower us to the tapestry. As the lock clicked and Da raised the glass on the skylight, I fastened the harness across my chest to Ma's rigging, and the three of us slowly descended on the ropes we'd lowered into the room. The room was pitch-black and as it swallowed us, I lost my bearings.

I slowed my descent and whispered, "Should I light a candle so—?"

"No!" Ma and Da said, a little too quickly and firmly.

I flashed on an image of the Castellan's burned house, a reminder of the last time I tried to light a candle, and fell silent.

I heard both my parents touch down lightly, and, thinking I was close, released my hold on the rope. And fell flat on my back with a thud. As Da helped me to my feet, Ma lit candles and handed one to each of us. We all leaned in close to the tapestry and reviewed the images and words Ma had woven.

"When you're good, you're good," I told Ma. "But I think, for once, you were too good."

Da reached out and felt the tapestry, pinching sections of it between his fingers. He ran his palm against the length of the weaving, up and down, side to side. Then he glanced over at Ma, who took the pack from her shoulder. Opening it up, she withdrew the Spider.

Ma had invented the Spider years ago to help her with the intricate detail in her forgeries. The Spider was a thick leather helmet with eight hinged legs attached to the front, each with a magnifying glass on its end. Da slid the Spider over his brow as I moved in close with my candle to give him proper light.

He pulled two Spider legs down, positioning one lens in front of each eye. His head moved back and forth, his eyes staring intently at the tapestry. He pushed those lenses out of his way and pulled down two more, this time both in front of his right eye. Still nothing. He did this several more times until he'd used each lens at least once. Sighing, he shook his head.

"Okay, let's see what we're up against." He held out his hand to Ma, who slid her fingers into a small pouch on the side of her backpack. From within, she pulled a red-tinted monocle in a thin brass frame. The one enchanted item we owned, it offered amazing magnification with the added bonus of being able to see hidden magic. We didn't use it much. We kept it hidden for special occasions, seeing as it wasn't exactly *legal* for anyone but a mage to possess a rubyeye. That's why we had to sneak in to study the tapestry.

Da removed a lens from one of the Spider's legs and replaced it with the rubyeye. Breathing deeply, he pulled the red lens over his eye and peered closely at the tapestry.

"Zoc!" he cursed, a mite too loudly. Wide-eyed, he

turned to Ma and me. "It's fateskein!"

Ma's hand went to her mouth. Without realizing, I took a step back from the tapestry, suddenly nervous. Our family had our code and we stuck to it. We never preyed on the weak or poor. We never filched from other thieves when their backs were turned. And we never, ever dealt in illegal, dangerous goods. There's decent money to be made in selling muskmoss, but we don't touch it because selling it's a direct ticket to Umbramore Tower, the High Laird's prison. And of all the prohibited substances in the Five Provinces, fateskein was the most dangerous. Possession of fateskein was the only crime, apart from treason, that was punishable by death.

Disbelieving, Ma pulled the red monocle toward her, looking through it at the tapestry. She gasped. "No . . . no, it can't be."

"How did you get fateskein?" Da asked, slipping the Spider from his head.

"I don't know!" Ma insisted. "You don't think I'd be so stupid as to do this on purpose?"

I took the Spider from Da and used the monocle to study

the tapestry myself. Through the tinted glass, the deep-brown fibers looked like massive strands of blood-colored rope. Fine golden strings wove in and out of the red fibers, binding them together. The gold strings seemed to pulsate. Looking again at the fabric with my naked eye, I saw only the brown, woven designs. But peering through the red lens, it became very clear to all of us what had happened.

As its name implies, fateskein, once woven, has the power to influence fate. Whatever images it depicts come true. That's all I really knew about it, as its illegal nature made it taboo to even discuss. Centuries ago, during the Great Uprisings, the reigning High Laird had narrowly evaded a bloody coup when a rogue mage attempted to use fateskein to make himself supreme ruler. The High Laird prevailed, the mage was executed, and fateskein had been illegal to make, possess, and use ever since.

And my mother had used it unknowingly to craft for our family a fate where we were supposed to save the town from a series of unthinkable disasters.

"We have to tell the Castellan," Ma insisted.

You knew the Grimjinxes were in a corner when they

considered turning to the authorities for help.

Ma continued. "Explain to him at once—"

"That you used fateskein?" Da asked. "Even if he believes it was an accident, we'll all be hanging from the gallows by morning if we tell him we destroyed the original tapestry and replaced it with a fake."

"Can't we just stop this?" I asked. "Destroy *this* tapestry. Shouldn't that break the—"

Before I'd even finished my suggestion, Da drew a small dagger from a sheath concealed on his wrist. The blade flashed in the candlelight as he brought it up and down in an arc, slashing at the tapestry. But the instant the blade touched the fabric, the magical light that had only been visible through the monocle flickered into brighter evidence, rippling across the tapestry like tiny bolts of golden lightning, and the steel dagger shattered like glass.

To confirm what we were beginning to suspect, I held my candle directly to the cloth and the flame immediately went out. There would be no destroying the fateskein tapestry. Not through regular means, anyway.

Da began his nervous pacing again as the thunderstorm

outside raged on. "Okay, Allia, think. Can we trace this back? Do you remember where you got it? Maybe whoever sold it to you can tell us how to undo this."

Ma's licked her lips nervously. "Of course I remember where I got it. We talked about it when we came up with this scheme, remember? I told you I couldn't just walk into Brassbell Promenade and ask for yarn the exact color of the tapestries. So we agreed I'd have to look—"

"At Graywillow Market," Da finished with Ma. He cupped his face in his hands and groaned.

Graywillow Market was an unofficial market upriver from Vengekeep. It sprang up every weekend, tents erected across a small clearing on the riverbank. The average person who came upon the impromptu bazaar might just assume they'd stumbled on a group of local merchants selling their wares to the countryfolk who lived outside the town-states.

But, in reality, Graywillow Market was known in thieving circles as a great place to unload stolen merchandise to unsuspecting customers, swap with fellow thieves, and make other unfortunate acquisitions go away.

A picture formed in my mind. Some two-bit vagabond

accidentally found himself in possession of fateskein and, desperate to pawn it off on someone before the authorities closed in, set up shop in Graywillow Market. It just happened that my mother became the mark. There was no way to trace the fateskein back to its source.

Ma pointed at the tapestry. "Those predictions are going to keep coming true."

I said, "And everyone in Vengekeep is going to look to us to keep them safe. What are we going to do?"

Da pulled himself up to his full height and stuck out his chin defiantly. "What we do is what Grimjinxes have done for generations when faced with insurmountable odds. A time-honored family tradition for con artists."

We all nodded.

"Run."

6

No Escape

"Triumph is the reward of a shrewdly timed exit."

—*The Lymmaris Creed*

Look, we just weren't the hero types. It's not like we *wanted* to see Vengekeep attacked by giant flying skeletons. Or overrun by hordes of killer vessapedes. If we stayed, it was only going to end with a bunch of dead Grimjinxes to clean up. Really, it just made sense to leave the defense of Vengekeep to the likes of Aronas and the stateguard. Fateskein or no, the Grimjinxes knew how to save only one thing: ourselves.

We spent the next day quietly packing the house. Da

brought our covered wagon around to the front door. Long ago, Ma and Da had converted the interior of the wagon into a miniature home: chairs, storage, hammocks for beds. "Just in case," they said. Which meant "just in case we ever have to leave in a hurry." Like tonight.

We tried to be discreet as we packed it with all our possessions. Once night fell, Ma made for the livery stable to "borrow" a couple mangs to pull the wagon. As Da, Nanni, and Aubrin finished packing, I kept watch on the street corner for Maloch or any of the other stateguards assigned to watch us.

"Oya, Jaxter!"

I jumped. Callie turned the corner, dressed in black breeches and a dark gray tunic.

"A mite late to be out, Callie," I said, my heart hammering in my chest.

She raised her eyebrows. "Could say the same for you."

"What's up?"

She shrugged. "Oh, I dunno. I'm feeling a bit restless tonight. I thought we could maybe start my lock-picking lessons. The town-state mage's house is empty until Talian gets back from the Trials—"

"Wait, how do you know Talian?" The apprentice mage had left Vengekeep before Callie had moved here.

She smiled. "He's my cousin, naff-nut."

Of course. The only son of the Keeper of the Catacombs. I should have remembered. Talian had become a bit of a local celebrity. At only eighteen, he was the youngest person ever to be appointed a town-state mage. *If* he passed the Trials.

"When he returns, the house will belong to him," Callie said. "But until then, it's just sitting there . . . like it's waiting for an apprentice thief to try her luck. What do you say?"

I glanced past her to the wagon parked in front of our house. Nanni and Aubrin were moving some of Ma's more sensitive equipment into a secret compartment under the driver's perch at the front of the wagon. It wouldn't be long now until we were off.

"Listen, Callie," I said, trying my best to sound disappointed. Which wasn't hard because I actually was. "Tonight's not the best time. . . ."

She noticed the wagon and asked, "You going somewhere?"

I nodded, summoning the lie that we'd created as our

cover story. "Just popping out of town for a couple days. Visiting family in Whitepiper Dell." Then I smiled and added, "Don't worry. We'll try to be back before any more bad prophecies come true."

In the dim light, her eyes fixed on mine. She frowned. "Jaxter Grimjinx, you might be able to take one look at me and deduce my family history, but one thing you don't know about me is I can always tell when someone is lying."

I looked down. Nanni had taught me years ago how to suppress all the body language that indicated a lie. Somehow, around Callie, I'd forgotten to do that. "Callie, I—"

"Are you leaving?" Her green eyes narrowed as she added it all up. "Are you and your family abandoning Vengekeep so you don't have to deal with the prophecies?"

I bit my lower lip. "*Abandoning* is such an ugly term—"

"Ugly?" she asked, anger tinting her voice as her hands went to her hips. "Well, what do you think of this word? *Cowards!*"

Like when Maloch said *cutpurse*, I flinched. But in this case, my reaction came from knowing that what she said was true.

My palms started to sweat. I wanted to say something—an apology maybe—but the words stuck in my throat.

"You and your family are all that stand between this town-state and destruction," Callie continued, her voice wavering with anger. "No matter what the people of Vengekeep used to think about the Grimjinxes, they *believe* in you now."

"Not everyone," I said meekly. "Maloch thinks we staged the whole thing just so we could look like heroes."

Her arms crossed her chest. "Did you?"

"No!" I tried another approach. "Callie, I'm no hero. I'm a thief. And not a very good one. If I thought I could help, I'd give it a try. But if I'm not good at the one thing my family excels at, how could I ever save anyone from anything?"

"No one just *is* a hero," she said. "You have to at least try."

She stared angrily at me for several moments. Behind her, Ma and Da were hitching the stolen mangs up to the wagon. Ma turned to me and wiggled her thumb. *Time to go.*

"Callie, look—"

"Leave, then," Callie spat. "I'm told the prophecies have been wrong before. The Twins usually knew what they were talking about, but they must have been having a bad day when they wove that tapestry. Because there's no way they could be right about Vengekeep needing the Grimjinxes."

Before I could say good-bye, she darted off into the dark. I heard the wagon come clip-clopping toward me. I waved into the black streets at Callie's back, then hopped on the wagon and joined Nanni and Aubrin in the back.

The guards at the gate never questioned our need to visit family in the dead of night. They simply raised the portcullis and we proceeded through.

The front of the wagon tilted upward as we climbed the rocky hill that led away from Vengekeep. Outside, in the driver's seat, I could hear Ma and Da singing a par-Goblin nursery rhyme about raiding the High Laird's vaults. I stared out the back window, watching the flickering lights along the town-state's perimeter walls growing smaller. Callie's final words stabbed at me. The more I thought about them, the angrier I got. What made her think thieves knew anything about responsibility? Let alone heroism.

"I'm no hero," I repeated quietly to no one.

I felt the wagon level out as we reached the top of the hill. It wouldn't be long before the uneven pavement gave way to soft dirt roads and we'd be rid of Vengekeep. I turned to join Nanni and Aubrin, already asleep in their hammocks, when the wagon came to a sudden halt. I froze, worried that we'd been pursued by Vengekeep's stateguard, who'd changed their minds about letting the town-state's "saviors" leave. But I listened and heard nothing until: "Zoc!"

Da's curse rang out. A hatch in the front wagon wall slid open and Ma peeked inside.

"Jaxter, look out the back and tell us what you see."

Confused, I opened the rear door and peered into the dark. Thick clouds hid both moons, robbing the blackened landscape of any features. I could see the hill descend into the valley and the lights along Vengekeep's borders twinkling below. Stepping outside, I walked around to the front of the wagon where Da and Ma sat, their faces racked with concern.

"Nothing unusual," I reported. "Just Vengekeep. Were you expecting an angry mob?"

It wouldn't be the first time.

Da and Ma shared a look, then Ma nodded forward. I turned and took a few cautious steps ahead of the mangs. The rocky road away from Vengekeep normally disappeared into the woods at this point. Instead, I could see from the light of the lantern Da hung on the front of the wagon that the road was now sloping downward. I stepped right up to the edge where the path slanted down into a valley that had not been there before, the forest nowhere in sight. My breath stopped as my eyes followed the path to a large, wooden gate.

"It's Vengekeep!" I told my parents, whirling around. "But how can it—?"

I ran to the back of the wagon again, where the hill disappeared into the darkness. There, still at our rear, was Vengekeep, sentry fires burning. I moved back to the driver's seat and stared up at my parents in disbelief.

"Is it a trick?" Ma wondered. "Some kind of illusion?"

Da shook his head. "There's no mage in town. You'd need a full-fledged mage to cast an illusion that strong."

They looked around, trying to spot another escape route. But as I stood there, looking back and forth at the two Vengekeeps, I came to understand what was happening.

"It's the fateskein," I whispered to them. "It won't let us leave. If we try, we'll always arrive back at Vengekeep." By weaving our family into the tapestry, Ma had secured our fate here.

Ma pulled her shawl tight around her shoulders. "We have no choice. We can't leave until the end of the year."

And, of course, I had to state the obvious. "If we live that long."

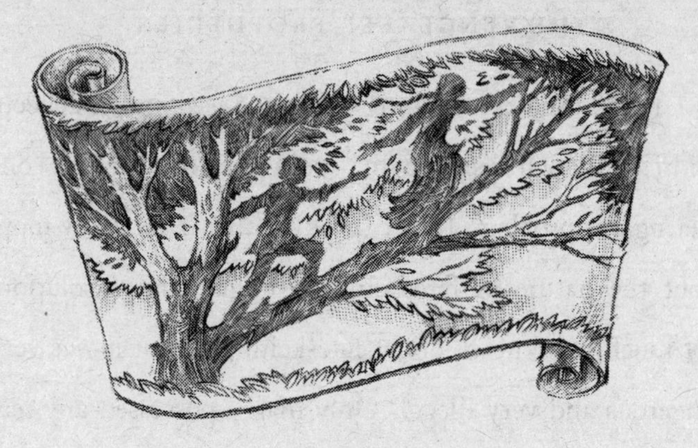

7

The Second Prophecy

"Truth is a poison of last resort."

—Ancient par-Goblin proverb

Say what you want about the Grimjinx clan—and believe me, people often did just that—you can't say that we don't know how to act in a crisis. True, our action of choice usually involves running far, far from danger. But on those extremely rare occasions when that *can't* happen—like, say, when an enchanted tapestry is magically preventing us from escaping—we hunker down and come up with a plan.

We don't have as much practice at that because the running away usually works.

I awoke the next morning in my bed back in Vengekeep. I didn't get much sleep, having spent most of the night considering our problem. I kept thinking that if we knew more about the nature of fateskein, we might find a solution. Not much was known about fateskein, just that it was very dangerous and very illegal. Only mages possessed any real knowledge of the matter and we couldn't ask the Palatinate without incriminating ourselves. That left us with finding ways to prevent, or lessen the effect of, any prophecies that were set to appear.

Running away was always so much simpler.

By the time I got dressed and went downstairs, I found Nanni and Aubrin in the kitchen, cooking breakfast. Ma and Da had just returned from an early morning trip to the town-state hall for another look at the "fake prophecies." Ma had taken a large piece of parchment and sketched an exact replica of the tapestry for us to study. After downing a plateful of gekbeak eggs and singetoast, we huddled around the dining room table and stared long and hard at Ma's drawing.

I'd forgotten just how many prophecies there were. And how horrible they all looked. Da pointed at the stick figures surrounding the four-point star and beamed.

"Well," he said with a laugh, "we've got one thing going for us."

"What's that?" Ma asked.

"The tapestry says we'll save Vengekeep, right?" Da said. "If the fateskein is forcing whatever the tapestry says to come true, I guess we're bound to do that, one way or another. We'll be heroes!"

"Da," I said uneasily, "wasn't it Vaster Grimjinx who said, 'A dead hero is indeed a hero but let's not forget he's also dead'?"

"Sorry, Son, what was that? I was too busy ignoring you."

Ma waved her hand dismissively at the drawing. "This probably looks much worse than it actually is. What are we really dealing with here?"

Together, we started counting. In all, we identified twenty-nine different prophecies. Nanni drew three columns onto a new piece of parchment and we separated the predictions into categories. The first was labeled Easy to Beat. This included minor disasters like food shortages and droughts, stuff we could easily prepare for. The second category—also the longest list—was Difficult to Beat. Here we listed things like a major flood and a vessapede infestation. It would take some work, and we'd need help from all of Vengekeep, but these were still things that could be overcome. The final category was How Will We Ever Beat This? Under that, we listed the flying skeletons that appeared to be tearing the town apart.

"There we are!" Ma said brightly. "It's better than I thought. Only one impossible-to-beat prophecy."

"But one is all it takes to destroy everything," I replied.

"Sorry, Son, I missed that," Ma said. "Ignoring you can be a full-time job."

The one good thing about the flying-skeleton prophecy was that it was the only one where we had a good idea *when* it would happen. While all the other prophecies could happen at any time, Ma had woven a single word under the picture of the skeletons: MOONCRUX.

Mooncrux happened every three months. Most nights, Velos, our larger moon, would rise from the west at sunset. Zelos, the smaller moon, would rise from the east. They'd cross the sky, passing side by side in the middle of the night, before setting on opposite horizons at sunrise. But during mooncrux, Velos passed directly above Zelos. Instead of appearing side by side, they would overlap and look like concentric circles. Superstition said that bad luck came at mooncrux.

Superstition had *no idea.*

"Mooncrux will occur four times this year," Nanni said, casting an eye at a nearby calendar. "Question is: Which mooncrux will bring the beasts?"

The way our luck was running, the question didn't need to be asked. The first mooncrux of the year was just over five weeks away. We all bet that Vengekeep had only that long before the impossible-to-beat prophecy came true.

"So," Da said, "we've got some time to think about the flying creatures. Let's figure out what to do about the rest of this."

We spent all day crafting ideas on how to beat the prophecies. We danced around the harder ones, tackling the Easy to Beat column first. Ma, Da, and I tossed ideas around as Nanni wrote down the good ones and stuck her tongue out at the bad ones. Aubrin drew sketches to suggest how we might store water ahead of the drought. By dusk, we'd come up with solutions for about half the predictions. We'd reached a point where we had no choice but to talk about some of the worst prophecies.

Da ran his finger down the Difficult to Beat list until it rested on a single word: *firestorm*. "This one seems pretty nasty. So, think! What do we do in the event of a firestorm?"

And that's when we heard the screams from outside.

Ma and I were the first out the door and into the street. Just as we emerged, the air above us sizzled. Bright orange light lit the dusk and we felt a wave of scalding heat. Looking up, we saw a great fiery ball shoot across the rooftops and plunge into a building across the way, sending a shower of brick and timber in all directions.

Nanni and Da, with Aubrin in his arms, came out next. We watched as more flaming rocks rained down all across the town-state, igniting buildings and punching craters into the roads. People ran everywhere, some falling as flying debris struck. The demonic hiss that announced the arrival of every fireball soon drowned out the screams as more and more flaming rocks fell.

Ma grabbed my shoulder and ushered everyone into the

narrow alley that separated our house from our neighbors. The neighbors, an elderly couple, had already taken shelter there. We crouched and watched the destruction, unable to do anything.

It took several moments of silence to realize the fireballs had stopped. We crawled from the alley. I gagged on the smoke that snaked through the streets, my eyes watering at the stench. The screams continued, mixed with the roar of fires. Somewhere, a few blocks over, we heard the alarm bells of the fire brigade. Then we saw a group of men and women in leather aprons running down the cobblestones, each carrying two buckets filled with water.

Ma pointed at Nanni. "Stay with the children," she ordered. She and Da ran off to follow the brigade, disappearing into the chaos of the streets.

Nanni tried to usher Aubrin and me inside, when a woman I recognized—a baker from down the block—stumbled through the haze, holding her daughter in her arms. The little girl was crying, clutching at her red and blistered hand. I called out to the baker.

"Bring her over here!"

I darted into the kitchen and grabbed a handful of the glass containers where I kept my herbs. Stepping outside, I met the baker and smiled at the teary-eyed girl.

"Oya," I said, "my name's Jaxter. Can I have a look at your hand?"

She winced but gave me her hand. I paged through the *Formulary* and began mixing bits of different plants, rubbing them in my hands until the oil from my fingers combined to make a gel that I applied to her burn. At first, she cried out, but then she smiled as the soothing effects of the salve set in.

"Thank you," the baker said.

Before I could say anything, the baker started directing more wounded people to our door. "We're gonna need more supplies, Jinxface," I said to Aubrin, who ran into the house and raided the herb cupboard. Suddenly, Aubrin, Nanni, and I were running a triage center, helping the injured and comforting those who'd watched their homes burn.

We did that until the moons rose. By then, I'd run out of the plants I needed to make burn salve. Ma and Da returned, blackened with soot from assisting the fire brigade. Ma couldn't stop crying. She looked around at the destruction and kept muttering, "I did this. . . . I did this. . . ."

Two days later, Vengekeep was still smoldering. A thin pall of smoke hung just over the city walls and nearly everything was covered in a veneer of ash. Some roads were impassable. About a hundred homes had been completely wiped out. Brassbell Promenade was nearly destroyed. Quite a few buildings on the Promenade had burned to the ground. The fire brigade had no water tower to draw water from.

While most praised us for helping burn victims during and after the firestorm, some people had gone back to resenting us. To them, the tapestry's promise of Grimjinx salvation was looking sketchy at best. Now when our family walked down the street, it was back to business as normal: glares and the occasional hiss.

We spent our days devising methods to beat the other prophecies. Each night, we went to bed exhausted and no closer to finding a way to defeat the flying skeletons. One night, after a particularly long planning session, I went for a walk to clear my head.

My tunic clung to my body in the humid evening air. I dragged my feet, but my mind raced. I'd never questioned the life my family lived. But if my parents had been bakers or millers, we'd live normal, quiet lives. I never knew what that was like. Truth be told, normal and quiet sounded *boring*. But boring, right now, seemed far better than what was coming to Vengekeep this year.

I got to the park, went to the tall mokka tree, and sank down against the trunk. As I tried to think of what to do next, I heard a rustling in the silhouetted leaves above.

A figure dropped from the lowest branch and Callie stepped into the moonlight. Her face shone as brightly as her eyes.

"It's true. You came back."

I sat there quietly, letting her believe that a sense of honor had won out over our cowardice and that we'd returned to take our rightful place as defenders of Vengekeep. She wanted a hero and, for those few moments, I got to play that part. But I knew that wouldn't last. Someone in this town finally liked me. I didn't want her liking me for the wrong reasons.

So I asked her to sit and I told her the whole story. The tapestry, the fateskein, how we weren't able to leave Vengekeep. I even told her about how my clumsiness started the fire that burned the Castellan's house down. I felt a mite sick to my stomach. My aunt Risella was right: "Honesty is a tonic for fools.".

Callie was fascinated by the tapestry switch, frightened by the fateskein, and disappointed that our return wasn't honor driven. But she made no judgments and just listened. It felt good to tell someone all this. Once I'd finished, she stood. "I owe you a tree-climbing lesson. Come on." She scaled the trunk to the lowest branch and reached down for me.

"Can't I be the kind of hero who doesn't climb trees?" I asked.

"You could. But where's the fun in that?"

I steadied myself and took her hand. Soon I was on the low branch. We didn't stop there. Together, we worked to go higher and higher. She scampered up with ease. I almost fell only twice. Or three times.

Okay, I lost count.

Each time, she grabbed my wrist and wouldn't let go. We disappeared into the thick, shadow-dappled leaves until we could go no farther and our heads popped out of the top of the tree.

"Bangers!" I whispered.

From here, we could see the whole of Vengekeep. The only buildings taller than the tree were the town-state hall to our right, the clock tower straight ahead, and the turret marking the town mage's house behind us. Twinkling candles in the streetlights dotted the empty roads. I could see the far watchtowers that guarded Vengekeep's southern borders, the farthest point of the town-state. And all I could think about were the people who still believed in us, sleeping soundly in the knowledge that the Grimjixes were here to protect them.

I wanted to vomit.

We sat on the highest branch, pushing the leaves out of our way to get the whole view.

"You did it," I said. "You got me to climb the tree."

"No, *you* did it," she said, poking me in the ribs. "If klutzes can climb trees, who says thieves can't be heroes?"

I blushed. "I suppose this means I need to start your thieving lessons. So tell me, Miss Strom, what will you do with your new skills?"

Her eyes sparkled. "I'll tear up all my lady dresses, say good-bye to the widow Bellatin, and become a night bandit. I'll roam the countryside, pillaging wherever I go."

We laughed and I almost fell. Almost. She grabbed my arm to hold me in place. And she didn't let go.

My eyes rested on the tall turret in the distance. If Lotha was still around, he probably would know a spell to stop this mess. But he was dead and Talian, his replacement, wouldn't be back for a while. So all we had to rely on was—

A lump caught in my throat. I thought about what Nanni had told me the other night about being valuable to the family. Everyone—Ma, Da, Aubrin—had their specialties and I had mine: beating magic with nonmagical means. In all our talk about plans to stop the prophecies, I'd forgotten about that. I *did* still have something to contribute.

"Callie," I whispered to the darkness, my gaze never leaving the turret, "you ready to learn how to pick a lock?"

8

Quarantine

"Slashing your own throat and sharing a secret produce the same results."

—*Lorris Grimjinx, inventor of the rubyeye*

"If this is my lock-picking lesson, I want my money back."

Shivering in the cool night air, Callie stood behind me, holding a candle near the lock on Lotha's front door. I knelt on the doorstep, rubbing a fresh batch of my blue paste on the lock.

"My great-aunt Illinda always said, 'You pay what you get for.'"

Callie scowled. "What does that mean?"

I shrugged. "Who knows? Mad as pants, old Aunt Illinda."

"You're not even picking the lock. You're . . . spreading goo on it."

"Patience, apprentice. It's a mage's house," I explained. "Magically sealed." I gave the lock a quick touch. The faint vibration had stopped.

Callie crouched at my side as I demonstrated the fine art of lock picking. I slipped my picks through the small hole and showed her how to feel around for the tumblers inside. My fingers twisted, moving the picks up and down, side to side. But each attempt to move the tumblers ended with the picks slipping from my fingers to the ground.

When I was just about to give up, Callie whipped her hair back and said, "I think I get the idea. Here." She handed me the candle and slipped the picks into the hole. Her thin fingers wiggled and a moment later, the lock gave a soft click and the door popped open. Callie grinned.

"Yes," I said, with a quick nod, "that was . . . well, not bad for, you know, your first time. Shall we go in?"

We explored the house. It was all very fancy—polished wood on the walls, everything lined with either copper or silver. Some of the fancier items—sculptures and paintings—bore protective sigils that told me not to bother stealing them. Touched by anyone but the caster of the spell, those sigils could do nasty things.

"So, what are we looking for?" Callie asked. "We can't use magic."

"Books," I said. "Journals. Notes. Any information Lotha might have had about fateskein. The more we know, the more likely we can use the *Formulary* to find a nonmagical solution."

Callie pulled a throw from the back of the sofa and tossed it over her head like a mage's cowl. "I believe Vengekeep is in need of a town-state mage. Pleased to be of service."

I bowed humbly. "Allow me to show you around, milady."

We played in the upstairs dining room, sitting at each end of the table, pretending to pass each other snifters of glintflower brandy and speaking of "the simple people." We took turns rolling on the very soft bed in the master bedroom. Finally, we got to the double doors at the end of the upstairs hall and walked into the room beyond.

The library. Easily the biggest room in the entire house. Bookcases thrice my size lined every wall, each one filled to bursting with ancient tomes. I hadn't expected there to be quite this many.

"It'll take forever to look through all these," Callie moaned.

"We don't have forever," I reminded her. "We have until mooncrux."

We spent a solid hour poring through the books. I started a pile on the small round table in the room's center for books that had potential. I had no idea how many I could realistically take with me. Talian would return from the Trials soon. With so many books filling the shelves, too many gaps would be conspicuous.

When we were too exhausted to open another book, we gathered five of the books I deemed most valuable and made our way downstairs again.

We slipped out of the house and into the streets. At the next crossroads, Callie turned left to head home and I turned right.

"See," she said, before leaving, "if you're not careful, Jaxter Grimjinx, you just might end up a hero after all." Callie gave me a wink and took off down the dark street.

Back at home, I went upstairs to my room, kicked off my boots, and sank into bed. I was just about to fall asleep when I finally saw the flaw in my plan. The information in the *Formulary* was good at negating low-level magic. The formulas were useless against anything more powerful. And fateskein was the most potent stuff I'd ever seen. The chances of finding an answer were slim.

I looked out the window. Across the alley, I could see the ruined buildings up and down our street. I knew the prophecies wouldn't stop until Vengekeep was destroyed. I closed my eyes and remembered what my cousin Kellis Grimjinx always said: *From slim chances come fat rewards.* For all our sakes, I hoped he was right.

Whenever we weren't researching fateskein, I was teaching Callie how to be a thief. I read her stories from the Grimjinx family album about my ancestors' greatest heists.

She took to her lessons immediately and, in no time, became better at picking locks than me.

I had to give her to Aubrin, who started teaching Callie sleight of hand. The pair would sit in the park while I rummaged through Lotha's books. Aubrin would hold up a blue stone. Callie had to pass her hand over Aubrin's and replace the blue stone with a red one without Aubrin noticing. It didn't come to her as naturally as picking locks, but it wasn't long before Callie could make the swap swiftly enough so that Aubrin didn't feel a thing.

But each time she succeeded, Callie would hold out the blue stone triumphantly and shout, "Ta-da!"

"Um, Cal," I said, as Aubrin shook her head, "just so you know . . . Real thieves? Don't say 'ta-da!'"

The stress of trying to think like saviors was taking its toll on the family. Late one afternoon, as Aubrin and I helped Nanni make supper, Da trudged in through the front door, exhausted from his day at the shop. He sank into his chair at the kitchen table.

"You know," he said, "I miss the old days. Back when people avoided the phydollotry shop. Or I could at least scare away anyone who was curious. Now that we're saviors, *everyone's* stopping by. 'How's the shop today, Ona?' 'Can I make an appointment, Ona?' If this keeps up, I'll have to figure out what phydollotry is. And that means I'll have to start . . . *working*! Who wants that?"

Aubrin passed him a glass of ashwine as he put his feet up. He'd just asked us all to pitch in ideas as to what phydollotry might be when Ma burst through the back door.

"I've got it!" Ma cried, going straight to Da.

We were all a bit surprised. Ma hadn't been the same since the firestorm. She'd become listless, hardly talking anymore, taking naps at the oddest times during the day and staying up all night, staring out the window. She mumbled constantly that "her" tapestry was causing this. For the first time in several days, she seemed back to her normal self.

"What's that, dear?" Da asked.

Ma turned to the rest of us. "The solution to our little prophecy problem. It's so simple. Jorn's only concern is the safety of everyone in Vengekeep. So let's get everyone out of Vengekeep!"

We looked around at one another, eyebrows scrunched.

"Come again?" Nanni asked.

But Da was catching on. "An evacuation. Of course. Sounds like a perfect idea. We get everyone to pack up their essentials and we start a massive caravan to . . . I don't know where. Surely some town-state will take in a few refugees."

The more we talked, the more the idea blossomed. Ma started writing down thoughts on how to approach Jorn. He wouldn't like the idea—he'd probably see it as a way for us to empty out the town so the Grimjinxes could have free pick of everyone's belongings . . . which actually wasn't a naff-nut idea. But if we used reason, he would probably come around. If he was going to buy it, we'd need a very specific plan, so we went about plotting the exodus of Vengekeep.

Just then, we heard pounding at our front door. I opened it to find Maloch, in his training armor, flanked by two full-fledged members of the stateguard.

"BYORDEROFTHECASTELLANTHEGRIMJINXFAMILYWILLCOME—"

"Why are you shouting?" I asked, grimacing and poking my ear with my finger. "We're right here in front of you."

"BYORDEROFTHECASTELLAN—"

"And could you slow down?" I said. "Really, Maloch, it's like you've got marbles in your mouth."

"BYORDEROF—"

Ma rolled her eyes. "Oh, please don't make him go through it again, Jaxter. I think we're supposed to go with him to meet the Castellan."

Maloch scowled at me, did an about-face with the state-guards, and led the whole family down the street. Moments later, we approached the city gate. I saw several guards gathered atop the main watchtower, looking down the other side. We followed Maloch up a staircase to the battlements. From the defensive walls, I looked out into the valley and up at the hilltops that surrounded Vengekeep.

"By the Seven!" I breathed. "Look!"

Rows and rows of armored troops formed a living wall along the ridge of the valley in the distance. Behind the barricade of soldiers stood an array of catapults, trebuchets, and battering rams. As I turned around in place, I saw that this wall of force had completely surrounded the town-state.

"Are we under attack?" Da asked. We all traded glances. *That* wasn't in the tapestry.

Maloch sniffed. "Hardly. They were sent by the High Laird."

I squinted into the setting sun. Sure enough, the standards the troops flew bore the purple and black colors of the Provincial Guard, the High Laird's personal army.

"There you are!"

Castellan Jorn, brow sweaty and crimson, marched over to meet us. Before we could speak, he grabbed my hand and pulled me toward the main watchtower. Looking over the edge of the wall, I saw four men atop mangs. Three were soldiers. The fourth was dressed in purple, flowing robes that identified him as a member of the High Laird's cabinet. He wore a feathered hat, shaggy beard, and pointed-toe boots.

"They're here, Chancellor Karadin!" Jorn declared to the herald. "This is the Grimjinx boy . . . Jazza."

"Jaxter," I corrected.

Jorn scowled. "Whatever. This is the family I told you about. The family in the tapestry."

The Chancellor seemed unimpressed. "Yes, I can see that," he called up. "It changes nothing."

"Castellan," Ma whispered, "what's going on?" The

Chancellor acted as the voice of the High Laird, enforcing his will throughout the Provinces. His arrival—and that of what looked to be the entire Provincial Guard—couldn't be good.

Jorn pointed down to the Chancellor. "Go ahead. Tell them what you were just telling me."

The Chancellor sighed a belabored sigh, removed a parchment from a leather tube, and made a great show of reading it. "'By decree of the High Laird, the town-state of Vengekeep is henceforth forbidden from making contact with the outside world until such time as the curse that has befallen—'"

"Curse?" Nanni called down to the Chancellor. "What are you talking about, Fancy Robes?"

The Chancellor glared. "News of Vengekeep's recent and forthcoming woes has reached the High Laird. He has consulted with the Lordcourt at the Palatinate, and the High Laird has come to the conclusion that the disasters afflicting Vengekeep are the result of a powerful curse. In order to protect the rest of the Five Provinces from becoming afflicted as well, it has been ordered that everyone who lives in Vengekeep shall be confined there until the effects of the curse as outlined in the prophecies have run their course."

The Palatinate had supreme control over all mages, but they answered to the High Laird. They acted as counsel in all things magical. Somehow, they'd come to believe Vengekeep was cursed.

Curses, like fateskein, were highly dangerous things. Very rare, but everyone in the Five Provinces took them seriously. Cursed people were often confined to their homes. Curses were like diseases: easily spread. So it was understandable that precautions were taken.

Only Vengekeep *wasn't* cursed. And quarantining an entire town-state had never been done before. Certainly not with as much firepower as the High Laird had sent to enforce the quarantine. But there was no way to convince anyone that there was no curse. The Palatinate wouldn't risk sending someone to investigate, because the investigator could become cursed as well.

"This is mad," Ma spat to no one in particular.

But her words reached the Chancellor's ears and he squared his shoulders. "This is the will of the High Laird.

He seeks only to protect his Provinces."

"As well he should," Jorn said, attempting charm to appease the High Laird's spokesman. "But as I explained, this family has been singled out as the . . . protectors"—he could barely say the word—"of Vengekeep." He turned to me and hissed. "Show him the birthmark."

"He'll never see it from all the way down—"

"Show him the birthmark!"

I glanced at Ma, who rolled her eyes. I pulled my tunic away from my shoulder and bent over so the Chancellor could examine me.

Jorn poked the four-pointed star until it became even redder. "Surely there is no evidence that a curse can be countermanded by the existence of a savior? Which clearly indicates that it's not a curse."

Jorn had abandoned the charm and was spitting words through his clenched yellow teeth. Still, the Chancellor seemed unmoved by Jorn *or* my birthmark *or* the Grimjinxes' alleged role as Vengekeep's redeemers.

"Instruct your people that they are not to leave this valley. The Provincial Guard has orders to kill on sight if anyone tries to escape. That is all."

Before Jorn could protest further, the Chancellor turned his mang, and he and his escort of soldiers made their way up the rocky road toward the army on the hilltop. Jorn's shoulders deflated and I actually felt sorry for him. It wasn't going to be easy relaying the Laird's decree to the populace of Vengekeep. How do you tell a people already under one threat that their own sovereign would rather see them die than give them a chance at survival?

Jorn dismissed us with a wave of his hands, and we took the stairs back down into the streets.

"So much for the evacuation," Ma mumbled. The sadness returned to her eyes, and she didn't say another word all the way home.

That night was quiet in our house. Ma didn't touch her dinner. She sat in the living room, staring into the empty fireplace. Da did his best to make her happy, cracking jokes and reminding her we had several strong plans in place to beat most of the prophecies. But after a few hours, Ma rose silently, went upstairs, and closed the bedroom door behind her.

I grabbed my satchel filled with Lotha's books and made for Cloudburn Park. Squinting as the light from both moons shone down, I dove into the books. I read and read until my eyes burned, more determined than ever to find an answer.

I had more than Vengekeep to save.

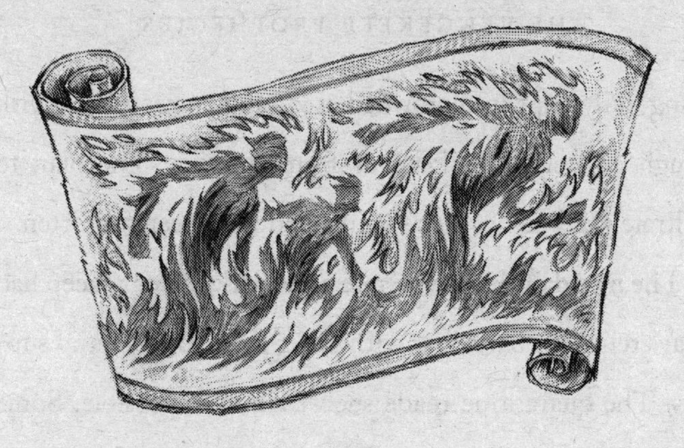

9

Reclaiming Fate

"If it's right for the con, it's right for you."

—*Ancient par-Goblin proverb*

Ma got worse in the following weeks. Her face grew thin, her eyes sunken. She spent most days in bed, barely able to lift her head. Nanni and I took over running the household, seeing that everything stayed clean and well stocked. Da closed the phydollotry shop until further notice and put all his energy into thinking up ways to fend off the prophecies.

We discovered that being saviors didn't pay much. Nothing at all, in fact. Aubrin became our breadwinner, taking daily trips into crowded areas and coming back with enough copperbits to keep us from starving. The plan to infiltrate the butcher Lek's vaults had long been forgotten.

The mood of the town-state grew darker. Vengekeep had always relied on bartering with other cities for essential supplies. The quarantine made such trading impossible. Some predicted we couldn't sustain ourselves for an entire year, that unless we were able to get provisions from the outside, we'd starve. Just one drought—something mentioned on the tapestry—or one bout of mag-plague to wipe out the cattle, and we'd be finished.

Da began meeting with Castellan Jorn daily to discuss ways to protect Vengekeep. Together, they devised a plan to deal with the flood forecast by the tapestry. Da oversaw a work crew who dug trenches at parts of the city prone to flooding during normal rain. The trenches would divert the rain to a special overflow tunnel being built under the city. The tunnel would then shunt most of the floodwaters away and directly into the nearby River Honnu. It became one of the few visible projects to give people hope.

The new trenches had come at just the right time. One

afternoon, just three weeks until mooncrux, black storm clouds appeared on the horizon. Thunder, unlike any I'd ever heard, ricocheted across the valley.

Callie and I had taken Aubrin to the park, where they continued to practice sleight of hand under the mokka tree. My nose remained in a book.

"Ta-da!" Callie cried, making another successful swap. Aubrin sighed. There was simply no reining in Callie's pride at her accomplishments.

There was a distant flash of lightning, and we all looked up at the storm brewing in the skies along the valley rim, past the Provincial Guard barricade.

Callie's eyes widened. "Look at the clouds churn. This could be it."

I nodded, clutching the book in my hands tightly. "I think we're ready for floods. It's a nice change from fire." Magma men, fire from the sky . . . What *were* Ma and Da thinking? At least two more prophecies meant we'd be dealing with fire. Couldn't an unseasonal snowstorm have been in the cards?

Finished with her lesson, Callie crawled over to me

while Aubrin went looking for stickworms. Callie poked at the stack of books by my side.

"I wish Talian was here. He's smart. He could help."

A week ago, the Palatinate had notified the Castellan via a magical parchment that materialized on his desk that Talian had successfully completed the Trials and was returning to Vengekeep. Talian had orders to help the town-state in any way possible. Every day, the Castellan waited at the gates, wanting to be the first to welcome our new town-state mage. But, a week later, Talian still hadn't arrived. And the Palatinate didn't seem very concerned about his continued absence.

Without him, Callie and I had no choice but to continue making visits to the mage's house in the middle of the night, swapping out books and hoping that the newest batch would provide a breakthrough. I was learning lots of great stuff but nothing very useful about fateskein. In all the books we'd borrowed, I'd only ever found one brief mention of the stuff.

"This is interesting," I muttered, pointing to a book on animals of the Five Provinces. "It explains how to make fateskein."

Callie groaned. "I feel safe in saying we've got quite enough already, thank you."

"When you see fateskein through a rubyeye," I said, "you see what looks like gold wires running through it. But it's not wire. It's the silk from a spiderbat's web."

Callie shuddered. "What good is that?"

"Well, you know how I can beat low-level spells by mixing a few natural ingredients? That works because certain plants and animals have a natural resistance to magic. Before they died out in the Great Uprisings, par-Dwarves were the most magic-resistant creatures in the Five Provinces. Now that the par-Dwarves are dead, spiderbats are the most resistant. And even they're dying out. The plants I use resist magic and cancel out its power."

"That doesn't make sense," Callie said, shaking her head. "Why would a magic-resistant substance be at the heart of a magical item like fateskein?"

"Actually, it makes a lot of sense. You take the most magic-resistant substance ever known—the silk from a spiderbat's web—and coat it in gold, a metal with magical properties so strong it's illegal for anyone but a mage to possess it." I held up the book and quoted directly. "'The energy produced by these two opposing forces in close contact is enough to disrupt fate.'"

"That's interesting and all, Jaxter, but how does it help us?"

I scowled. "It doesn't. The stupid chapter ends by saying that if you destroy fateskein, you cancel out anything that was to come. But it doesn't say *how* to destroy it."

Nearby, Aubrin cried out. She sat with her back to the tree, tears welling in her eyes, breathing through teeth clenched in pain. Callie and I went to her side. Aubrin held out her hand. A dark red welt marked where her forefinger joined her hand. Atop the welt was a layer of clear, thick mucus. Looking around, I verified my suspicions. Lying next to Aubrin was a stickworm, long and thick as my tallest finger, its clear, gelatinous body wriggling slowly as it left the scene of the crime.

I smiled at her as I undid the pouches around my belt. "Hurts, doesn't it? I've gotten stung by my share of stickworms too. But you know what? Stickworms are the best things to get bitten by because they leave you something to make you feel better."

Callie started stroking Aubrin's hair to calm her down. Gently, I ran my finger around Aubrin's welt, scooping up as much of the clear mucus as I could. "See," I explained, "this is the stickworm's venom. That's what's making the bite feel like it's on fire. They always spit out too much when they sting. And the great thing about that is you can use venom to make antivenom."

I took pinches of salts and herbs from my pouches. Kneeling down, I picked a few clovers from the ground, crushed them until they became pulp, then mixed everything in the palm of my hand with the venom.

Aubrin looked at me uncertainly. "I know," I said, "it sounds weird that the same thing that hurts you will be what helps you. But that's how it works. These other ingredients change the venom just enough to make it soothing and . . ." I rubbed the antivenom on the wound. At first Aubrin flinched, but her gap-toothed grin returned as my concoction cooled the burning.

Thunder growled in the distance, and it was as if the accompanying lightning strike had gone off in my head.

There, explaining the properties of antivenom to Aubrin, my mind exploded. For weeks, I'd felt I was getting nowhere reading Lotha's books. But, all that time, my brain had been cataloging bits of arcane facts that were now suddenly coming together like a giant puzzle. As the picture formed in my mind, I thought, *We have a chance.* A chance to beat the fateskein.

"We have to go," I whispered, standing.

Callie threw a glance at the oncoming storm. "Right. The rain will be here soon." We each took Aubrin by the hand and raced back to our house.

When we arrived, we found Da, Ma, and Nanni at the kitchen table, eating a spot of dinner. Nanni beckoned us in.

"Just in time for roast panna casserole. Callie, you're welcome to join—"

"I know what to do," I said loudly. "I know how we can fix things."

Everyone—Ma, Da, Nanni, even Aubrin and Callie—stared at me like I'd gone naff-nut. I pulled the satchel from my back and extracted the green leather book I'd just been reading.

"I've been studying up on fateskein," I said, paging through to the section on spiderbats. When the family cast cautious glances at Callie, I admitted sheepishly, "It's okay. Callie knows."

Callie nodded. "I won't tell anyone."

Da glowered at the book in my hands. "Where did you get a book on fateskein?"

"From Lotha's library," I said.

Nanni frowned. "But Lotha's house is locked. How could you—? Oh. Right. Sorry, forgot who we were for a minute."

I held up the page. An illustration showed one of the rare spiderbats. The size of a large infant, it had the many-legged body of a spider with the leathery wings and pointed ears of a bat. I passed the book around while I grabbed a sheet of parchment and began scribbling as I continued to explain.

"The book's not *about* fateskein. Most books only mention it in passing. And those that do only suggest magical solutions. They all agree that you need several high-ranking mages to perform a long, complicated spell that eventually weakens the fateskein's hold and breaks it down."

Nanni sighed. "Well, that's nice, Jaxter, but we're a mite short on mages of late."

I nodded. "Right, well, that's just the *official* way to beat fateskein." I quickly told them about the antivenom I'd made for Aubrin. I then explained about the spiderbat silk used to make fateskein.

"I've been giving this a think," I said slowly, not wanting to get anyone's hopes up, "and I'm pretty sure I can make a solvent that will dissolve the tapestry and prevent the rest of the predictions from coming true." I held up the list of ingredients I'd just composed. "It would be hard to make and, of course, we'd need a lot. A bucketful at least. But I really think this will work."

Ma studied the list. My chest grew warm to see her taking part with even a small amount of energy. "We can get some of this here in town, but I haven't heard of half these items. The sap of an ernum tree?"

"Ernum trees only grow in Yonick Province," I noted. "That's the first problem: we'd have to get most of the ingredients from outside Vengekeep." I pointed to a sketch in the book, showing a large, bulbous spiderbat hanging upside down from a stalactite. "The second problem is that, even if we figure out how to get stuff from outside Vengekeep, the ingredient that would really go to work on the fateskein is the milk of a spiderbat. Just like how venom is needed to make antivenom, we'd need something from the spiderbat to combat the silk thread. Wouldn't need a lot, just a couple vials full. But it's what will make this all work. Thing is, spiderbats are nearly extinct. The only place where we can find them is in the aircaves outside Merriton."

Merriton. The town-state on the exact opposite side of the Five Provinces from where we were.

But Da's face lit up optimistically. "Not a problem. We simply tell the Provincial Guard that we've discovered how to end the curse and ask them to fetch the ingredients."

I shook my head. "Technically speaking, only a mage or a cursebreaker can end a curse. They know Talian's not here, so claiming we can stop it would be suspicious. And any mage would look at this list and know it has nothing to do with cursebreaking. So that means we have to get the ingredients *ourselves*."

At this, everyone's faces fell.

"Well, that's that then," Ma said ruefully. "Even without the Provincial Guard blocking the way, the fateskein's not going to let us leave anytime soon, is it?"

"The thing about fateskein," I mused, removing my glasses and chewing lightly on one of the legs, "is that it's quite literal. You have to be very specific when you use it or there could be, well, nasty consequences."

Indeed, one of the factors that had led to the outlawing of fateskein was this unpredictability factor. The bards who traveled the land often sang tales of those who attempted to use fateskein and how it backfired. There was the story of Xol, who made a pair of magic mittens with fateskein that he hoped would give him a million copperbits, but the moment he put them on, he was immediately crushed to death when a million copperbits fell from the sky on top of him. And the lovely lady of Yonick who wove a blanket depicting her as the most beautiful woman in the Five Provinces and spent the rest of her life mopping blood off her doorstep as suitors from across the land slaughtered one another in her presence in an effort to possess her.

"What's hard to judge," I said, pointing to Ma's sketched

replica of the tapestry, "is how literal it's going to be for us." I pointed out the star and the four stick figures in the center, then I underlined the accompanying text with my finger. "It might mean that only those of us with the star birthmark have to stay."

Immediately, all eyes went to Ma, a Grimjinx by marriage and the only one of us without the birthmark on her shoulder. She shook her head. "You can forget it. I'm not leaving any of you behind—"

"Allia," Da said, taking her hand, "if you can go and get help—"

"I'm not leaving!" Ma insisted through gritted teeth. "If that's the only way, we'll just have to think of something else."

"It might not be the only way." I touched each of the four figures one by one. "Ma wove four figures into the tapestry. It could be that only four Grimjinxes have to stay. *One* of us could go get the ingredients for the solvent."

I expected there to be lengthy discussions about which of us should attempt to leave. But Da quelled all debate by saying, "Jaxter, it has to be you."

I blinked. "You're sending the klutz for help?"

"Neither your Ma nor I is willing to leave the family to face whatever's coming next without us," he reasoned. "Nanni wouldn't make it far and Aubrin's too young. Only you can quickly identify the rare plants. If someone's going to try, it has to be you."

My hands grew cold. Of course they thought I could do this. Here I was, confidently spouting off the plan of attack. But that was because I *knew* the plants involved. I *knew* I could make the solvent. I had no idea how to venture out to find everything. That was beyond what I could do.

"No," I said, feeling my chest tighten. "I'll only mess it up. I can write up detailed descriptions of the plants, explain where they can be found—"

Before I knew it, I could barely breathe. I closed my eyes and felt cool hands press gently against my cheeks. I opened my eyes to find Ma staring at me. Her face was calm and reassuring.

"Jaxter," Ma said, "we're running out of time."

A thunderclap sounded overhead, underscoring Ma's point. She was right. We didn't have time. I swallowed, then gave a nod.

"All right then," Nanni said quietly, "that just leaves getting him past the Provincial Guard."

No one said a word. Largely because the only words to say related to my natural clumsiness and how all of my past attempts at stealth, even hiding in the darkness of night, were miserable failures.

"I know how he can get out."

Everyone turned. We'd forgotten Callie was still with us. She brushed away her honey-colored bangs and smiled. Da returned the smile and pulled out a chair for her.

"Do tell, Miss Callie. Do tell."

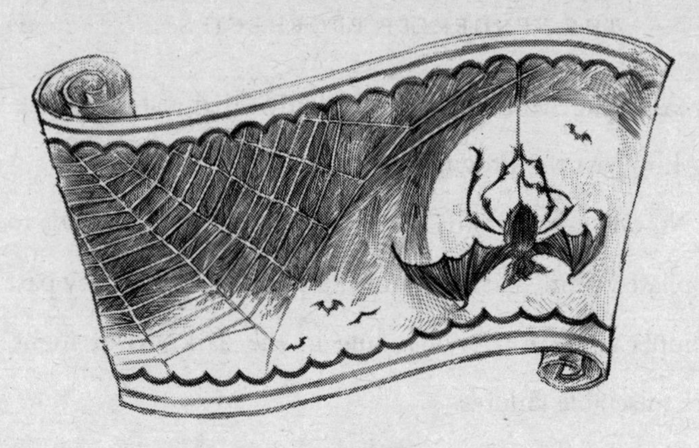

10

Into the Catacombs

"If you must steal from a wise man or
a foolish one, steal from the wise. You'll leave him
with something he'll value: a lesson."

—*Onarta Grimjinx, creator of the Grimjinx family album*

To beat the floods, I had to leave immediately. For our plan to work, Callie needed to go home. She left, promising to meet me at the town-state hall. The Grimjinxes, returning to form, sprang into action. Ma and Da filled my backpack with equipment for the trip. Nanni and Aubrin prepared food. I joined them in the kitchen, grabbing the jars where I kept my herbs and supplies, and began restocking the pouches on my belt.

While everyone seemed excited with the plan, Nanni wouldn't have been Nanni if she didn't raise some concerns.

"What do you know about milking spiderbats?" she asked, wrapping a small singemeat pie in parchment. "Even if you find them, how do you plan to get their milk? I doubt they'll just let you walk up and take it."

I filled one of my pouches to the brim with amberberry powder. "I don't know, Nanni. But mooncrux is three weeks away. This is our best chance to stop . . . you know what." We both looked to the wall, where Da had hung the tapestry sketch. The flying skeletons continued to stand out as the biggest threat.

Scoffing, Nanni finished packing the food and skulked from the kitchen. I knelt near Aubrin and handed her a thin, black leather book. "Okay, Jinxface. You're in charge while I'm gone." I poked her nose and she giggled. "Write down everything that happens so I'll know what I missed. Take care of everyone for me."

She cradled the book in her arm and leaned forward to kiss my cheek. Then her lips moved to my ear and I heard a faint, scratchy whisper.

"Be . . . safe."

My heart leaped as Aubrin pulled back and gave me a sly wink, placing her finger to her lips. I mimicked the gesture, grinning like a mad fool. Then I kissed her on the forehead and we joined the others at the kitchen table. Da and Ma gave me a tour of my pack.

"Maps," Da noted, pointing out a side pocket. "One for each province."

"Vials," Ma said, pointing to the concealed pouch on the satchel's underside. "For spiderbat milk."

They pointed out a few other necessities—a tinderbox for lighting fires, a tiny lantern, a blanket—then added Nanni's food pack. The supplies that wouldn't fit inside the pack were tied with rope to the outside. The weight of the backpack nearly toppled me over as I threw it on my shoulder. One by one, they kissed me good-bye. As Ma held my shoulders, she said, "I'd say 'Make us proud' but you already do that every day. So I'll just say 'Come back soon.'"

As I stepped outside, the storm hit. I ran through the streets, dodging raindrops the size of fists. By the time I got to the town-state hall, the rainfall was so thick I couldn't see the buildings around me, and water had pooled up to my heels in the streets. Callie was waiting for me outside the hall doors. On her back was a large pack.

"Okay," Callie said, "once we get down to the catacombs, we can make our way—"

"Sorry?" I asked. "*Our* way?"

She grinned. "I'm coming with you. Ta-da!"

A very large part of me wanted her to come. I didn't like the idea of doing this on my own. But traveling across the Five Provinces would be dangerous enough, and I didn't want to feel responsible for bringing her along.

Seeing I was going to shoot her down, her hands went right to her hips. "What happens if you need a lock picked? I can do that, Jaxter. You know I can."

The rain fell harder and crept up the town-state hall steps. Arguing didn't seem like a good idea. "I can't stop you. Can I?"

She guffawed. "Oh, please. Like you had a chance."

We ducked into the town-state hall, where a skittish clerk manned the front desk. He looked up, saw us, and on meeting my eyes, his hand shot to defend the money pouch at his waist.

"My uncle forgot his glasses today," Callie announced to the clerk. "He sent me to grab them."

Everyone knew Callie's uncle, Masteron Strom, was Keeper of the Catacombs. He oversaw the safe handling and security of the Twins' tapestries in the chambers below the town-state hall. Nothing like his niece, he was a meek and forgetful man. This wouldn't be the first time that Callie had been sent to retrieve something he'd forgotten.

When the clerk made no move, Callie crossed her arms and glowered at the man.

"This is Jaxter Grimjinx," she said icily. "He is my guest and, in case you hadn't heard, one of the saviors of Vengekeep. He has as much right to accompany me into the catacombs as anyone, if not more."

"Right this way," the clerk squeaked. He escorted us down a hall to a narrow, ornately decorated wooden door on the right. He went to unlock it, but Callie produced the key ring she'd gotten from home.

"I've got my uncle's keys," she announced. "Thank you." The clerk scuttled away as Callie opened the door, revealing a long, winding staircase that dropped into the floor.

We made our way down, a series of small oil lamps lighting our descent. Our footfalls echoed back to us with each step.

"It might take some looking," she said quietly, "but my uncle once told me that there's a small tunnel hidden in the catacombs, behind one of the tapestry racks. The catacombs were much bigger when Vengekeep was young, but the town-state council sealed off some of the tunnels because of a problem with vessapedes."

I shivered. Vessapedes were nasty, burrowing, many-legged creatures, as wide as I was tall and long as a city block. I remembered that one of Ma's prophecies involved a horde of them invading Vengekeep. With any luck, we'd be back to destroy the tapestry before that happened.

"The abandoned catacomb tunnels come out somewhere near Glenoak Falls, just beyond the valley," she said. "That should be well past where the Provincial Guards are stationed."

The bottom of the stairs led directly into a mammoth room, the biggest room I'd ever seen. A soft, green-blue light—enchanted fire that would burn until extinguished—flickered from slender candles embedded in copper candelabra that towered over me by two heads at least. The room was longer than it was wide. Wooden racks made with thick, vertical dowels in neat rows lined the walls. Jutting up from between the dowels were slender glass tubes, each end sealed with a thick clot of red wax that shimmered in the light. Inside the glass tubes, rolled up tightly, were all the tapestries ever spun by the Twins. Each tube bore a small, brass plaque identifying the year the tube was to be unsealed.

"All right," Callie said, pointing to the racks, "if the hidden tunnel is behind one of them, we should be able to feel a breeze from the back. You look in here and I'll look in there."

She moved through a doorway that led into an identical room. I knelt at the nearest rack, running my hand along the space where the rack met the blackstone wall. Cool but no air. I continued like this, scurrying back and forth between tapestry racks. The room was seemingly endless and I grew tired quickly. I sat down to rest and, looking up, noticed that the green-blue flames on the nearest candelabrum were flickering. I slipped my hand behind the closest rack and felt a breeze.

Crouching down, I pressed my shoulder to the rack and pushed with my entire body weight until it budged a bit. I continued grunting and shoving until I'd exposed a small crawl space in the wall. Frigid, moist air spilled into the catacombs. I peered down the tunnel. Even crawling, there would be just barely enough room for me and my pack.

I stood to call out for Callie, when I got hit around the waist by a fast-moving blur. I slammed into the floor on my stomach, the air driving from my lungs. Strong hands gripped my shoulders and turned me onto my back. Before my eyes could focus, a fist grazed my temple, once then twice. My vision blurred with tears as I felt myself straddled, powerful legs locking my arms to my sides.

I shook my head and found myself staring up at Maloch, his fist cocked in the air for another strike. I should have known he'd followed us here.

"Maloch?" I rasped. "What are you—"

His fist came down again, a light, glancing blow across my chin.

"You're under arrest," he growled, "for breaking into the catacombs, for tampering with tapestries, for . . ."

As he continued to list charges, I tried to move my hand. If I could just reach the pouch at my hip, I could end this with some ground roxpepper seeds, which doubled as blinding powder. But his knees dug into my forearms, keeping them immobile. I had to buy time to figure a way out.

"Maloch," I said as calmly as possible, "we used to be friends. I know you're not like this." Actually, this was exactly what he was like.

Maloch sneered. "You don't know anything about me, Jaxter."

"Well, why not tell me about yourself? I've got the time." My fingers wiggled, just able to skim the edge of my pouches. But he weighed a ton. I wasn't going to budge him anytime soon.

"I'm taking you right to the Castellan for—"

I never got to hear what he'd planned. From the side, a large backpack flew through the air, knocking Maloch off my chest. I snatched a handful of roxpepper dust and tossed it in his face. He screamed in pain as the gray powder burned his eyes and blisters formed on his cheeks. He writhed blindly on the floor as Callie appeared, retrieving her pack.

"I said you'd need me. I didn't think it would be *this* soon." Callie grinned.

"Bangers, Callie, thanks for the save," I said, nodding at the hidden tunnel. "I found it."

"What do we do about him?" she asked, pointing to Maloch.

Down the other end of the room, we heard the report of armored boots on the stairs and the hysterical voice of the clerk screaming, "He's down there!"

Callie and I looked at each other. The clerk had raised the alarm. We had no choice. Ignoring Maloch's pained cries, I let Callie enter the hidden tunnel, then followed close behind. Pulling the lantern from my pack, I passed it ahead to her to light our journey.

We crawled along on all fours. Slime from the tunnel floor squished between our fingers. Thin roots dangled from the tunnel ceiling like spider legs, tickling our faces as we moved forward. When the noise in the catacombs had become a low murmur behind us, our tunnel emptied out into a much larger passageway, big enough that we could both finally stand.

Callie held the lantern up. "This must be one of the old catacomb tunnels. If we follow it"—she looked back and forth, to get her bearings—"that way"—she pointed to the right—"we should be at Glenoak Falls by sundown."

"Let's go," I said, and we made our way down the tunnel.

We marched along, casting the occasional eye over our shoulder to make sure we weren't being followed. "Isn't your uncle going to notice you're gone?" I asked.

Callie didn't seem concerned. "I left him a note saying I was going to find Talian. Don't worry. He'll never follow us. That would mean breaking quarantine and Uncle would never go against the High—"

Callie stopped suddenly and looked around. "Is that," she said, cocking her head to listen better, "rushing water?"

I listened closely and heard what she heard: a low, dangerous rumble behind us.

"Sounds like it. Maybe it's the waterfall at Glenoak Falls."

Callie looked unconvinced. "There's no way we've gone that far."

"So, then what . . . ?"

We listened and the ominous sound grew louder. And it was getting closer. A sudden realization hit and my jaw dropped. I thought about the heavy rains in Vengekeep above us. I thought about Da and his trenches, the ones meant to keep Vengekeep from flooding. The trenches drained into a shunt that sent the water underground. What if that shunt had tapped into these old catacomb tunnels?

As if to confirm my theory, the rumble became a roar and was now the unmistakable sound of a wall of water bearing down on us from behind. Callie's face filled with a mix of terror and excitement. I slipped my belt and pouches into the leather backpack, knowing we were sunk if they got wet. In the dim light, my hand found Callie's and our fingers locked as we both yelled:

"Run!"

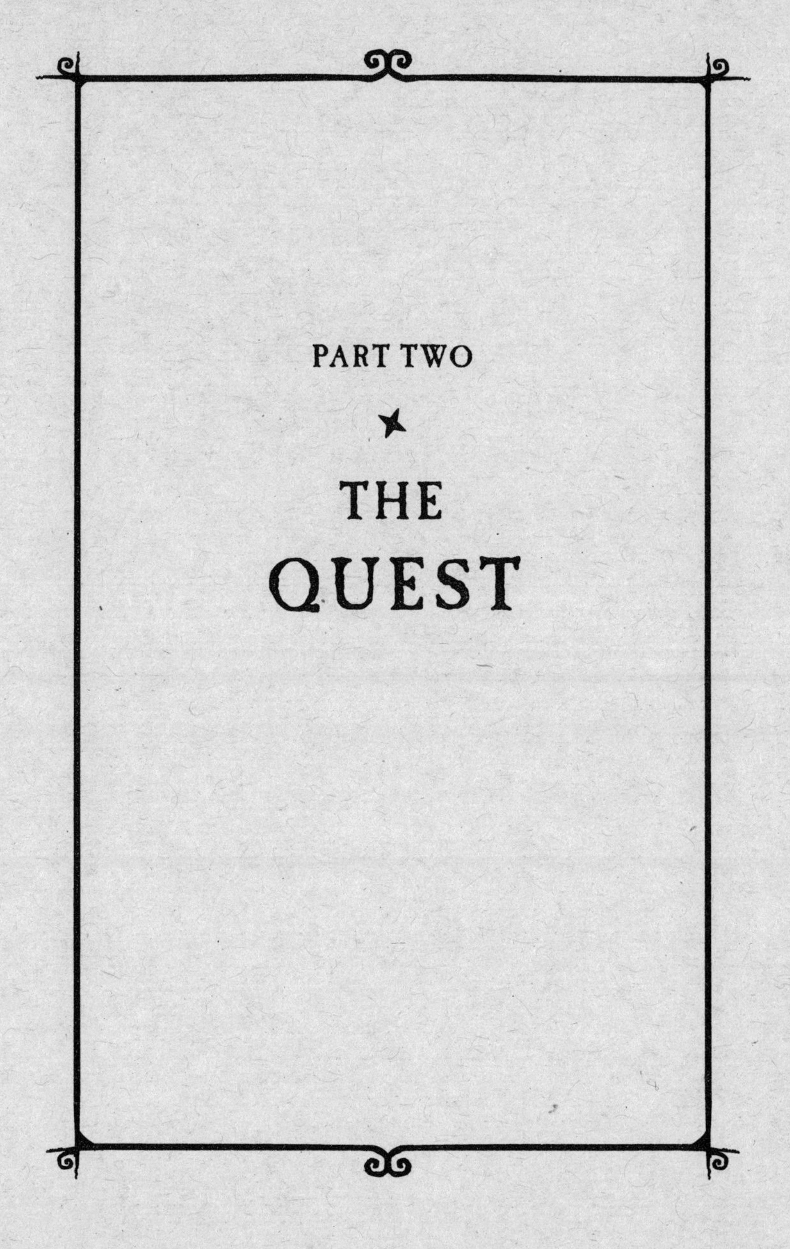

PART TWO

THE QUEST

11

The Search Begins

"Fear is just Bravery's older, wiser brother, leading the charge away from danger."

—The Lymmaris Creed

Ma and Da raised me on stories of their exploits. Before I was born, they traveled the Provinces as carefree rogues, moving from town to town, bilking marks wherever they went. I always imagined living a similar life, full of intrigue and danger on the open road.

In all their stories, Ma and Da never mentioned that the open road sometimes involved being covered with sparkleeches.

"Ow!" I cried.

"Hold still," Callie said, "and it won't hurt. At least, not as much."

The sun had just started to rise. I knelt near the edge of our campsite on Glenoak Lake, shirtless and cowering. Dark red splotches dotted my body, marking where dozens of sparkleeches had previously attached themselves. Only two of the parasites remained. Callie reached out to my chest and grabbed one by its thorny tail. "Ready?"

I whimpered. The sparkleech, with its hard yellow shell atop a green gelatinous belly, squirmed between Callie's fingers. I could feel its mouth pinch tighter to my flesh. Callie gave a quick yank. As the sparkleech detached, a blue spark jumped between its mouth and my skin. I yelped. Again. Callie held her arm back, then pitched the sparkleech back into the lake as she'd done with all the others.

Nearly drowning as the wall of water in the underground tunnel swept us away wasn't bad. Being forcefully ejected through a small hole that came out beneath the powerful waterfalls at Glenoak wasn't bad. Setting up camp on the banks of a lake and falling asleep, soaked and shivering, wasn't bad. But waking up to find our tent infiltrated by dozens of sparkleeches—most of which had gleefully attached themselves to our bodies in the middle of the night—was absolutely terrible.

That's a lie. All of it was bad. But the sparkleeches were the worst.

Callie, not even a little squeamish, had immediately ducked out of sight behind the tent to doff her clothes. She emerged later, fully clothed and sparkleech free. Meanwhile, I stood in my underclothes, too paralyzed with revulsion to do anything. Callie took the liberty of wrenching them from me, spark after painful spark.

I cringed as she reached out for the last one.

"Maybe we should leave it," I suggested. It was just one sparkleech, right? A little blood seemed a small price to pay to avoid another excruciating shock.

"Do something to take your mind off it," Callie said. "Quiz me again."

Callie's thieving lessons weren't limited to lock picking and sleight of hand. Ma insisted that if I was going to teach her, she should get a well-rounded education. Lately, we'd been studying thieving history.

I looked away so I couldn't see her grab the sparkleech. "Erm . . . Who are the Seven?"

"The seven thieves who created the Lymmaris Creed after the Great Uprisings," she answered automatically.

"And their names are . . . ?"

"Unimportant, except Quorris and Harjina Grimjinx, who probably wrote most of it themselves."

I laughed. "You're a quick study. If you're not careful, we might have to make you an honorary Grimjinx."

I felt a tug and an electric jolt that turned my laugh into a howl. Callie held up the last sparkleech. "Now you see it"—she threw it into the lake—"now you don't. Ta-da!"

I rolled my eyes. "Every time you say 'ta-da,' you make my little sister cry. I think we can assume your sleight of hand career is over before it's started."

Callie stuck her tongue out as I put my shirt back on. Together, we packed up our camp and marched around the edge of the lake until it turned into the River Honnu, snaking its way north. We followed the riverbank for hours, taking a short detour to climb a hill to get our bearings. At the top, we could look south and see the back of the Provincial Guard barricade surrounding Vengekeep at the rim of the valley. They were small, nearly invisible on the horizon. But they were a reminder that we had a lot farther to go.

With the midday sun beating down on us, we sat for a quick break. As Callie downed water from her flagon, I pulled two parchments from my pack. The first was a still-soggy map of the Five Provinces. The second was the list of solvent ingredients. I'd already crossed off the ingredients I knew we could get in Vengekeep. That left five we needed to acquire:

~~horvax~~

wraithweed

sap of an ernum tree

~~naxis root~~

~~mardagan~~

~~stems of a corraflower~~

minzgrass

~~powdered veezus horn~~

seeds of a firestalk

~~emion~~

rankstamen

~~musewood~~

I indicated the missing five ingredients, then pointed to the map of the Provinces. "We've got two things making this difficult. First, these items are very, very rare. Second, they're scattered all over the Provinces, tucked away in forgotten valleys, rocky crags. . . . You get the picture. Once we get to all these locations, it could take us days to find the actual plants."

Callie nodded. "But just traveling all over will take weeks. Or months."

"Which we don't have. We've got three weeks to scour the Provinces, track down the plants, and return to Vengekeep. Three short weeks . . ."

"Until mooncrux," Callie finished.

I was starting to see the problem with leaving before we had a solid plan. I sighed. "It'll take too long to do this on foot. We need to hire some sort of transport."

Callie groaned. When the wall of water dumped us into

Lake Glenoak, the supplies tied to the outside of my backpack scattered. We lost all the food Nanni and Aubrin had packed. We also lost the moneypurse Ma and Da had given me. We currently had six copperbits between us, not nearly enough money to hire so much as a mang to carry us around.

I rolled up the map and tucked it into my pack as Callie studied the list of ingredients.

"You forgot the spiderbat milk," she said, handing me the list back.

I checked. "Oops. Guess that one's important. Got a quill?"

She crossed her arms. "Does it *look* like I have a quill?"

"Well, I'm sure we'll remember it." I folded the list up and returned it to my pack.

Staring off into the distance, Callie suddenly pointed north. "Look," Callie said.

I followed her finger to a meadow, near where the river bent. A thin trail of campfire smoke rose up from a cluster of ragged-looking tents. We could make out people and animals.

"Sarosans?" she asked.

I shook my head. The Sarosans rarely came this far south. Nomads by nature, they wandered the land, living simple lives. They abhorred all forms of magic and wandered from town-state to village preaching against it. They stuck to the Northern Provinces, where magic use was more abundant.

I squinted. "No. That's Graywillow Market." I explained the improvised clearinghouse for thieves to her and her eyes lit up as her imagination took hold.

My stomach growled and Callie looked at me sadly. "I'm hungry too," she said. "Think we can eat at the market?"

I reached into my pocket and pulled out the little money we had. "Six copperbits. It'll buy us a decent dinner at Graywillow Market. We should be careful, though. Given the market's reputation, we might look like a couple of easy marks to everyone—"

"That's it!" Callie cried, jumping up. "We're going to a marketplace, right? A marketplace that we know will be crawling with thieves."

"Right," I said, slowly.

"That paste of yours," she said, eyeing the pouches around my belt. "The stuff you use to help open magical locks. That *must* be valuable to other thieves, right? Why don't we sell some of that?"

That had never occurred to me. I'd only ever made the paste for family use. The formula for the paste wasn't widely known. We could probably make a mint selling the stuff to other thieves and buy transport anywhere we wanted. My pouches had been safe inside the leather backpack when we ended up in the lake. That meant the ingredients were still dry . . . and usable.

"Help me," I said, taking off my belt and selecting the necessary pouches. "We're about to go into business."

12

Graywillow Market

"The bitter ashwine of a coward's chalice is soothed by the sweet dawn of a new day."

—Ancient par-Goblin proverb

Ma had packed eight empty glass vials. We quickly mixed several batches of the paste and filled six of the vials, saving two for the spiderbat milk. With our new wares in hand, we packed up and followed the riverbank toward Graywillow Market.

We decided to charge two silvernibs per vial. A bit pricey but, as Callie pointed out, many thieves would find the ability to break into a magical lock priceless. If we sold out, twelve silvernibs would pay for a coach to Yonick Province *and* supplies to make more blue paste to sell for our next trip. If this worked, we could easily travel the Provinces and back in three weeks.

If this worked.

Even before we rounded the bend, we could hear the chatter of merchants and the smell of roast panna wafting downstream. Turning the corner, we got our first up close look of the market. The ragtag bazaar consisted mostly of tattered tents, rickety tables holding up sketchy-looking merchandise, and vendors whose wares fit neatly into nearby wagons. Nothing permanent, everything meant to be quickly and easily packed in case a squadron of the Provincial Guard should wander by.

"Is it just me," Callie said, her gaze darting everywhere uneasily, "or does everyone here look . . . suspicious?"

Everywhere we looked we saw shifty eyes, scarred faces, and permanent scowls. I'd grown up around people like this. But it was all new to her.

"Callie," I said softly, "I guarantee that everyone here is either recently out of gaol, plotting a crime that could send them to gaol, or both. Of course they look suspicious."

We strolled among the makeshift alleys, acting as if we always visited markets for thieves, but our arrival drew suspicious stares almost immediately. The clamor of buyers and sellers talking business fell silent as we walked past, replaced by nervous whispers once we'd gone ahead. Still, we kept our heads up and pretended we belonged.

Callie poked me and nodded to an old Satyran woman selling clay pots filled with highly illegal muskmoss out of a wheelbarrow. The Satyran scratched her wiry beard, which matched the silver hair on her haunches. Before I could stop her, Callie sauntered over. At Callie's approach, the Satyran took a cautious step back, her hooves tramping in place nervously.

"Good morning, ma'am," Callie said cheerily. "How are you today?"

The old faun, one eye permanently shut while the other assessed us up and down, grimaced. "Who wants to know?"

Callie looked flustered. "I didn't mean anything by it, I just— Well, we were wondering if we might be able to do some business."

The nicer Callie acted, the more suspicious the old woman became. I wanted to thank her and turn away before things got worse, but Callie pressed on merrily, taking a vial of blue paste and holding it up for the woman to see.

"We're offering you this unique item," Callie said. "It can be used to open magical locks. Well, you still need to pick the lock, but if it's magically sealed, this paste will . . ."

I didn't hear the rest of Callie's sales pitch. I was too busy watching all the brawny, menacing-looking denizens of the market who'd taken an interest in our presence. A semicircle of thugs had formed to our rear. Some held wooden spoons and tent stakes the way you might hold a club.

The old faun turned quickly, gathering her pots and stacking them into the wheelbarrow. Without another word, she gripped the wheelbarrow's handles and hobbled away.

"But I think two silvernibs is a very fair price!" Callie called after her, holding the vial over her head.

I locked elbows with Callie, walking her quickly away from the prying eyes of those assembled.

"In case you'd forgotten," I whispered, "we are surrounded by people whose lives revolve around doing things discreetly. You're acting like a bunknug."

"A what?"

"It's what we call someone who pretends they're interested in buying stolen goods, but who's really working for the Provincial Guard to expose a thief," I explained. "We've got to be more subtle."

She huffed. "Fine then, O Master of All Things Subtle. Show me how it's done."

"First," I instructed, "we have to pick our buyer carefully." I looked over my shoulder. The group who'd watched us talking to the Satyran had dispersed, but we still drew wary glances. I scanned the marketplace, searching for the perfect buyer.

"There," I said, nodding just ahead. A wizened man, a long staff tucked under his arm for support, hunched over a three-legged table. A tall, sleek sprybird with tawny feathers and pointed beak perched on the old man's shoulder. Its oval, yellow eyes, surrounded by a thin tuft of gray hairs, stared down the crowd. Holding a needle and thread, the old man slipped beads along the string to make the necklaces laid out on the table. "If he's a necklace salesman, then I'm a four-earred cargabeast."

Callie squinted. "What's so special about him?"

"For one thing, he keeps a sprybird," I noted. "They can be trained to steal. Thieves love 'em. And see how nimbly he threads the beads? He's a pickpocket. And pickpockets also need to know how to pick locks. He's old and his fingers aren't what they used to be." I pointed as the old man dropped a bead and struggled to pick it up. "If anyone could use our paste, it's him."

We approached the old man, who immediately stopped threading and greeted us with a warm smile.

"A gracious good morning, young ones!" he said, his ancient voice cracking. "Looking to buy a small bauble for this fine lass, sir?"

I heard Callie snicker. I picked up one of the necklaces and held it up to the sunlight. "Very pretty. How much?"

The old man cackled with delight. "For you, sir, a single copperbit."

I laid the necklace down and pretended to continue browsing the selection. "Sell a lot, do you?"

He nodded. "Oh, yes, sir. They come from all over to buy

Henren's beads." The sprybird gave a small squawk.

I paused. *Henren* was par-Goblin for trust. I wasn't sure if he was testing my knowledge of the language and trying to tell me I could trust him or if it was simply a fake name he used for marks.

"Great quality. It must be getting harder for you to make them," I said, giving him my best sympathetic stare.

"Henren" lowered his head and frowned. "True, sir, true. These fingers used to do amazing things." He wiggled his thin fingers to demonstrate.

Leaning in, I said in hushed tones, "Ever have trouble with *senj wahr*?"

The old man's eyes narrowed. By using the par-Goblin phrase for "magical impediments," I'd tried to communicate I knew the language of thieves. It must have worked because the man nodded once and looked at me, eager for more information.

I produced a vial of the blue paste. "It's a special blend. You spread this on a magical lock and you'll have it picked in no time."

The old man moved toward me, a noticeable limp forcing

him to wobble as he walked. He took the tube and stared at the paste inside. "Really?"

I nodded. "I mean, it works on low-level locking spells. I haven't found anything to work on a stronger spell, like a powerlock charm. But I think you'll find that most enchanted locks will open if you use it."

"And quite a bargain at only two silvernibs a vial," Callie said quickly under her breath.

Henren looked intrigued and I thought he was about ready to haggle. But then he threw back his head and howled. "All my problems are over!" he bellowed. "I never have to worry about picking magical locks! These young folk have all the answers."

"What are you—?" I cried, snatching the vial back from him. The sprybird bent forward and nipped at my fingers, then leaned back and screeched. The old man continued to carry on and people began to surround us again, scowling. "Keep it down!"

But the old man only got louder. "Gather 'round, everyone! We have a master thief in our presence. Only two silvernibs to sample his genius! Quite a bargain!"

The crowd muttered to one another. I'm pretty sure I heard mention of rope, tar, and feathers. Callie pressed against me as the mutinous rabble closed in.

"Zoc," I cursed softly. Reaching into a pocket on my left hip, I withdrew a small, black pellet. "Take a deep breath," I whispered to Callie, who quickly obeyed. Holding my own breath, I held the pellet up over my head and threw it to the ground. There was a crack, a brilliant flash, and a plume of thick white smoke sprang up from the ground. As everyone around us started coughing, I grabbed Callie's wrist and pulled her through the smoke.

Running blindly, we could hear what sounded like the whole of Graywillow Market mobilizing to pursue us. I thought I felt the sprybird's wings graze the back of my head. I batted at the air to keep it away. We didn't stop running until we were deep in the forest and completely out of breath.

13

An Unlikely Alliance

"You can only fail to pick the Castellan's pocket once."

—*Corenus Grimjinx, clan father*

I tossed the last of our firewood on the dying embers, causing a few flames to leap up as the fire came to life again. The night air sent goose bumps up and down my arms, the coldest night we'd felt since we first left Vengekeep. Shivering, Callie hugged herself tightly as she sat as close to the fire as she dared.

My stomach growled, a not-so-subtle reminder that neither of us had eaten anything all day. Tomorrow, I could find us some edible plants to keep our strength up until we could make it to a town where we could use the last of our money for food. For tonight, though, we'd go to bed hungry.

"We're lousy thieves and terrible merchants," Callie sulked, teeth chattering. "Remind me why we think we'll be able to save Vengekeep?"

I propped my backpack up like a pillow and leaned against it. "Corenus Grimjinx, the man who started our clan, once said: 'You can only fail to pick the Castellan's pocket once.'"

"What does that mean?"

I smiled uneasily. "Well, the vote's split on that, actually. Optimists think it means that after you fail to pick the Castellan's pocket, you learn what you did wrong so you don't make that mistake the second time."

Callie nodded in approval. "And the pessimists?"

"They think it means that the Castellan catches you picking his pockets and orders your hands chopped off so you never succeed—or fail—at picking pockets again."

Callie laughed and threw a handful of fallen leaves at me. "So what does that have to do with us?"

I shrugged. "If we believe the optimists and failure breeds success, we're due for a whole lot of success any day now."

She poked at the fire with a stick. "We succeeded in escaping. That's something. What was that cloud thing, anyway?"

I pulled another black pellet from my belt pouch. "Something I invented. By themselves, arros root and yellin grass are nothing. But mash them together in a mortar with a pestle and they get rather . . . explosive. Great diversionary tactic. Da used them to get away from an unruly mob once or twice." Or maybe ten times.

Callie grinned, eyeing my collection of pouches. "How is it that you always seem to have exactly the right kinds of herbs in your pouches at any given time? It's awfully convenient."

I reached into my backpack, pulled out *The Kolohendriseenax Formulary,* and passed it to Callie.

"Nanni gave me this," I explained. "It tells all about twelve different types of magic-resistant plants. What each one does by itself and how you can combine them all to make new substances. It's how I learned to make the antimagic paste. And the flashballs."

Callie thumbed through the pages. "I've never heard of this before. If it's so amazing, why isn't it better known?"

"Well," I said, smiling slyly, "the book was written by the Sarosans."

Callie snorted. Living on the fringe as they did, the Sarosans weren't taken seriously by many people. It was no wonder hardly anyone knew of the book. And given how much the Sarosans hated magic, it was hardly surprising how well they understood plants with magic-resistant properties.

She handed the book back. "Well, if it works, it works." She took out the list with the five remaining ingredients that we needed for the solvent. "I just wish there was a way you could combine the things in your pouch to make these ingredients magically appear."

"Can't do that, but how about this?" I asked, flicking my wrist. In one of my very few successful bits of sleight of hand, I made a small beaded necklace appear between my fingers.

Callie gasped. "Did you . . . steal this from the old man?"

I grinned. "Grimjinx custom: taking souvenirs from your most memorable heists. I thought we should start a collection from our own little adventure."

She smiled as she slipped the beads around her neck. "So . . . what do you think the real tapestry looked like? You know, the one your parents nicked."

"Given everything that's happened," I mused, "it was probably just one giant picture of the entire Grimjinx brood with a big red *X* through us."

We laughed but fell quickly silent when we heard leaves shaking in the nearby trees. Looking up sharply, we saw the silhouette of a man stepping from the darkness. As he emerged into the glow of our meager fire, we found ourselves face-to-face with the old man from Graywillow Market. Callie and I traded looks.

Henren stood there, leaning on his staff just at the edge of the clearing. The sleek sprybird, perched on the man's shoulder, stretched its wings, then relaxed. Out of the corner of my eye, I saw Callie's hand slide to her ankle, where she'd strapped a small dagger under her trouser leg, our only weapon. We stared at him and he stared at us. No one moved.

"*Graeta meshek*," the old man called out, locking his eyes on mine.

Callie leaned closer to me. "What was that?"

"It's ancient par-Goblin," I explained in a whisper.

Callie frowned. "No one speaks that. Not even par-Goblins."

I nodded. "Thieves do. It's like our adopted language. How we communicate with one another."

"Okay, then, what did he say?"

I sighed. "There's no direct translation. It's a code between thieves. He's asking for sanctuary. Something thieves say when they want to share camp. It means, 'You don't stab me in my sleep, I won't stab you in yours.'"

"Lovely," Callie drawled, voice burnished with sarcasm. "Now what do we do?"

Ma had taught me the Lymmaris Creed and all the protocols that went with it. I knew vaguely of the sanctuary plea but had never been in a position to grant it.

The old man stood there patiently, waiting for our reply. Following procedure, I stood and bared both hands, turning them first palm up, then palm down, then palm up again. I nodded and said, "*Shivak.*"

Henren chuckled, slung his staff over his shoulder, and

walked unaided to our fire. Callie glanced at me; curiously, his pronounced limp had vanished. The old man crossed his ankles and lowered himself into a seated position. He didn't seem nearly as frail as he had earlier that day.

The sprybird hopped and came to rest on a fallen log near the fire. He looked from Callie to me and squawked.

"Be nice, Perrin," the old man said, shaking his finger at the bird. Like his limp, his withered voice was gone. In its place was a more robust, youthful voice with a hint of a Yonick Province accent. "These two are very kind to share their camp with us." He tossed a piece of bread at the bird, which it greedily ate. The "old man" smiled at Callie. "I wasn't sure you'd let me stay, what with all the trouble I caused for you back at the market."

"We let you stay so we could find out where you got the nerve to ask in the first place," Callie said before I could respond.

Henren raised his hands. "I deserve that. But I come bearing gifts." He reached into a ruddy leather satchel on his hip and pulled out a hemmon. The bird had been freshly plucked and already had a spit sticking through its body. The man reached over and set up two Y-shaped rods on either side of the fire, then laid the spit across them. In moments, our anger vanished as the scent of roasted hemmon promised to end our hunger.

"Really," the man said as he removed a small tin box from his pack, "I was just having fun. I saw a couple of whelps trying their hand at a con and wanted to show you that it takes nerves of steel to pull something like that. You should be careful trying to con people at Graywillow Market. They can be a rough crowd."

As he spoke, he opened the box and laid it on the ground. He tugged at his wild sideburns, peeling them slowly from his face. He set them in the box, which held two small glass jars filled with clear liquid and a couple of artist's brushes. Next, he removed his false eyebrows, then rubbed at his face, the cavernous wrinkles disintegrating into the raw putty from which they'd been formed. When he was done, he'd grown considerably younger, looking more Da's age than Nanni's.

"It wasn't a con!" Callie protested, holding up one of the vials of blue paste. "It really works."

"Oh, I know." The man smirked. From his belt, he pulled

an identical vial, which he held up to the firelight. Half the blue paste was gone. Callie growled, checking our supply. One of the vials was missing. I nodded to the sprybird. He'd managed to snag one in the confusion of our getaway.

"I didn't believe you at first, but I thought I'd give it a try. Helped me get into a chest I'd been trying to open for weeks."

He reached into his pack and pulled out a small chest, sleek and polished. The lock on the front was smeared with blue paste. He popped the lid open to reveal a jeweled tiara. As if to show there were no hard feelings, the man produced three silvernibs and tossed them at Callie, who quickly pocketed them. "You could make a lot of money with that stuff," he continued.

"We know," I said. "We *tried.*"

He shrugged. "Hey, how was I supposed to know it really worked? I'd have bought some if I'd known."

Callie folded her arms. "Then maybe you can come with us to the market tomorrow and tell your friends about it so we can sell the rest."

The man shook his head. "Market's already gone. Most

of the stuff being sold there . . . well, it's dangerous to keep in one place for too long without the Provincial Guard coming to look for someone's 'lost' property." With the hemmon fully cooked, he slid it from the spit and gave us each a meaty wing. Callie and I dug in greedily. The man smacked his lips. "So, you seem awfully young to be prowling the forests of Korrin Province at night."

Neither Callie nor I looked up from our meals and I cursed myself. Coming up with a cover story—a fake explanation to tell anyone who asked why we were out on our own—was part of basic thieving skills, and I'd completely forgotten to do this. Callie continued to stare at the ground, indicating it was up to me to decide what and how much to tell our new friend.

"Right now, we're trying to raise money," I said, which was basically the truth. "We're going on an expedition. We need money to arrange transport across the Five Provinces."

Henren nodded. "And you're hoping to sell your pretty blue paste to make your way?"

"That's the idea," I said.

The man considered our plan, tearing off more hemmon

meat and passing it to me and Callie. "It could definitely work. At two silvernibs, you're practically giving it away. You could charge much more. Much, *much* more. But you can't approach this as naff-nut as you did at the market today. Try to sell this to the wrong thief and he'll cut your throat and take your supply before you can even start to barter. What you need is someone with connections. Someone who can help you sell it to the right people for the right price."

Callie leveled a wary gaze at him. "Let me guess. That someone is you."

Henren gasped in mock rage. "You could do a lot worse than me, missy. I know where the thieves who could use this sort of stuff hang out, I can talk the talk, and I won't even take a cut of what you make, so you can use all the money for your 'expedition.'"

"If you don't want money," I said, "then what do you want?"

He shrugged, as though he hadn't really considered it. "I don't know. . . . How about detailed instructions on how I can make that paste myself?"

The look on Callie's face told me she didn't trust him. I

didn't exactly trust him either. Our agreed sanctuary meant we could sleep easy in the night without him betraying us. But the bonds of the sanctuary lasted only until the sun rose. The memory of his antics in the market was still fresh in our minds.

On the other hand, even though the Sarosan text from which I'd gotten the recipe was rare, it wasn't exactly hidden knowledge. Sharing the formula with him wouldn't be giving out a trade secret. If he could get us the money we needed to hire a coach to Yonick Province, we could take it from there.

"All right," I agreed, pushing my glasses up my nose. "Come with us to Bejina. It's a town-state not far from here."

He nodded. "I'm very familiar with Bejina. Lots of contacts there. If I can't get you sixty silvernibs for the rest of your stock in under half a day, you can keep the instructions and we go our separate ways."

I looked to Callie. She didn't appear convinced, but we both knew we couldn't say no to sixty silvernibs. That kind of money would almost pay for our entire trip. The man reached across the fire, offering his hand to Callie.

Reluctantly, she took it, adding, “I’m Callie Strom.”

“A pleasure,” the man said, turning to offer his hand to me.

“And I’m Jaxter Grimjinx.”

As I took his hand, he squeezed tightly and a broad grin cleft his face. He looked into my eyes, almost as if he couldn’t believe I was there.

“Well, now,” he said softly, “I’m especially pleased to meet you, Mr. Grimjinx. My name is Edilman Jaxter. . . .”

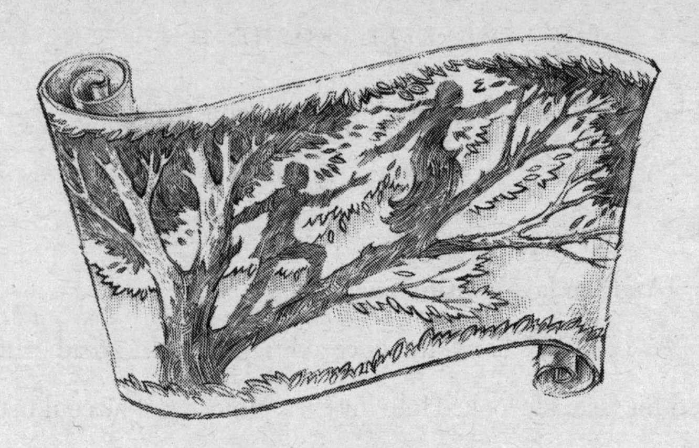

14

Darkraptor Hamlet

"Keep your enemies close, your friends closer,
and let them fight it out."

—*Callux Grimjinx, creator of the Grimjinx Conspectus*

Long after Callie had dozed off, my namesake and I stayed up talking. Edilman begged for news about Ma and Da. He smiled as I told him about our lives in Vengekeep, the phydollotry shop, and my first solo burglary. I learned that if you leave out the arson and our capture—as I did—it's an impressive story. I also left out the bits about the tapestry, the prophecies, and all the other horrible things that had happened of late. When you don't mention all that negative stuff, I come out of it looking pretty good.

He returned the favor by reporting on the years he'd spent thieving with Da and all the trouble they got into. As he gave detail after detail, I wondered why Da had never told me these stories. Even if they'd grown apart, he and Ma cared enough about Edilman to give me his name. It seemed odd to never speak of the man.

We were still chattering away at dawn when Callie awoke and let us know with an icy stare that our jabbering had kept her up most of the night. Bleary-eyed, the three of us ate what remained of last night's hemmon, and then, with Perrin atop Edilman's shoulder, we headed off to Bejina. As we crossed the border into Urik Province, Edilman led us deeper into the woods, saying he knew a shortcut. Callie walked ahead of us, mainly because I think she was sick of listening to Edilman and me talk.

"So, Jaxter," Edilman said lightly, "when I arrived at your camp last night, Callie was talking about some list you had. Ingredients or something? What is it you two are after?"

I looked at my feet. Callie and I had agreed not to tell *anyone* what we were doing. We were fugitives, defying the

High Laird's quarantine. If we told anyone what we were after, they could be seen as an accomplice and share our punishment if we were caught. And while I believed we could trust Edilman, I wasn't ready to make him an accomplice either. The less he knew, the safer we'd all be.

Seeing my hesitation, Edilman nodded. "I know. According to the Lymmaris Creed, it's really bad form for me to be asking in the first place. Forget it."

I thought about it and realized it wouldn't hurt to tell him about the ingredients, as long as I didn't tell him *why* we needed them. I showed him the list of the plants we needed. "It's for an experiment," I said.

Edilman glanced over the parchment. "Pretty rare stuff. You've got your work cut out for you."

I pocketed the list and agreed. "And we're on a bit of a schedule, so the faster we can sell the paste—"

Edilman suddenly stopped. He pounded his staff on the ground and announced loudly, "We're here."

Callie, who was still several steps ahead of us, turned when she heard him and glanced around. "Here? This isn't Bejina."

She was right. We were still deep in the forest, surrounded by trees so tall their tops were hidden by the thick foliage above.

Edilman said, "I've been thinking about it since we talked last night. You don't want to go to Bejina. It would take another full day to get there. I get the idea you're in a hurry to make some money. Fastest way to do that is here."

He jerked his thumb at a nearby tree. The trunk was as wide as our house back in Vengekeep. Starting at the base, a series of wooden planks jutted out, rising higher as they spiraled up around the outside of the tree like a staircase. Perrin squawked softly as Edilman began climbing upward.

Callie joined me. "This wasn't part of the deal," she said quietly. "He was supposed to take us to Bejina."

I shrugged. "My uncle Garax always says, 'The baker's coin spends just as well as the Castellan's.' What does it matter *where* we get the money, so long as we get it? Edilman's better at this than we are. We should trust him."

I could tell by her face that Callie was still unsure, but she followed me when I climbed the stairs after Edilman. The planks were wide, but I hugged the trunk of the tree the higher we went. And we went *very* high. Soon, we were pushing aside twisted branches, thick with fat, blue leaves, and fighting to ascend.

"*Shedan tu verros,*" Edilman said to Perrin. The sprybird squeaked, then took off, disappearing into the dense treetops.

"Is Perrin okay?" Callie asked.

"He's doing a bit of reconnaissance," Edilman replied. "He'll be back."

Just as we could no longer see the ground by looking over the edge of the stairs, my legs started to shake from exhaustion. I was about to suggest taking a break when we came to a clearing in the foliage and Edilman stopped.

"Welcome," he said, "to Darkraptor Hamlet."

Callie smiled widely as she looked around. "An Aviard nestvillage!"

All around us, massive teardrop-shaped clusters of intricately woven sticks—nests—dangled from powerful branches. A system of thick vines and pulleys hung throughout the village, attached to large wooden platforms that could be used to raise and lower supplies from one level to the next. A series of bridges made of planks and rope spanned the widths between the stick-cluster nests and the trees. But hardly anyone was using the bridges. Everywhere we looked, Aviards were flying in between the giant nests, using the plank pathways only when they touched down and entered a building.

The people in this nestvillage looked like the Aviards I knew in Vengekeep: tall; broad-shouldered; talons for fingers and toes; and feathers that covered the head, chest, arms, and legs. The only difference was the wings. I'd only ever seen wingless Aviards before. Everyone here had long, wide wings that expanded greatly while in flight and huddled close to their backs when at rest.

As we stepped onto one of the bridge pathways, we immediately drew stares. Suspicious, unfriendly stares. Sunlight filtered through a layer of blue leaves above, casting mottled azure shadows in our path. As we strode past the village's inhabitants, Callie and I noticed the same thing.

"Not many humans here," Callie whispered. A pair of brown-feathered Aviards flew past and clicked their beaks at us.

Edilman nodded. "The Aviards who live in nestvillages

are notorious for disliking strangers, especially of other species. They don't shut anyone out, but they don't fall over themselves to make visitors feel welcome either."

Edilman led us through the web of rickety pathways. Most of the people stopped staring, and soon we were all but ignored. We heard a short squawk just as Perrin returned to Edilman's shoulder. Perrin nipped at Edilman's ear, then took off again. This time, the sprybird flew slowly, doing circles around us but clearly driving us forward. He was leading us somewhere.

"By the way, Callie," Edilman said softly, "I don't know if Jaxter's told you, but you probably shouldn't mention to anyone here that he's a *Grimjinx*."

Edilman whispered my surname very quietly and I blushed. He just had to bring *that* up.

"Why not?" Callie asked.

"Erm," I said, eyes shifting nervously, "long story. Family history. Pillaging nestvaults, angry words exchanged, brink of war. But everything's been fine since the peace accords."

"The Grimjinx family has peace accords with *the entire Aviard race*?"

"Like I said . . . long story."

We arrived at a stick-cluster building that was wrapped around a tree trunk. We ducked behind and Edilman started rummaging through his pack. He pulled out what looked to be the lavender and black robes belonging to a member of the High Laird's court. Throwing them on, he then took his makeup case and began creating a disguise.

"Should Jaxter and I start mixing up some paste to sell?" Callie asked, giving me a puzzled look.

"Hmm?" Edilman asked, distracted. "No, no, not here. Not many thieves here."

I frowned. "But you said you were going to help us sell the paste."

"I will, I will," Edilman said, staring into a hand-sized mirror and gluing a large mustache to his upper lip. "We're just going to get a little money here to buy transport to Bejina. And *there* I can help sell the paste and get you enough silvernibs to buy a carriage to take you anywhere in the Provinces. I promise."

He pointed to one of the nests that hung from a nearby branch. "That there is the Aviard tax collector. And I'm about to go 'collect a tithe' for the High Laird."

Callie's brow furrowed with worry. "But the tax collecting happened last month. Won't it be suspicious?"

"When people see these robes, they get all nervous and do whatever I ask. Relax, Callie. I've done this hundreds of times."

Callie tugged at my arm, pulled me aside, and whispered. "Jaxter, we don't have time for him to be pulling cons. Another prophecy could be hitting Vengekeep right now."

"Let's give him a chance," I said. "If this works, it'll save us a lot of time."

"And if it doesn't work?"

I couldn't answer that.

His disguise complete, Edilman pointed to one of the rope bridges. "I won't be in there long. Wait for me here. Shout if you see anything unusual."

Edilman straightened his back and began walking regally toward the tax collector's office. Aviards in his path barely looked at him, giving scant nods to the power they knew his robes represented. Edilman ducked as he entered the office.

"Jaxter!"

Callie tugged at me, pulling us both behind a thicket of leaves. She pointed to where two more humans—members of the Provincial Guard—had just entered the village. The Aviards cast only short, unhappy glances at the soldiers, just as they had when we arrived. The soldiers took no notice. They scanned the village quickly, then turned to nail a poster on the side of a large nest.

"Cal," I said, peering through the leaves, "why are we hiding? It's not like anyone *knows* we're from Vengekeep."

"I don't know," she said. "Isn't this what thieves do when you see the law?"

She had me there.

The soldiers moved on, crossing bridges and hanging posters until they ran out. Then they returned to the stairs that led to the ground and left. Once they were gone, Callie went to read the poster while I kept an eye on the tax collector's office. I wondered what was taking Edilman so long.

Suddenly, a large piece of parchment appeared in front of my face. Callie held the poster she'd just torn from the side of the nearby nest.

WANTED

Jaxter Grimjinx

&

Callie Strom

It included our descriptions along with very unflattering sketches of us both. The bottom of the poster warned people not to approach us because we were "cursed."

"Do I really look like that?" I asked, feeling my ears to make sure they weren't nearly as big as they were on the poster.

Callie fumed. "My uncle! He must have gotten word to the High Laird that we escaped Vengekeep. The Provincial Guard will be looking for us everywhere!"

Well, that made things complicated. I tried to focus on the positive.

"Your first wanted poster, Cal!" I said. "Barely a few days into your career as a night bandit and you're already being hunted. Bangers!"

"This is *funny* to you?"

"No," I said. "This is my life. And it's what you said you wanted. Remember?"

Callie pursed her lips, clearly regretting her expressed desire to become a thief. She crumpled up the poster and tossed it aside. "How can we find the ingredients if we're—"

Below, angry shouts rang out from within the tax collector's nest. Edilman finally emerged . . . his arms held behind his back by two muscular Aviards wearing copper breastplates and bearing spears.

"Oh, zoc!" I said, moving to where I could get a better look. The Aviard guards were dragging Edilman, who struggled to free himself from their grips. As he yanked and pitched about, their talon fingers sliced open his sleeves, leaving his arms bare. But he wasn't getting away.

"Should we help him?" Callie asked, looking around.

I studied the network of bridges and platforms and got a horrible idea. "All right, listen," I said to Callie. "I'm going to create a diversion. When the guards release Edilman, go to him and hide in there." I pointed down to a small, ovoid nest that hung below. I'd seen people go in and out. I guessed it was an inn.

"What are you going to do?" she asked as I moved away.

"Something really, really stupid," I said glumly. I scurried quickly up a combination of stairs and bridges until I was near the highest bridge in the village. Below, I saw the guards had forced Edilman to his knees. By now, passersby were watching the situation closely. This was going to have to be a *big* diversion.

From what I'd seen, the Aviards flew too fast for me to outrun them. If I had any hope of making it out of this, I was going to need a little extra help. Unobserved, I took a jellyweed flower from a pouch on my left hip. I walked to the middle of the bridge and wrung the flower. Great blogs of orange jelly oozed out. I slathered it all over the bottom of my boots until they were completely coated. Then I pulled out a fresh flower and squeezed until my hands were full of the orange jelly.

Just as they were about to take Edilman away, I threw my head back and yelled: "Hello, Darkraptor Hamlet!" My voice echoed off the gigantic trees. "I appear to be lost. Could you help me? My name is Jaxter *Grimjinx!*"

Every Aviard head within sight spun in my direction.

I could feel dozens of yellow eyes burning through me. Mutters that sounded like irritated squawks started rising from the streets.

"Grimjinx . . . *Grimjinx!* . . . Grimjinx . . ."

As I predicted, the two guards holding Edilman suddenly lost interest in him. One of them opened his beak and let out a terrifying screech. His partner did the same. Soon all the nearby Aviards were making the same noise. The guards tossed Edilman aside. Their wings spread and they launched themselves up at me. I remained still just long enough to see Callie dart out to help Edilman. As the guards flew higher, I grabbed the rope railings of the bridge and threw myself forward. When my jelly-coated feet hit the planks—whoosh—I slid across the bridge like an arrow from a crossbow.

The two Aviard guards began crisscrossing in the sky above, taking swipes at me with their razor-sharp talons. But I bent my knees and kept skidding along, faster and faster. The jelly made my feet frictionless, allowing me to accelerate the longer I slid. As the guards flew parallel to the bridge, I tossed fistfuls of jelly at them. It stuck to their wings, making it hard for them to flap. The guards wavered. They veered away, attempting to land safely elsewhere. I continued gliding faster than a charging cargabeast, all the way to the platform at the end of the bridge.

That's when I realized I had no idea how to stop.

I tripped on the platform, flew headfirst, and tumbled down the stairs. I hit the bridge one level down, dazed. Before I could get up and run to the meeting place, I found myself surrounded by three Aviard women who'd heard me identify myself and weren't waiting for the guards to recover. Talons raised, they advanced.

I cowered, scrambling to get to my feet. Just before they reached me, I heard a shrill call. Perrin swooped down between me and the women, flapping his wings and shrieking. When the women paused, it bought me enough time. I reached into another pouch, pulled out three flashballs, and tossed them onto the stairs. *Flash!* A white cloud swallowed all four of us, allowing me to sneak around the coughing Aviards and continue down to the meeting place.

Ducking inside the nest, I nearly fell over at the foul stench. Looking around, I saw crude copper pipes and a wall of dull, lead basins. It wasn't an inn. It was a public latrine.

Edilman, shaken from his experience, breathed heavily in the corner. Callie stood on the other side of the room, glaring at Edilman.

"I knew they wouldn't be *happy* to learn I was a Grimjinx," I said, "but I think they overreacted. All the wingless Aviards in Vengekeep do is ruffle their feathers at my family. Too bad we don't—" Neither Callie nor Edilman responded. They just kept staring at each other. "What's wrong?"

Fear in her eyes, she pointed a trembling finger at Edilman. "He's—he's marked!"

I looked over at Edilman's forearm, exposed after the Aviards tore his clothes. A raised symbol in pink flesh—the *S* from the High Laird's family crest—had been burned into the muscle just above his wrist. When Callie and I couldn't stop staring, Edilman finally turned away from us.

"That's the mark of the High Laird," I told Edilman.

"I already knew that," he spat, still cowering from us.

A moment later, Perrin flew into the room and landed on his master's shoulder. He gave Edilman a sympathetic nudge with his head.

"Only prisoners under a death sentence are branded," I continued. "What did you do, Edilman?"

I didn't need to ask. The only two ways to earn a death sentence were treason or possession of fateskein. And I guessed he didn't have the guts to commit treason.

"I made a mistake," he said, turning to us with tear-filled, pleading eyes. "A stupid mistake that I'm still paying for. I'm condemned to die and there's no reprieve. Only a pardon from the High Laird can reverse a death sentence and, given my background, I'm not likely to earn that any time soon, am I?"

Callie moved toward the door. "We've got to get away from him, Jaxter. We'll only call attention to ourselves by being with a condemned man."

"No, no, please listen," Edilman begged, falling to his knees as I stood to join Callie. "I need you. I need you both. The Provincial Guard has been tracking me all across the Provinces and they're getting closer every day. But they're looking for a criminal traveling alone. They won't suspect a man traveling with two kids."

I looked at Callie and we shared the same thought. Now

that we knew the Provincial Guard was onto us too, we'd attract less attention travelling with Edilman. I could see in Callie's eyes that she hated the idea.

Edilman used the tatters of his sleeves to cover his branded arm. "I just need your help getting to Port Scaldhaven in the north. There's a ship there that leaves in a few weeks. It'll take me far away from the Provinces, where I'll be safe. I made a stupid, stupid mistake. I don't deserve to die for it."

If it had been anyone else, I wouldn't have cared. But I couldn't shake the fact that this man had been a close friend of my parents. I thought of Maloch. We were no longer friends, but I wouldn't wish this on him. Despite growing apart, I wasn't convinced my parents would want to see Edilman hunted like this.

Callie turned away and I went to her side.

"I know what you're going to say, Jaxter," she said quietly. "I think it's too dangerous."

"Callie, we have to," I whispered back. "You saw the guards. They covered this village with posters. By sundown, those posters will be in every Province. If we're by ourselves, it's only a matter of time before someone turns us in."

Edilman took a deep breath and said, "What if I told you that I knew a single place where you could find every item on that list you're carrying?"

Callie whirled on me, shocked that I'd shared the list with him. Then she said, "He's bluffing. He'll lead us on a wild chase, all the while promising to do just 'one more job.'"

Edilman shook his head. "Not true. I swear by the Seven." Then he looked directly at me. "I swear on the kinship of your parents. I'm telling the truth. I'll take you to a place where you can find everything you need. All I ask in return is that you continue traveling with me to throw the Provincial Guard off the trail. Once you have those plants, just get me to my ship in Port Scaldhaven and you'll never have to see me again."

I looked to Callie, but she still hadn't changed her mind. She wanted us to sever our ties once and for all right there. And even though the possibility of every item being located in a single place seemed far-fetched, as rare as these ingredients were, I couldn't turn my back on the chance to save Vengekeep quickly.

"You've got three days," I told him. "Three days to take

us to where we can find everything on the list. And if you don't, we'll call the Provincial Guard ourselves."

Exhaling with relief, Edilman rose, a thankful smile on his lips. Callie shook her head in disbelief.

"Three days?" Edilman asked, peeling off his fake mustache. "I can get you there in two."

15

The Dowager

"There's a word for a thief
who doesn't know danger: poor."

—Minaeris Grimjinx, founder of the Tarana Thieves Alliance

The tall, imposing wall around Redvalor Castle loomed ahead of us. The two Provincial Guards at the gate, halberds in hand, watched us warily as we approached.

"Everyone ready?" Edilman whispered. He was nearly unrecognizable in a scraggly wig, false nose, bushy eyebrows, and dentures that gave him a pronounced overbite.

Callie tugged at the high collar on her dress. "This will never work."

"You knew what we were doing when you left Vengekeep," I said to Callie. "Why did you pack a dress?"

Before she could answer, Edilman interrupted. "It's good that she did. We need to look presentable."

"This will never work," Callie repeated. She'd said little else in the two days it had taken us to get here.

Edilman pointed ahead. "Behind that gate is everything we both need. You get your plants, I get whatever I can grab in the castle vaults. Wait here."

We paused while Edilman went to speak to the guards. A moment later, they unlocked the gates and allowed us through. We walked across a courtyard paved with sparkling stone until we arrived at the huge front doors of the castle.

Redvalor was a castle in name only. It bore none of the battlements or reinforcements of a proper castle. In reality, it was a lavish mansion that had been in the High Laird's family for centuries. Mostly it had been used as a vacation home for the royal family. However, rumor had it that some years ago, the High Laird's sister, the Dowager, had a falling out with her brother and had moved into Redvalor permanently.

Edilman tugged on a rope, and a bell sounded. Moments

later, the door opened, revealing a tall, stern-looking Aviard.

We jumped, the nestvillage still fresh in our minds. But we quickly recovered and pasted large, fake smiles on our faces. The elderly majordomo looked down the length of his ample beak at us with an air of supreme caution. "May I help you?"

"Greetings!" Edilman trilled in a very high, overenthusiastic voice. "I am Professor Quintas Wenderkin from the Urahl Academy. I do believe the Dowager is expecting us."

Edilman produced a pince-nez with lenses so thick I couldn't imagine he could see through them. He parked them on the end of his nose and elbowed Callie. Callie curtsied while I clutched the sides of my vest proudly, as I imagined a student at the "Urahl Academy" might do.

On hearing Edilman's fake name, the majordomo nodded. "Of course, Professor. Do come in."

With the setting sun at our backs, we stepped over the threshold into Redvalor Castle. I'd been in some fancy homes in my life. I always imagined that royal residences would put them all to shame. Looking around, I was right.

Sort of.

In the cavernous main hall, where I expected to see a floor of shiny, swirled marble, I found a field of soil. A blanket of transparent grass covered the entire floor. Tall, thin trees sprouted up, their long branches twisting up and around the shiny copper chandeliers. Large bushes changed from green to red as we walked by. Overhead, a small black cloud hung over a grove of trees, raining down on them. A moment later, the cloud stopped raining, and it floated over to a hedge along the far wall, where it started raining again.

Amid the miniature forest, contraptions made of metal and wood whirred and clicked. Squatting down, I peered into the nearest, a boxy machine. Inside, I saw pairs of small animals running on wheels that moved conveyor belts that churned the innards of the device. Every so often, a pipe at the top shot a jet of steam into the air.

The majordomo led us through all this—stepping over knee-high mushrooms with squinty eyes, stubby arms, and several pairs of knobby feet—and acted as though everyone had a small jungle filled with contraptions in their foyer.

The Aviard held up a taloned hand to stop us in the middle of the room. "Please wait here while I announce your arrival to the Dowager." He turned smartly and went up a wide staircase that led to a second floor landing.

Edilman gave a low whistle. "Well, isn't this . . . ? Help me out here, guys."

"Where have you brought us?" Callie asked, fear creeping into her voice.

I quickly changed the subject. "Will Perrin be okay?"

Edilman nodded absently, his eyes never leaving the mushrooms that continued to stare at us. Prior to our arrival, Edilman had sent the bird off into the forest. Talented as he was, Perrin enjoyed stealing a bit too much. Edilman had decided we couldn't risk having him with us in the castle and exposing who we really were.

"Why would the Dowager be looking for intelligent children?" I asked. I should have brought this up when Edilman first told us about the scheme. But he seemed so sure we'd find all the solvent ingredients here, I'd let it slide.

"All I know," Edilman said, "is that several months ago, the Dowager sent word to schools across the Five Provinces saying she was looking for the best and the brightest students the land had to offer. She didn't say why, only that she wanted to meet with them. I contacted her, posing as a professor, promising to bring my finest protégés for her consideration. Even found a couple of youthful-looking accomplices to play the roles."

"What happened to them?" I asked.

He shrugged. "Little bunknugs got greedy. We were a day's journey from Redvalor when they decided they wanted a bigger cut of whatever we stole from here. In the end, we couldn't come to terms and the plan fell apart. That is, until I very luckily came upon you two. It was fate, really."

Callie frowned. "So, for all you know, she might be some insane person who thinks she can gain youth and intelligence by eating the brains of smart children." She gave a little yelp when a nearby machine squealed and spat oil across the lawn.

Edilman shrugged and raised his bushy fake eyebrows. "Erm, I doubt it. She comes from a good family. Good families tend not to feast on the young. Still, let's hope it doesn't come to that."

This didn't please Callie. She was already angry that we had to pull another con to get the ingredients. During the trip to Redvalor, whenever Edilman wasn't looking, she would pull out a calendar and make a show of reminding me how close we were to mooncrux. As of today, it was two weeks away. She folded her arms. "And where is Urahl Academy?"

Edilman considered. "What sounds good to you? How about Abon? Lovely seaside village. Good location for an academy."

Callie looked to me, perplexed. "*Urahl* is par-Goblin for 'bogus,'" I explained.

Before we could agree on an appropriate setting for our imaginary alma mater, a thunderous boom echoed in the room. My head snapped around to find the majordomo standing on the second floor landing, bearing a large silver staff that he used to strike the floor twice more. Once he had our attention, he announced, "The Dowager Annestra Soranna."

The Aviard stepped aside as a tall figure joined him on the landing. From the neck down, the figure wore a one-piece leather suit like the kind a worker would wear in the Kaladark crystal mines. The suit was covered with pockets that bulged with unseen contents. A large, black glass bubble covered the figure's head like a helmet. The figure carefully walked down the stairs, gripping the polished brass railing for support. Reaching the soil below, the figure removed the bubble helmet, revealing a regal-looking woman.

I guessed her to be slightly older than Ma, with a touch more gray in the dark hair that wove around her head like a large cotton ball. The smile on her face was crooked but earnest. Her oddest feature was her uncanny eyes. Wide and unblinking, they never seemed to settle on any one spot for long, constantly flitting about in their sockets like agitated birds. All this combined to give her an ethereal quality, compounded when we heard her airy, lilting voice.

"Professor Wenderkin!" she said in a singsong tone. She set the helmet down and held out her arms to take Edilman's hands. Edilman squeezed the fingers of her bulky leather gloves, crossed his feet, and performed an elaborate bow. The Dowager blushed. "How good to finally meet you. I feel as if I know you already from your kind and effusive letters."

"Dowager Soranna," Edilman squeaked humbly, "the honor is completely mine. You do me such service to grant us this audience." Edilman came out of his bow and placed his hands on Callie and me. "As promised, I'd like to present to you the two top students that Urahl Academy has to offer. Veelie," he tapped Callie, who launched into a very elegant curtsy, "and Tyrius." In response to my phony name, I offered a polite, stiff bow from the waist.

The Dowager tossed us both a strange, toothy smile, and I began to wonder if Callie's idea of us being eaten wasn't far from the truth. The Dowager's continually shifting eyes and the way her head swayed from side to side, as if she were daydreaming, did nothing to shake off that image.

"Please excuse the state of the hall," the Dowager said, her arm sweeping to indicate the madness around us. "My work became more than my laboratory could contain."

Callie squeezed my elbow as we thought the same thing. *What does the High Laird's sister need with a laboratory?*

"I had just about given up hope," the Dowager said, taking Edilman by the arm and leading him across the hall. Callie and I fell in step behind them. "Several professors have brought their most promising pupils to call, but I'm afraid none of them quite measured up. From your letters, I was sure I would find what I need in the students you promised to bring. But I was expecting you several months ago."

Edilman nodded. "My apologies, Dowager. We would have arrived on time were it not for the fact that poor Veelie here came down with a bout of sagpox." The Dowager winced at the news and Edilman hastily added, "But she's completely cured now and eager to see if she can serve your royal needs."

"We shall see," the Dowager said, with a somewhat dubious glance at Callie. "I was happy to receive your recent missive, announcing your imminent arrival. We've prepared rooms for you. I'm sure you must be tired and hungry." The Dowager turned to the majordomo, who had been quietly following our small entourage. "Oxric, please take them to their rooms and then escort them to the dining hall."

Oxric, the majordomo, nodded. Edilman kissed the Dowager's gloved hand as Callie and I repeated our curtsy and bow. The three of us left the Dowager in the main hall to follow Oxric up the grand staircase to the second floor. We were relieved to find that the second floor was more . . . normal. Callie and I waited at the top of the stairs as the majordomo took Edilman down the right-hand hallway to his room.

"I still don't like this," Callie muttered. "I don't trust him, Jaxter. Do you?"

"I don't know."

"Selling fateskein," she tsked. "How stupid is that? And dangerous. For all we know, he's the one who sold the fateskein to your mother."

I hadn't thought of that. It was possible. In one of his disguises, he could have very easily sold Ma the yarn she was seeking, not mentioning it was really fateskein. Was the problem that had come between him and my parents so great that he would have endangered them like that? I made a note to keep a closer eye on him. At the first sign of treachery, Callie and I would bolt.

Callie nodded down to the Dowager, who hadn't moved. The lady seemed transfixed by one of her sputtering machines, her head continuing to sway to unheard music. "Not what I expected from someone whose family rules the land," Callie whispered. "She seems . . . not quite all there."

I shrugged. "Should make this an easy job. We get what

we need for the solvent, Edilman nicks whatever valuables he can find, we all go our separate ways."

A moment later, the majordomo took us down the left-hand hall, stopping first to show Callie her room, then taking me to my room next door. It was massive. My room was the size of the entire first floor of our house in Vengekeep. Polished glenoak furniture. A four-poster bed with shiny, red silk sheets. A copper-trimmed fireplace. A small terrace overlooking a sprawling garden with fountains and hedge mazes. A selection of dress clothes in various sizes had been laid out on the bed. I tried each one on until I found a sharp set that fit perfectly. I studied myself in the mirror and had to admit that I looked every bit the dashing rake. I couldn't pick a lock or forge a coin to save my life, but how could the Dowager resist that smile?

Resist it she did.

When we joined the Dowager in the lavish dining room, her demeanor had changed drastically. She was suddenly cold and distant. Edilman had warned us this might be the case, that she might force us to do the talking in an effort to impress her.

We sat at the table as the knee-high mushrooms waddled in with our salad plates atop their caps. When we took the plates, the mushrooms waddled off, muttering to themselves.

"They don't seem very happy," Callie noted.

The Dowager shook her head. "Well, you wouldn't be happy if you'd been turned into a mushroom, I dare say."

My eyes widened. "You mean . . . they're not really mushrooms?"

The Dowager flushed. "Of course they are. Now. But they used to be my servants. Some of my research went a mite awry. The Palatinate had lent me a braincube and I . . . Well, I don't want to talk about that. I hope to get them back to normal soon."

Callie looked sick but I was curious. *Research?*

As we ate, Edilman bumbled his way through a lengthy and highly imaginative account of the curriculum at the Urahl Academy and how "Veelie" and I had proven again and again to stand head and shoulders above the other students. But the Dowager spent most of the salad course frowning, pausing only to ring a small bell that summoned the mushrooms back. They bounced up and down at our sides, holding out their stubby arms and grunting until we placed our salad plates atop their heads. They staggered away, returning in a moment with soup bowls.

By the time we'd finished our soup, Edilman had given up trying to impress the Dowager. We waited for the next course in silence, Callie and I trading glances, unsure of what to make of the strange woman or what to do next.

The muttering mushrooms returned, taking away our soup bowls and replacing them with fine bone plates heaped with generous helpings of roast panna, potatoes, and a steaming purple vegetable I hoped was monx. One mushroom scurried over to the Dowager with a covered silver bowl on its head. As the Dowager took the bowl and removed the domed top, I caught the distinctive scent of aramon leaves. The smell, like rotting blackdrupes, churned my stomach. I watched, fascinated, as she took a large spoon and covered her meal with a generous portion of the chopped leaves.

As the Dowager began eating, I felt a tug at my elbow. I leaned toward Edilman, who whispered, "The entire plan rests on you two making like you're smart. Go on. Say something intelligent."

I sighed through my nose and pushed up my glasses. Command performances were never my strong point. I turned to our hostess and said, "If I may ask, how long has your stomach been upset, Dowager?"

The fork she'd lifted to her mouth stopped halfway there and her flittering eyes rested on me briefly, her childlike face confused. Even Edilman and Callie eyed me for asking the seemingly strange and random question.

"Come again?" the Dowager asked, lowering her fork and smiling in an "I don't know what you're talking about" sort of way.

I nodded at her plate. "I see that you've seasoned your food with aramon leaves. They're quite pungent and not all that tasty. I can't imagine someone flavoring their food with them without a good reason. The Satyrans on the island of Rexin use aramon to settle an upset stomach. From the amount you used, I guessed you've had problems for some time."

Her eyes glistened as she regarded me with curiosity. I

smiled. She straightened her back and began playing with her food. "Well, yes. I've suffered a bit of indigestion these past few weeks. The aramon has helped a great deal. It's not a commonly known remedy." This last bit betrayed the admiration my simple observance had earned me.

"Of course," I went on, "the problem with aramon is that it's very bitter. I would recommend letting fresh leaves dry out for a few days, shredding them, and mixing them with oskaflower honey. Takes the edge off the taste and the honey doesn't leave you with the bad breath that aramon does. And you can spread it on toast. No need to coat your entire meal with the leaves."

For a moment, I felt like I'd channeled my silver-tongued father. I knew exactly what to say and how to say it. The Dowager's eyes widened with each suggestion I made, and behind those eyes, I could see her thinking about what I'd said and realizing that it was all true.

"I'd never thought of that," the Dowager said, a hint of eagerness in her voice. "Are you studying to be an apothecary?"

I shook my head. "Most of what I know about remedies I

got from a book. *The Kolohendriseenax Formulary.*"

The Dowager cried out, clapping with approval. "The Sarosan text. I know the very book! It's marvelous, isn't it?"

And that's how it started. She began asking me about what I'd learned from the book and soon we were discussing other titles. Without realizing it, I'd forgotten my hunger as our conversation grew deeper. My initial impression of the Dowager as tottering drifted away the more engrossed we became in sharing our theories about combining various tree saps to heal wounds caused by a darkshrike bite and about the numerous uses for mokka tree bark. Soon, our words were overlapping each other as we spoke, and my face started hurting. I hadn't realized I'd been grinning the entire time.

I've no idea how long we'd been talking, but at one point someone cleared their throat. The Dowager and I suddenly realized we'd forgotten about Callie and Edilman. I poked the food on my plate and found it was cold. I also noticed that Callie and Edilman had finished their meals. I snuck a peek at the Dowager, who gave them a small smile.

"Please forgive us," the Dowager said, ringing a bell. The mushrooms waddled into the room and bounced until we put our plates on their heads. "Young Master Tyrius and I have been rude in neglecting everyone else."

"Not at all," Edilman sang, forgiveness mixing with delight in his voice. "I had a feeling you two might hit it off." Under the table, Edilman gave my leg a congratulatory pat. "But it is rather late and the children have had a tiring day of travel. It might be best if we turn in. We can all start fresh in the morning."

"Tomorrow," the Dowager said, as we all rose, "I shall take you to see the East Gardens. I think you'll enjoy it quite a bit."

"I'd like that very much, ma'am," I said earnestly. Then, with Edilman's hand clamped on my shoulder, we turned and left the dining room.

Edilman, Callie, and I moved across the indoor forest in the foyer. We took each step of the staircase slowly, huddled close together, speaking in hushed tones.

"Bangers, Jaxter!" Edilman enthused. "That was brilliant. You've got the old bird hooked."

We reached the top of the stairs. "So what do we do tomorrow?" I asked.

Edilman said, "Keep our eyes peeled, don't ask too many suspicious questions. We'll let her continue showing us around and let her call the shots." He tapped his forehead. "But pay attention. We need to know this place inside out. Got it?" He gave us a salute and bounded down the hall.

Callie and I continued toward our rooms. I looked over my shoulder to where Edilman had disappeared. "You have to admit his plan is working."

She pursed her lips, not quite ready to give Edilman any slack. "If we get the ingredients, I'll give him a pat on the head." We stopped outside the door to her room. "You and the Dowager really hit it off."

I swallowed hard. "What? That? All part of the con."

She squinted at me. "Sure it was. G'night." And she slipped into her bedroom.

In my room, I changed into the silky nightshirt the servants had laid out for me and buried myself in the most comfortable bed I'd ever known. Lying there, I stared at the patterns the bright moonlight cast on the wall, unable to sleep.

I kept replaying my conversation with the Dowager in

my mind. I recalled how my chest tingled with excitement to be able to have a very serious discussion about plants and animals on a level that challenged me. Ma and Da had always listened politely when I'd talk about some exciting new book I'd read, trying to get them as enthused as I was about what I'd learned. But in the end, they'd smile and nod. The Dowager, however, listened *closely* to what I had to say and could respond in turn with something equally interesting. I loved it and it was obvious.

Pulling the blankets tighter to my chin, I wondered what tomorrow would hold. Would I be able to enjoy more conversations with the Dowager without feeling guilty, knowing how this had to end? Tonight it didn't matter. For the first time since I started doubting my abilities to continue in the family trade, I felt at home.

Looking back, it was probably that sense of satisfaction that made everything fall apart as badly as it did.

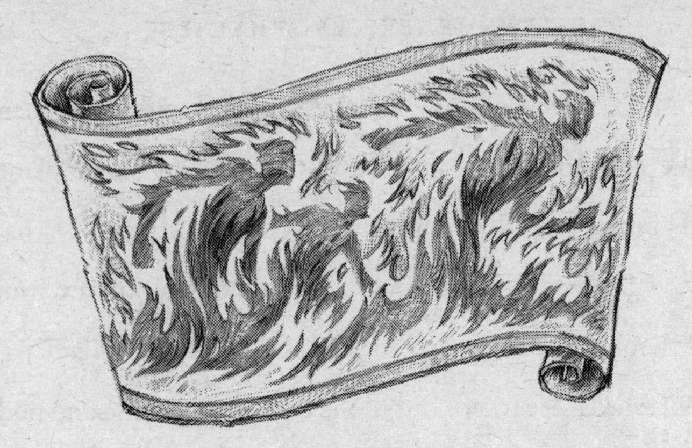

16

The Greenhouse

"The honor binding thieves
is colder than a gaoler's shackles."

—*The Lymmaris Creed*

Over the next two days, the Dowager never left my side. Each morning began with the four of us enjoying a hearty breakfast and the Dowager recommending several books I'd never heard of. Then, she would take me by the arm and lead me from the dining room, Edilman and Callie quietly following us at a polite distance.

The first day, she gave us a tour of the mansion. The third floor, like the foyer, was a mixture of opulent and odd.

The art gallery, featuring works by the most famous artists throughout the Provinces, was filled with more of the Dowager's experiments. Glass kettles, filled with multicolored water, hung from the ceiling by hooks. When you placed your finger in the water, the liquid emitted a hum. The pitch varied, depending on which color you touched. The Dowager proudly proclaimed it a "liquid organ." But she admitted that it wasn't very practical for musicians at present.

Next she showed us the ballroom. Sparkling chandeliers floated and twirled magically above. A copper-trimmed bandstand, covered with instruments just waiting for musicians to play, sat against the far wall. It would have all been very beautiful if it weren't for the towering mounds of sludge and dirt that covered the dance floor.

The Dowager reached into the sludge and pulled out what looked like a shining ruby the size of her fist. I'm sure Edilman nearly passed out. That ruby would probably pay for a ship of his very own to take him from the Provinces. But then the Dowager cracked the gem open on her knee, revealing a gooey, wormlike creature inside that squirmed in her hand.

"I'm breeding slithervox," she proclaimed. "Wonderful little things. They sing, you know."

As if to demonstrate, the newly hatched slithervox bleated a slow, eerie tune.

"Between them and the liquid organ," Edilman said, "you could start an orchestra."

He was being sarcastic, but the Dowager took in a short, sharp breath, as though the idea hadn't occurred to her . . . but she liked it. A lot.

We moved to the second floor and came to a darkened passage just down the hall from my room. I peered into the shaded corridor lit by enchanted candles emitting pale green-blue light. Stone statues representing honored generals of the Provincial Guard lined the narrow passage. The passage ended in a massive door covered in a series of locks and dials.

"How interesting," Edilman said, pushing the pince-nez closer to his eyes. "And what's down there?"

The Dowager waved her hand. "Nothing of interest. My vaults where I store valuables. It's not nearly as interesting as our next stop."

We moved along but not before Callie, Edilman, and I shared a knowing glance. We'd found one of our two objectives: the vaults. Now we had to locate the ingredients for the solvent that Edilman was so sure were here.

Continuing the tour, the Dowager led us to the mansion's library. I felt a tingle as we entered, like I was standing on hallowed ground. The tomes that lined the scores of bookshelves ranged from freshly bound and barely read to antiquated and crumbling but lovingly shelved. The Dowager glided from shelf to shelf with childlike excitement, reminding me of Aubrin weaving in and out of a crowd as she picked pockets.

I wiped the lenses of my glasses clean and sat with the Dowager as we paged through book after book. I have no idea when Edilman and Callie left us. I only know that one moment they were there and the next, it was the middle of the night and they were gone. The Dowager had dozed off. I helped her to her bedchamber, then slipped back to the library to continue reading.

At breakfast the second day, Callie and Edilman sat quietly by as the Dowager and I talked nonstop about aquatic life, geological formations, studies of the heavens, and other topics that went far beyond my simple love of magic-resistant plants. Whenever I could, I threw them a sympathetic look. But Edilman only ever responded with a touch to his temple. He understood. It was all for the con.

Later, after a stroll through the East Gardens, we sat down to a sumptuous dinner.

"What a bright boy Master Tyrius is," the Dowager remarked to Edilman for perhaps the fourth time that day. "When you return to the academy, you can be assured that I will be making a sizable donation toward its continued well-being."

Edilman bowed his head respectfully and I'm sure I caught him smiling to himself, no doubt thinking, *You certainly will, Dowager.*

As dinner finished, Edilman suggested we retire for the evening, but the Dowager took my arm. "You two go on ahead. I have something special to share with Master Tyrius."

Callie and Edilman bowed and exited as the Dowager took me through the kitchen to a door I'd never seen. We went down a long, well-lit corridor ending in a narrow spiral staircase. "Watch your step," the Dowager warned as she took a green-blue flame candle from the wall and led the way up. We climbed and climbed before coming to a closed door.

The Dowager produced a small key from a hidden pocket on her sleeve and we entered. The meager candlelight did little to tell me where we were. Handing the candle to me, the Dowager turned to the wall to our right, where I spotted a large wheel. Grabbing the wheel, the Dowager cranked it hard several times to the left.

As the wheel spun, I heard the clattering of metal above. Suddenly, a vertical slit of light appeared opposite us, high above the floor. The slit widened with every crank of the wheel, letting in the fading purple twilight. I could see now that we were in a large domed chamber, the dome opening as the Dowager continued to turn the wheel. In the center of the room stood a massive telescope.

The Dowager stopped turning the wheel and led me over to the telescope's base. My heart raced as I took it all in. Spinning some small wheels near the telescope's base, the Dowager bent over and peered into the eyepiece. Smiling, she stepped aside.

"Take a look."

Closing one eye, I peered in. I saw a small cluster of stars against the encroaching midnight-blue sky. It was the constellation Xaa, but I'd only ever seen it as a dim speck before. Here, in the telescope, it was huge and brilliant.

"Bangers," I whispered.

The Dowager nodded her approval and moved toward the slit in the dome. I followed her. From this height, we could see far across the forest-covered lands that surrounded Redvalor Castle. We stood at the railing and surveyed the grounds.

"I came to Redvalor Castle to research the natural world," the Dowager said in her lilting, dreamlike voice. "For the last five years, it's been absolute bliss."

The smile on her face slowly melted and her flittering eyes grew sad. "Do you know much about mag-plague, Tyrius?"

I knew it had wiped out Vengekeep's cattle several years ago, but beyond that, I knew little, so I shook my head.

The Dowager sighed. "When I was your age, I caught mag-plague. It's very nasty. They weren't sure I was going to live. But I persevered and I survived . . . at a cost." The regret in her voice hung heavy in the room. "You can recover from mag-plague, but it leaves you in poor health for the rest of your days. The life expectancy of a mag-plague survivor is quite a bit shorter than that of a healthy person."

She turned to me and her face became gentle again. "I've worked hard to do my research here and I don't like the thought of dying without someone to pass it on to. So I sent letters to some of the finest schools across the Five Provinces, searching for the knowledge hungry. Hoping to find someone who might serve as my intellectual heir, willing to carry on my studies once I'm gone."

A lump gathered in my throat, the cool night air adding to the chill I felt as I realized what she was saying. The Dowager laid her thin, bony hands on my shoulders.

"I think, Tyrius," she said with a smile, "that you might be the brilliant young mind I've been searching for."

My face smiled, but my gut sank. In the back of my mind, I heard Ma's lessons about not becoming emotionally attached to a mark. Over the past two days, I'd almost forgotten completely that our purpose in coming here had been to trick this woman. Now, as she sat here offering me a heartfelt confession, "Tyrius" was forced to beam while Jaxter tried not to throw up.

Unable to speak, I looked out over the grounds. As my gaze fell to the south, I stiffened and my jaw dropped. Below, I saw a long, large building with glass walls and ceiling. A soft white light flickered inside, making the glass sparkle. Even from up here, I could see the room was filled wall-to-wall with plants.

The Dowager gasped. "Of course! I can't believe you've been here two days and I haven't taken you to see the greenhouse. My pride and joy! Come."

She took my hand and we descended the spiral stairs.

I breathed in a deep lungful of sweet, earthy smell as the greenhouse door closed behind us. The damp air covered me like a shroud as the miniature jungle crowded the narrow footpaths. Magical white globes hovered in the corners, providing a nurturing light.

"There's no finer and more complete collection of rare

and unusual plants anywhere in the Five Provinces," the Dowager boasted, her arm sweeping the room. We strolled along, studying the unusual leaves and spotted-bark flora. Each individual plant bore a small copper plaque that identified it. I saw the aramon plant from which she harvested leaves to settle her upset stomach. I saw the plants that I kept in the pouches around my belt. I saw plants that I thought had gone extinct.

As we got midway through the greenhouse, I turned a corner and froze. A twisted mass of black leaves and vines jutted up out of a brown clay pot on the floor. A series of large purple, teardrop-shaped pods covered in bulbous, dark-ochre pustules poked out between the leaves. I swallowed and glanced down at the copper plaque.

Wraithweed.

As I reached out, the Dowager said, "Be careful. The pustules contain a very strong acid."

I nodded, pulling my hand back. After the spiderbat milk, that acid was the key to destroying the fateskein.

The Dowager had taken a small watering can from near the door and gave the wraithweed a healthy drink. "This may be one of the last remaining wraithweed plants. They used to grow plentifully in Jarron Province. Now they're dying out. A lot of magic-resistant plants have been dying out in recent years. I tried to tell my brother about it, hoping he would look into it and perhaps act to preserve what was left of them. But he's too busy with affairs of state and other meaningless jabber. . . ."

Guilty as I felt about betraying the Dowager, I had to think of Vengekeep's plight. I steeled my jaw, feeling for the first time in a long while that we might be able to pull this off. *We could save Vengekeep.*

"Tyrius," the Dowager said, shaking me from my reverie. I turned to see that sad, serious look back on her face. "I want you to consider what I've told you tonight. We're cut from the same cloth, you and I. If you accept, I would ask you to leave your studies with Professor Wenderkin and move into Redvalor Castle to apprentice under me."

As much as it pained me, I gave her a smile and said, "I—I'd like to think about it. May I?" The idea was tempting. But I was a Grimjinx. A thief. And even if I wanted to study with her, saving Vengekeep meant betraying the

Dowager. There could be no turning back.

She smiled warmly. "Of course. It's a big decision, I understand."

We said good night and when I returned to my room, my head spinning from all that she'd said, I found Callie and Edilman waiting for me.

"Look, Edilman," Callie said with a playful smirk, "he remembered we exist!"

"And he wants to talk to us," Edilman said, playing along. "I can only hope we're worthy."

"Very funny," I said, and they laughed. If nothing else, all my time with the Dowager had allowed the two of them to bond. I wasn't sure I liked that.

After making sure the door was secure, I told them everything the Dowager had said.

"Intellectual heir?" Callie asked. "What's that?"

"She wants me to carry on her research," I said. "I'd become her apprentice."

Edilman cleared his throat. "I think we've enjoyed the Dowager's hospitality for long enough. It's time we do what we came here to do. Tomorrow night, we strike."

We reviewed our plan. Callie would get the plants from the greenhouse. Edilman would pillage the vaults. And I'd keep the Dowager busy.

They left. I changed into my nightshirt and lay awake for much of the night. I focused on everything my parents had ever told me about pulling off a successful con. For years, I'd lived these lessons and, my clumsiness aside, helped them complete some of the greatest scams imaginable. That night, surrounded by the warmth of the down-stuffed blankets, I found it harder than ever to ignore perhaps the smartest par-Goblin saying I knew.

Think twice about the con, not the mark.

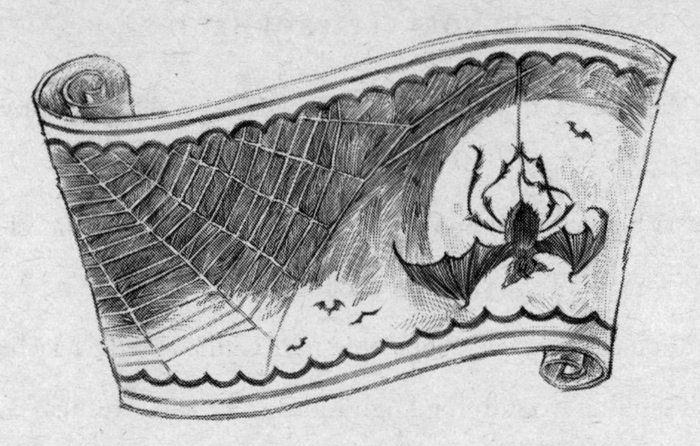

17

Escape from Redvalor Castle

"Proof should be as solid as a ripple in a pond."

—*The Lymmaris Creed*

The first sign that the day would end in disaster came at breakfast. As Callie, Edilman, and I sat at the dining room table, we couldn't help but notice the Dowager's absence. The grumbling mushrooms brought us plates of eggs and singebacon as Oxric entered.

"The Dowager sends her regrets and will not be joining you today," he announced. "She invites you to enjoy her continued hospitality and hopes that she'll be able to rejoin you tomorrow."

We nodded respectfully and hunched over our food once he left.

"What do you suppose that's all about?" I asked, shoveling a forkful of eggs into my mouth.

"You don't suppose she's onto us?" Callie asked. "Maybe she's sending word to the High Laird so he can arrest us."

Edilman shook his head. "She's got plenty of Provincial Guards staked out around the manor. If she wanted us arrested, she'd have them do it. She's probably just under the weather. Focus on what's good. We've got free rein today. Callie, I suggest you check out the greenhouse and find where all the plants you need are located. Will save you time searching for them later tonight."

I handed Callie the parchment with our list of ingredients. "Everything in the greenhouse is clearly labeled. Be careful near the wraithweed."

Edilman turned to me. "I'll watch the grounds, figure out the guards' patrol schedule. Jaxter, you've got the most important job. Keep an eye out, in case the Dowager decides to put in an appearance."

And that's how we spent the day. Callie took a walk

through the greenhouse, locating the position of each plant on our list. Edilman tracked the Provincial Guards, noting when they patrolled the perimeter. I spent my time wandering the halls, hoping for a sign of the Dowager.

But by sundown, we still hadn't seen her. After dinner, Callie, Edilman, and I met in my room. Edilman paced, clearly upset.

"We have to know where she is," he muttered. "We can't make a move unless we're sure her attention is elsewhere."

I balanced an unlit candle on the terrace railing outside my window. I looked down and found a perfect line of sight to the greenhouse. My lighting the candle later that night would signal Callie to leave the greenhouse and sneak over to our meeting place near the perimeter wall.

"I'll go find her," I said, turning to them. "I'll make sure things are clear for you to do your jobs."

Callie left for the greenhouse and Edilman made his way to the vaults. I ventured upstairs to the third floor and the Dowager's bedroom chambers. Taking a deep breath, I rapped on the door.

"Dowager?" I called softly. "Dowager Soranna? It's

Ja— Tyrius. I wanted to see if you were all right. We're all worried about you. Are you in there, Dowager?"

Silence. Just as I was about to descend the stairs, I heard the faint sound of music coming from the ballroom. I arrived to find the ballroom door ajar. Stepping inside, I spotted the Dowager sitting at a small table next to a mound of sludge. A large music box on the table, its lid open, played a haunting waltz. A glass and a half-empty bottle of ashwine sat near the Dowager. Her right hand swayed gently in time to the music, and as I got closer I noticed her face was stained with tears.

"Dowager?" I approached gingerly.

She made no sign that she'd seen me, just kept listening to the sad music. I knelt at her side and took her limp left hand in my own.

"We used to come here in the summer," she croaked in a voice much heavier than her usual airy tone. "My father—the *real* High Laird—brought us here. He taught me to dance in this room. I stood on his feet as a little girl. This music box would play and we'd dance."

As the crank on the music box slowed, so did the music.

The notes sounded far and few between. It was eerie. "I was meant to be High Laird, you know," she said, looking at me finally. This was the first time since our arrival that her usually manic eyes, glancing scattershot across the room, stayed focused on a single point. "I was the eldest child, and Father spent most of his life grooming me to succeed him. He indulged my need to know about the world, believing it would help me be a better High Laird, but he never took my studies seriously."

"What did you do?" I asked.

She reached over and closed the music box. "Oh, I thought about it. I thought about succeeding my father and starting a benevolent new regime, dedicated to education and inspiring others to learn. But then I realized that I'd be bogged down in the administration of it all. Others would be doing the research. Not me. I couldn't let that happen.

"So I went to my father on my eighteenth birthday and said, 'This isn't something that I *want* to do, but it's something I *have* to do.' He argued with me, right up until the day he died. And when that happened, I stepped aside and allowed my brother to become High Laird. To this day, I wonder how disappointed my father was. That I didn't follow in his footsteps."

That's when it hit me. The *real* reason I couldn't accept the Dowager's offer. It wasn't because I was a thief. It hurt to admit, but I was a *terrible* thief. I couldn't become the Dowager's apprentice because I was *sure* it would disappoint my family.

The Dowager squeezed my hand. "I don't regret it, Tyrius. I still believe there are things that you *have* to do, even if you don't *want* to. I didn't think I'd find someone like you. Other professors brought their students. I suspected some of them were frauds, merely posing as professors and students to gain the stipend I promised for a qualifying school."

I bit my lip.

"But you're the real thing," she said with a sigh, leaning back in her chair. "I hope you'll consider my offer, Tyrius. We're a rare breed, you and I. We're so much alike."

In that moment, I almost told her everything. My real name, the truth about why we were there. Everything. I reasoned she'd forgive our intent to rob her because she'd be more excited about the challenge of defeating the fateskein.

I imagined us working side by side in Vengekeep, experimenting to find the precise combination of ingredients for the solvent. I could picture us celebrating our success. And I *would* have told her everything—I'd even opened my mouth to speak—if it hadn't been for the howling.

The noise started low and ominous, like sick cattle. Then it rose in pitch to a mighty bellow that echoed down the corridors and across the foyer. The howling warbled, and I clenched my teeth to ward off the painful noise. In an instant, I knew what it was. A warncharm. Very powerful magic that acted as an alarm. Its tremulous volume could incapacitate would-be prowlers until help arrived.

I knew that Edilman had failed.

The Dowager was on her feet, her eyes going wild as she went to the door. "The warncharm. That's—that's coming from my vaults."

I stood as she turned to me. Looking past her at the mirrored wall, I saw the concern on my face, the doubt, the guilt. The Dowager took one look at me and instantly knew what was going on. Her face hardened, lined with betrayal. She backed away from me.

"Dowager," I pleaded, "I can explain—"

"Guards!" she screamed, running from the room. "Guards!" Once the door opened, the howls of the warncharm swallowed the Dowager's screams.

"Zoc!" I cried, bolting from the room. The Dowager had already disappeared down the stairs. I ran to my room on the second floor. Grabbing my pack, I paused only to light the candle in the window, and then went off in search of Edilman.

Dashing as fast as I could, I arrived at the entrance to the vault corridor. A wave of nausea came over me and I shoved my fingers in my ears to ward off the sound. The dim corridor lanterns flickered. I peered down and saw the vault door wide-open. A moment later, Edilman, his arms wrapped around a small wooden box pressed to his chest, charged from the vault.

As he passed the first pair of stone statues, an incandescent flash filled the corridor. Slowly, the statues moved, their heads turning to watch Edilman run away. Granite swords in hand, the statues stepped down from their plinths and lumbered after him.

Flash! Edilman passed the next pair of statues and they, too, stirred from their slumber, leaping to the ground, weapons raised. As Edilman passed each statue, another flash brought it to life until he had a small stone army in pursuit, silent except for the scraping of rock on marble.

As Edilman emerged from the corridor, a stone arrow whizzed past his head and sank deep into the banister along the landing. "Move!" he ordered, and we took off for the stairs. Down in the foyer, the front doors to the mansion flew open and a half-dozen members of the Provincial Guard stormed in, swords at the ready. We paused. To our right, the statues were closing in. The guards looked up, spotted us, and charged the stairs.

"Come on!" I shouted over the howling, tugging Edilman's arm and pulling him into my bedroom. Slamming the door, we threw our shoulders into moving the enormous bureau so it blocked the entry. A moment later, wood splintered as a mighty stone fist slammed into our barricade.

Edilman thrust the box he'd stolen into my arms and pulled two ropes and a large metal hook from his pack. Hastily, he wove one rope around me, tying the heavy box to my back. As a combination of living and stone warriors chopped at the door and bureau, he lashed the other rope and hook to the terrace railing and dropped it to the ground below.

I looked down. "Are you naff-nut? Edilman, I can't take two steps without tripping. You expect me to—"

A stone ax broke through the bureau, creating a hole through which stone arrows zipped. I ducked as Edilman grabbed the rope and jumped over the side. "It's do or die, Jaxter," he called, scaling down the side of the mansion.

"Why can't it ever be 'do and live'?" I muttered.

Certain I was about to die, I grabbed the rope, stepped over the terrace, and followed Edilman down. I teetered with the weight of the box pulling at my back. I slipped, the rope burning into my palms. Concentrating, I closed my eyes and continued down, hand over hand. I heard Edilman touch down, then cry, "Jaxter, look out!"

I looked up to see a stone archer statue on the balcony, taking aim at my head. I tried wiggling but couldn't fling myself out of the way. Just then, the statue with the stone ax brought his weapon down on the rope, severing it.

I fell the rest of the way into Edilman's arms and we tumbled to the ground together. Up on the balcony, we saw the statues regroup and bolt back into the room. On our feet, Edilman and I turned and ran across the grounds, hiding behind trees and hedges as best we could. The warncharm continued howling in the distance, growing fainter the farther we got from the mansion. Finally, we found ourselves at the perimeter wall near a giant glenoak, where Callie was waiting for us, torch in hand.

"I heard the howling before I saw the candle," she whispered. "What happened?"

"Slight complication," Edilman said breathlessly, staring up at the wall that stood between us and freedom.

"Did you get everything?" I asked, casting a glance back to the mansion. The Provincial Guards were searching the grounds.

Callie nodded. "Every ingredient. I could only fit two wraithweed pods in here. I hope it'll be enough." I hoped so too.

"At this point," Edilman said, "I'll entertain suggestions on what to do next."

Callie whirled on him. "What do you mean? You said you had rope we could use to scale the wall."

Edilman pointed to the balcony we'd just descended from. "We had to use it to escape. The hook's back there."

"Oh, great!" Callie growled, throwing her arms up. The sound of hedges being hacked to bits alerted us to the approach of the statues. I could only guess the living guards weren't far behind.

I ground my teeth. I had a way out, but it wouldn't be pretty. I handed the heavy box to Callie and gave her torch to Edilman. I took my belt off and emptied the contents of several pouches into a mound of powder and sap on the ground. I kneaded it all together with my hands.

"Those Sarosans really know their stuff," I muttered. "*The Kolohendriseenax Formulary* lists twelve magic-resistant plants. Did you know that there are four thousand and ninety-five ways to combine those twelve plants? Each combination does something different."

"Yeah, that's great," Edilman muttered. "Any chance that you're doing one of them to help us?"

"Grass, Callie," I whispered. "I need a tall blade of grass."

As Callie searched, I emptied my entire pouch full of flashballs into the gooey mess on the ground, mixing them in to give it all a lumpy texture. Then I gathered up the slime I'd created and smeared it in a large circle on the wall. "As a matter of fact, Edilman, yes!"

Callie returned with a medium-sized blade of grass—shorter than I wanted but it would have to do. I buried half of it into the goo, bending it upright so it stood perpendicular to the wall.

"Stand back," I warned, grabbing the torch from Edilman, who took Callie by the arm and led her a safe distance away. I cast a final glance over my shoulder to Redvalor Castle.

My eyes went directly to the observatory. There, silhouetted in the dome opening, I saw the Dowager's outline against the telescope. I forced myself to think about the danger my family was in. "I'm sorry," I whispered to no one.

In my head, it all made sense and worked brilliantly. I meant for the blade of grass to act as a fuse. I'd light it, head for cover, there'd be a massive explosion, and we'd run through the resulting hole. That's what would have happened if anyone else had tried this. Me? I reached forward to light the grass and touched the flames directly to my explosive goo by mistake.

The last thing I remembered was a deafening roar and a flash.

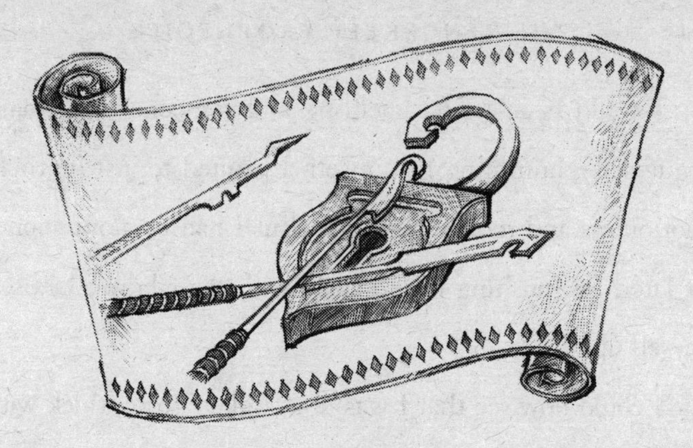

18

Trouble in Cindervale

"May your ironclad alibi never know
the corrosion of trust."

—*Ancient par-Goblin proverb*

My hands hurt. They hurt to move, flex, touch. My head was in no better shape. When I dared open my eyes, pain shot through my temples at the first sight of the soft morning light. I lay there, afraid that any other movement would be similarly punished. My only clues as to my location came from staring straight up into a thick cover of trees and from the rich aroma of roast gekbeak. We were in the forest.

I could hear a fire crackling and someone—Edilman, I guessed—humming to himself. I wanted to just lie there motionless and mostly pain free. But I had to move sooner or later. So, pushing back gently with my elbows, I raised myself up.

I could now see that I was in a sunken grove, thick with wide-bodied trees. Perrin, his head against his chest, slept on a tree branch above. My movement caught Edilman's attention. He crouched over a small fire, turning a slowly browning gekbeak on a makeshift spit. Smiling, he crawled to my side.

"Welcome back," he whispered, slipping my glasses up my nose. "Just in time for breakfast."

"Morning," I grumbled, and then winced. Even talking hurt. "Any sign of the guards?"

Edilman cocked his head. "No, I imagine they've given up trying to find us by now."

I tried to chuckle, but it came out as a cough. "Not very persistent, giving up after a night."

Edilman rubbed his chin, a look of uncertainty crossing his face. "Jaxter, you've been unconscious for nearly four days."

Stunned, my hands dropped, hitting the ground. Pain shot up my arms and made me see white for a moment. I looked down. From my wrists to my fingertips, my hands were wrapped in tattered strips of cloth. I knew immediately what had happened. I'd used my hands to smear the explosive goo on the wall and when the wall exploded, the residual gunk on my hands must have caught fire.

I looked around for my belt and pouches, hoping to make a burn ointment to relieve the pain. I spotted the pouches, empty, near the fire. I remembered using nearly everything I had to blow an exit hole in the wall. I didn't have what I needed for the ointment. Groaning, I examined the improvised bandages closer: a pale tan weave with red and blue accents. It took me a moment to realize they were torn from Callie's dress.

"Callie!" I ignored the pain as my head spun. I searched for a sign of her, afraid she'd also been injured in the explosion. Edilman laid a calming hand on my shoulder.

"She's fine," he assured me. "There's a small village not far from here called Cindervale. We wanted to lie low for a few days or we would have taken you to a healer. We've been taking turns nipping into town and swiping medicine from the apothecary. She should be back soon."

I smacked my dry lips. Edilman helped me drink from my flagon, then unscrolled my map of the Five Provinces and indicated Cindervale. "Quiet little town. Often a haven for thieves. Now that you're awake, we can get rooms at the inn, blend in quietly, and I can sell a few of these." He pointed to the box he'd stolen from the vaults, now open to reveal a mound of assorted jewels that sparkled in the morning sun. "I can get more than enough to hire us two coaches."

"Two?" I asked.

He nodded. "One to take you and Callie back to Vengekeep, the other to take me to Port Scaldhaven, where my boat is waiting. A deal's a deal."

I studied the map. Cindervale was on the border of Yonick Province. Just over the border were the aircaves, home of the spiderbats. Provided everything in Callie's pack had survived the explosion, we had all the components for the solvent. Except the essential spiderbat's milk. We were now closer than ever to succeeding.

Edilman added twigs to his dwindling fire. "You know,

Jaxter," he said, "I've stuck to the Creed and I haven't pushed you about what you and Callie are doing out here, scavenging for strange plants, so far from Vengekeep. What you need those plants for is your business, but I'm guessing it's not for a school project. You know you don't have to say anything, but since I'll be leaving the Provinces soon, I don't suppose you'd care to tell me what this little adventure was all about?"

I leaned forward and shifted to a kneeling position. Edilman had done exactly what he'd promised: he'd helped us get everything on our list. He'd earned the right to know exactly what was going on. So, taking a deep breath, I told him the whole story: fateskein, quarantine, and all. I explained my plan to make a solvent and how the plants we'd taken from the Dowager would help.

It was on the tip of my tongue to tell him about the spiderbat's milk, but I stopped. I guessed that he'd insist on accompanying us to the aircaves to acquire the milk. But this wasn't his fight. It was mine. Callie and I had to see this through, and the longer he stayed in the Provinces, the more danger he was in. I wasn't ready to risk that. It was better to let him catch his boat while Callie and I finished what we'd started.

He listened to my story with rapt attention and bowed his head humbly when I was done. "I'm honored that you chose to trust me. And I'm proud of you, taking on this challenge by yourselves. Are you sure I can't come with you to Vengekeep to make sure you get back safe—?"

"No!" I said. "You've done more than enough already, Edilman. It's too risky to come to Vengekeep. Callie and I will be fine."

He sighed and clicked his tongue. Perrin woke instantly and came to his master's shoulder. Edilman fed the bird a stickworm he'd plucked from the ground. "Quite a team you two make. Reminds me of me and your da. I only wish I could see the hero's welcome that awaits when you return to Vengekeep."

"Oya!"

Before I could react, Callie bounded through the forest, threw herself down next to me, and wrapped her arms around my neck. I gritted my teeth to keep from screaming in pain.

When she pulled back, she was scowling. "Four days, you naff-nut! Four days of forcing soup down your throat. I thought you were dead!"

I smiled weakly. "The way I feel, I kind of wish I was."

She shook her head. "That's nothing compared to how you look. Dr. Callie prescribes no mirrors for you for a few more days."

How kind.

She pulled her pack off her shoulder, dug around inside, and pulled out a small glass jar filled with a viscous, yellow slime. The label read "Essence of Yaiobean."

"Compliments of Cindervale's apothecary. Let's see those hands." She gently unwrapped my bandages.

Underneath, my palms were charred and red. The cool morning air stung the raw flesh, and I took in a quick breath to ease the pain. Callie did her best to be careful, but tears ran down my face as she applied the soothing salve. Edilman served up his gekbeak for breakfast as Callie removed what remained of her dress from her pack and tore it into long strips to make fresh bandages.

"You wanted to know why I brought a dress," she said,

her eyebrows raised mischievously. “Because I hate this ugly thing and this is *exactly* what I hoped we’d use it for.”

They took turns—Callie feeding me a forkful of gekbeak, Edilman holding the flagon for me as I drank—and with a little food in my belly, we were ready to break camp. They led me out of the grove to a winding dirt road, where we headed north.

Trudging along, I took my mind off the pain in my hands by trying to calculate the right amount of each of the ingredients. Although we had almost everything we needed, making the solvent would still be difficult. My mind flashed to the Dowager. I bet together we would have come up with exactly the right formula.

As we rounded a bend in the road and saw the edge of town, Edilman handed what little money we had left to Callie.

“Staying together helped us in the past,” he said, “but it’s too dangerous now. If the Dowager sent out a warning, they’ll be looking for a man with two kids. Best split up and regroup later. There’s a small inn on the north side of town called the Wily Leathersmith. Kind of a shady place. They won't think anything of two kids showing up and booking three rooms. Get us set up there."

"Where are you going?" Callie asked.

"I'm going to find the livery stable and hire the coaches we need to go our separate ways," he said, flashing a handful of jewels. "Go on now. I'll meet you in the pub next to the Leathersmith in a while."

Callie shook Edilman's hand, and together she and I headed down the path toward town. Cindervale was so small I was afraid two strangers would attract attention, especially one who—according to reports—looked very much the victim of an explosion. But no one paid us any mind as we wandered the streets. We kept watch for those wanted posters with our poorly drawn faces but saw none. Everyone was going about their business.

"Don't mind if anyone stares," she said matter-of-factly. "It's probably just the large, scabby gash on your forehead."

"Swell," I said. "I hope the rock that hit me at least split in two."

Callie laughed. "I think the score stands: Exploding Wall, one, Jaxter Grimjinx, nil."

We stopped at a fountain and Callie knelt to refill our flagons. "I have to say," she muttered, "I was impressed with Edilman. After the wall exploded and you were thrown back, he had this look of panic on his face. I expected him to bolt and leave us both behind. But he didn't hesitate. He buried your hands in dirt to put out the fire, then slung you over his shoulder and led me through the smoke. He really came through for us, Jaxter. I was wrong about him."

"He came through for us twice," I reminded her. "If he hadn't known about the greenhouse at Redvalor, we'd still be plodding around the Provinces, trying to find everything."

"So," Callie said slowly, "are you going to miss the Dowager?"

I gnawed on my lower lip and looked down at my feet.

"Come on, Jaxter," she said, "admit it. All that talking you two did . . . That wasn't just a con, was it?"

I hated being so transparent. "Sure, I enjoyed talking to her. I enjoyed talking about something other than how to break into a vault or the proper way to distract a mark for a change. So? Is it important?"

Callie hooked her arm around mine. "I dunno. You tell me. Is it?"

We walked on quietly. Mainly because I didn't have an answer. At least not one I was ready to admit.

We found the Wily Leathersmith along the northern border of the town. The innkeeper, a dour looking par-Goblin, stood on a stool behind the inn's registration desk. Half my height and plump, his moist green-gray skin glistened as he turned to look at us. The pointed tips of his hairy, slender ears reached up over his head, while the lobes drooped below his chin. Under his lower lip, he sported a pool of excess saliva, which his tongue occasionally flicked out to lap up.

He didn't so much as blink at two kids hiring three rooms, just as Edilman had predicted. We ran upstairs, stowed our stuff in our rooms, then headed out into the street to the pub next door.

Hundreds of antlers hung from the pub's ceiling, some sporting candles, but most just as thorny decorations. We made our way through the crowd to a small table in the corner from which we could keep an eye on the door. The only strange look we got was from the barmaid, who raised an eyebrow when we each ordered mangmilk. Apparently, she didn't get a lot of orders for mangmilk.

The patrons, a mix of burly men and rowdy women, fixed their attention on a small alcove near the window. A petite blond woman in a leather tunic and matching breeches strummed a niolyre and sang in one of the most gorgeous voices I'd ever heard. As Callie helped me drink my mangmilk, we listened to the bard tell stories of happenings from across the Provinces. We froze in place as her song turned somber and she sang of Vengekeep.

According to her song, two more disasters had recently struck our hometown: an infestation of vessapedes and a massive earthquake that had produced no magma men but had collapsed most of the buildings on the town's west side. When she finished the dirge, the crowd erupted in applause, showering her with copperbits and the occasional bronzemerk. Callie and I drank our mangmilk in silence, our thoughts far away with the families we'd left to deal with the aftermath.

I pulled out the Provinces map and showed Callie our

location in relation to the aircaves. "We've got a week until mooncrux. It'll take us a day to get to the aircaves, get the spiderbat milk, and then a day back to here. Then we use the carriage Edilman's hiring for us to get back to Vengekeep."

"Will we make it back in time?"

"It'll be close."

Really, it would be *very* close. And we both knew it.

"Jaxter," Callie whispered urgently. I looked up, following her wide-eyed gaze to the door. The patrons of the pub had fallen silent as a group of men wearing light armor and brandishing swords entered. Their patchwork leather armor suggested that they were members of the local constabulary. They surveyed the room before resting their eyes on us. I felt Callie's hand close on my forearm under the table as they surrounded us, weapons raised.

"You have been accused of fleeing the cursed town-state of Vengekeep," one of the men barked at us. "You are under arrest!"

19

The Missing Mage

"Investing in luck squanders skill."

—Ancient par-Goblin proverb

I actually found myself wishing for the gaol back in Vengekeep. Much cleaner, less stinky, and far more comfortable. The cell they threw Callie and me into stank of rotting hay and the ghostly odor of past, unbathed inmates. The only other occupant sat huddled in the corner, shrouded in layered black clothes. His or her shaggy head fell forward limply, and we weren't entirely convinced he or she wasn't dead.

As the door slammed shut behind us, my hand went to

my belt and pouches. Which were no longer there, having been confiscated on the way in. It wouldn't have mattered. I'd used up nearly all my supplies making the explosive that freed us from the Dowager's compound. Escape would have to wait.

"I don't know how the law works here," Callie shouted at the back of the departing constable, "but they don't lock up children where we come from!"

"Oh, yes, they do," I corrected.

Callie paced. "How did they know? There's no way they could tell just by looking at us!"

I sat on a broken bench near the cell's third occupant. "Relax," I said. "We won't be here long."

Callie grabbed the closed door and gave it a good yank. "Unless you've got a key, I beg to differ."

I sighed. "When Edilman can't find us at the pub, he'll follow standard protocol."

Grumbling, Callie leaned her back against the bars. "And what's 'standard protocol'?"

I glanced at our cell mate, who had not moved. From time to time, gaolers left snitches disguised as prisoners in cells, hoping to get information. I looked for signs that this person was a mite too eager to hear our conversation. Seeing none—in fact, seeing no sign that this person was alive—I continued.

"It's in the Lymmaris Creed," I said simply. "When someone you're supposed to meet up with goes missing, first thing you do is check out the local gaol. Edilman's probably on his way here now."

"How's he going to get us out?" she asked. "They think we're cursed. The constable probably plans on shipping us right back to Vengekeep."

"Vengekeep?"

The gravelly voice came from the dark figure sitting in the corner. He shifted and, for a moment, I worried we had an informant on our hands after all. He raised his head, peering out through curly black bangs that masked his eyes.

"Did you say you came from Vengekeep?" he asked.

Callie and I looked at each other. When the guards arrested us, we'd denied up and down that we had anything to do with our hometown. We claimed to be tourists from Tarana Province, just back from an expedition to the aircaves. Our lack of spelunking equipment must have given us away because they escorted us directly here. If this was an informant, it wouldn't do us any good to admit anything.

Then Callie's eyes narrowed, staring at our cell mate. She knelt down and her face brightened slightly. "Talian?"

The young man reached up and parted the curtain of hair in front of his face. A memory flashed in my mind. I'd seen Talian, Lotha's apprentice, around Vengekeep. He was bright-eyed, friendly. But the person in front of us was sallow skinned with a haunted face, looking much older than his eighteen years.

Talian cocked his head and peered back. "Callie?" The two cousins met in the middle of the cell and hugged.

"The town's been worried to death about you," Callie said, pulling back and smiling. "You were expected in Vengekeep weeks ago." She looked him up and down. His sooty, ragged clothes hardly befit a newly appointed town mage. "Last we heard, you'd completed the Trials and were being sent to help us with our little . . . problem."

Talian looked away, clasping his hands behind his back. "Yes. Well. I got . . . diverted."

A thought occurred to me. "This is bangers!" I told Callie, jerking my thumb at Talian. "We've got a mage on our side. Even if Edilman can't find us, Talian can get us out of here."

Callie reached out and gripped her cousin's arm. "Jaxter's right. You can help us. We have to go to the aircaves and then return to Vengekeep."

Talian scoffed. "Haven't you heard? The High Laird's quarantined the whole town-state. No one gets in or out."

"We got out," I said. "And we can get back in."

Talian regarded us both. Then he quietly returned to his corner and sank down, bowing his head again. "Well, good luck to you. I won't be going."

Callie looked to me, then at her cousin. "But . . . why, Talian? Vengekeep's been without a mage for months. You're not worried about the 'curse,' are you? Because, there's not really—"

Talian laughed grimly. "Curse? Hardly. There's no curse on Vengekeep."

I folded my arms. "How do you know that?"

Talian grinned up at us cynically. "Curses are strong,

potent magic. Hard to break. But they're localized. You can curse a person; you can curse an object. The most powerful curse on record occupied a small house. There's no way to muster the energy to curse an entire town. Anyone at the Palatinate will tell you that."

Callie sat next to me on the bench. "But then why would the Palatinate tell the High Laird it was a curse?"

Talian shook his head. "They didn't. Not really, anyway. The Lordcourt danced around an explanation when the High Laird asked for one. They let him *infer* it was a curse without actually saying it."

"That doesn't answer the question," I noted. "Why would they do that? Why let the High Laird send most of his troops to keep Vengekeep sequestered?" To surround the whole of Vengekeep must have taken nearly the whole Provincial Guard. Much of the Five Provinces was unprotected because of what the High Laird believed.

Talian shrugged. "The Lordcourt doesn't take the High Laird seriously. Most of them see him as a buffoon. They enjoy watching the High Laird stumble over himself."

Outraged, Callie was on her feet again. "This is a joke to

them? Curse or not, Vengekeep is in danger. The Palatinate could put an end to it. Instead, they're tucked away in their palace, laughing at the High Laird? People could die."

Talian wrapped his arms around his chest and hugged himself. "Well. Strictly speaking, the Palatinate *did* try to put an end to it."

"How?" Callie demanded.

Talian pointed to his own chest. "They sent me. I finished the Trials and they said, 'By the way, some sort of magic is attacking Vengekeep. Go look into that, would you?' Gave me a mang and sent me on my way."

The three of us sat there silently. Callie stared hard at the floor, her fists tightening. I knew she didn't want to ask the next logical question, so I made it easy on her and asked myself.

"So what happened?" I whispered.

Again, Talian offered his haunted grin. "I was halfway to Vengekeep, thinking of everything I'd heard about the terrible things happening there, and I said to myself, 'What are you doing?' The Palatinate wasn't even willing to send a more accomplished mage with me to investigate.

If they didn't care what was happening in Vengekeep, why should I?"

Callie clapped a hand to her mouth, her eyes brimming with tears.

Talian leaned back. "So I came to Cindervale instead. Got myself a job working at the docks, repairing boats. Things were going pretty well until the Palatinate figured out I'd abandoned my duty. They covered the Provinces in wanted posters. Somebody recognized me and the constable showed up at my door. Right now, a messenger is on her way to report me. Within minutes of delivering her message, the Lordcourt will retrieve me and then I'll be facing Palatinate justice."

Before I could stop her, Callie lashed out, swiping her hand across her cousin's face. Talian yowled, his hand covering the bloody streaks Callie's nails had left behind.

"You traitor!" she screamed. "You coward! I looked up to you. I was proud when you were selected to be the town mage's apprentice. Everyone in Vengekeep was praying you'd come back and sort this mess out and instead you abandoned us!"

Callie turned and ran to the opposite corner of the cell, sobbing quietly to herself. I put a gentle hand on her shoulder as Talian, stunned by the violent attack, wiped his face clean.

"You're a mage," I said quietly. "What do you know about fateskein?"

Talian looked at me curiously. "What?"

"Are you powerful enough to counteract the effects of fateskein?" I asked harshly as Callie continued to sob.

"You shouldn't be messing with—"

"Just answer his question!" Callie said, her back still to her cousin.

Talian shook his head. "It would take several mages working for days to counteract anything that fateskein set into motion. Why are you—?" He stopped. Realization spread across his face. "Of course! Fateskein. That explains everything about Vengekeep. I can't believe no one at the Palatinate came up with that! But how did it happen?"

For the second time that day, I reluctantly relayed the story of the tapestry, my plan to create the solvent, and everything that Callie and I had been through since escaping from

Vengekeep. Talian nodded as I spoke, stroking the stubble on his cleft chin.

"Brilliant plan, Jaxter," he muttered, admiration coloring his voice. "I don't think anyone in the Palatinate could have come up with something like that. A nonmagical remedy. Bangers!"

By now, Callie had stopped crying. She turned back and glared at her cousin. "You can't breathe a word of this to anyone. If anyone finds out, Jaxter's parents will be—"

"I know the punishment for using fateskein," he said gently. "I won't tell anyone. I promise. And if you succeed with what you're planning, you won't have to tell anyone either. The tapestry can be destroyed, Vengekeep will be saved, and no one will be any wiser."

"There's just one problem," I noted, pointing to the bars. "We might be headed home sooner than we thought."

Talian shook his head glumly. "I wouldn't worry about that. The people of Cindervale are terribly superstitious. If they think you're cursed, they won't go through the trouble of shipping you back to Vengekeep. They'll want to make sure you don't spread the curse. The constable's probably having a magistrate sign the execution order right now."

Callie looked horrified. A small part of me got excited, thinking I would add another execution order to our family collection.

"Even if we could get out of here," Callie said, "we still need the last ingredient for the solvent."

Talian closed his eyes and laughed. "Spiderbat milk. Again, Jaxter, you are a genius."

Callie seethed. "If you want to be useful, maybe you could suggest how we might get out of this."

"Yeah," I said, "I don't suppose they let you keep your spellbook when they locked you up in here."

At this, Talian raised his eyebrows rakishly. He gave a quick glance around to make sure no guards were about. Then he said quietly, "If you get out of here, you're going to find the spiderbat milk and save Vengekeep, right?"

Callie and I nodded. Talian yanked at the hem of his tunic until it tore and an iron ball the size of marble fell out, clicking as it hit the stone floor. He picked it up and held it in the palm of his hand.

"It's a spellsphere," he said. He uttered something in a language I didn't understand. A small fire lit up within the steel, causing the entire ball to burn with a hot, white-blue light. Callie leaned forward, her pupils shrinking as she stared into the heart of the light. But I noticed that when Talian stared into it, his pupils grew larger, obscuring the green of his eyes.

"I don't see anything," Callie muttered.

"*You* don't see anything," Talian said, "but *I* see all the spells I've learned since my first day as an apprentice, whirling around in there. Only old-fashioned mages keep spellbooks anymore. Today, most mages use a spellsphere to hold the sum of their magical knowledge. I sewed it up in my tunic when I first came to town. I knew if I used it, the Palatinate Sentinels would be able to track me down. Well, they're about to find out where I am, so using it can't hurt anymore."

The Sentinels were elite mages, trained to find rogue mages and illegal magic use. Everything I'd heard suggested these were mages we didn't want to find us. Talian stared deeply into the glowing ball, his lips moving. I didn't want to interrupt his concentration, but I had to ask.

"Talian," I said, "it's great that you're going to help us get out, but what are *you* going to do?"

His eyes remained fixed on the scorching light, and for a moment I wasn't sure he'd heard me. Then he said, "I'll face the Palatinate. Don't have much choice."

I took a deep breath. "No. Come with us."

Callie's jaw dropped and even Talian looked away from the sphere.

"Jaxter—" Callie cautioned.

"Listen," I said, "he can go with Edilman. They can both sail off on the boat and leave the Five Provinces. I agree. He's a coward." Talian blanched at this. "But if he can get us out of here, the least we can do is send him off with Edilman. He may have left Vengekeep to rot, but I've heard stories about 'Palatinate justice.' It's horrible. We can't leave him to face that."

Callie bit her lip, then gave a single nod. I asked Talian, "Will you come?"

Talian flushed but agreed. "It could be dangerous for you," he warned. "The Sentinels have been waiting for me to cast a spell since I went rogue. As soon as I do, it won't take them long to trace the magic here. If they catch you helping me . . ."

"We'll stay hidden," I promised.

Talian stared into the sphere, looking for the right spell. When he found it, he cried out.

He pointed to the wall at our backs. "Behind this wall is an alley. I'm going to remove part of the wall, we'll go through, and we'll find your friend."

I remembered how I'd managed to get through the wall at the Dowager's estate. "It won't be, you know, loud, right? Something to attract the guards?"

He shook his head. "Completely silent. We'll slip away unnoticed. Ready?"

Callie and I prepared to run as soon as the hole appeared. Talian held the sphere out at arm's length and hissed in that unfamiliar language. The sphere pulsed, sending a cone of bluish light into the wall. The bricks shimmered, and when the light from the sphere vanished, a perfectly round hole had punctured the wall.

But Talian had been wrong. Behind that wall wasn't an

alley. It was the chief constable's office. And we stood there, looking blankly at the constable and his officers as they stared in amazement at us, no one moving.

"Always had a lousy sense of direction," Talian muttered.

20

Double Cross

"The unknown thief revels in her cash. The known thief basks in her cunning. Only one will buy food."

—*Lyama Grimjinx, Master Thief of Jarron Province*

Talian gathered his wits first. As he hissed another command, the cone of light shot from the sphere again, replacing the missing section of wall. Whirling around, Talian barked another magical command. This time, a torrent of green lightning shot from the sphere, melting the bars and tearing down the wall beyond. The hole led to a street full of confused citizens, who quickly gathered around.

Callie grabbed my arm as we ran out with Talian leading the way. "We do like our spectacular exits, don't we?" she said. Ducking into the assembled crowd, we could hear the constabulary mobilizing behind us. We kept our heads low as we dove down a side street.

"We need to go to the Wily Leathersmith," I told Talian, who guided us on a zigzag path through the village streets. The mage nodded and took a sharp right. Callie and I kept an eye behind us, searching for signs of pursuit.

The chaos was behind us, but Cindervale was small. It wouldn't take long for the constable and his deputies to track us down. Talian led us up a side street that intersected with the inn. We slipped around to the back and darted through the rear entrance. The par-Goblin innkeeper was spit-cleaning his countertop as we came in.

"Excuse me," I said breathlessly, "did our friend show up for the third room yet?"

The innkeeper paused to think. "Skinny guy? Yonick accent?"

I nodded. "That's him."

The innkeeper pointed upstairs. "Came a while ago."

I thanked him and the three of us darted upstairs. Callie and I each went into our rooms to grab our things as Talian stood near a window, watching for signs of the approaching law. I threw my pack over my shoulder, feeling naked without my belt and pouches, now forever in possession of the Cindervale constable. I was just about ready when I heard Callie cry out. Talian and I met her in the hall outside her room.

"My pack!" she said, pointing to the room. "It's gone!"

I peered inside her room. The entire place had been ransacked; bed overturned, sheets askew.

"I hid it in the closet and now . . . ," she said.

"Zoc!" I cursed and pounded on Edilman's door. "Edilman? We've got trouble. The ingredients are gone." When he didn't respond, I opened the door. The room was immaculate, with no sign of his gear anywhere.

"Callie," Talian yelled, pointing out the window. "Village guards!"

The innkeeper had said Edilman was here. So where . . . ? A dark thought formed in my mind. I understood what had happened. Sadly, we didn't have time to do anything about it. "Come on," I ordered them. We bounded down the stairs to find the innkeeper also eyeing the approaching guards out his window.

I took a chance. "*Klaeva surrin ta noda?*"

The par-Goblin frowned and I worried that my accent was really bad. But, as I suspected, he understood my plea for assistance in escaping unseen—which meant he was a fellow thief.

The innkeeper scurried across the room and bolted the door shut. He nodded toward a rack displaying ancient halberds on the wall. "There," he grunted. "Down the stairs, through the tunnel. Go."

I pushed against the rack and found a secret door beyond. As the village guards began pounding on the inn's door, I ushered Callie and Talian into the dark compartment beyond, sliding the rack closed behind us. Talian spoke and his spellsphere started to glow, lighting our path. We took the creaky stairs down to a musty, hand-dug tunnel, reminding me instantly of our initial escape from Vengekeep. At top speed, we ran down the tunnel, unsure if the guards would find us.

The tunnel was a straight shot under the village, and, as the innkeeper had promised, ended in another hidden door near the city docks on the River Honnu. Once outside, Talian led the way.

"Come with me," he said, and we followed closely, trying our best not to look conspicuous. Talian led us up the gangplank of a small sailing ship. Once on board, he looked around and then took us belowdecks, where we hid among burlap bags that smelled of burr oats.

"In about an hour," Talian whispered, "this ship will sail north into Yonick Province and dock near Merriton."

"How do you know?" Callie asked.

"I've worked on these docks for weeks. I know that this ship goes there every day." He looked to me. "Didn't you say you needed to get to the aircaves?"

I nodded, but Callie continued to fume.

"We can't go too far," Callie cautioned. "We have to find Edilman—"

"We're not going to find Edilman," I said quietly. "He's the one who turned us in."

Callie stared at me, slack-jawed. I thought back to the innkeeper, telling us he'd seen Edilman and I remembered how Edilman's room had been untouched. He'd never gone in there. He'd gone into Callie's room instead.

I nodded. "I keep thinking about something Edilman said. Only a pardon from the High Laird can reverse his death sentence."

Callie and Talian looked at me, brows furrowed in frustration, and I had to come clean.

"I told him everything, Callie," I said. "About the tapestry, how we were going to use the plants for the solvent."

Callie stiffened. "He's going to try to make the solvent himself and save Vengekeep. He wants to earn the High Laird's favor and get his death sentence removed."

"And he couldn't let us take the credit," I added. "So he tipped off the constabulary that two refugees from Vengekeep were roaming the town. With us out of the way, he walked into the inn and—"

Callie's balled-up fists slammed into the wall. "But he has no idea what he's doing! He'll waste all the ingredients. And he doesn't even have the spiderbat's milk!"

I nodded, glad I'd never revealed the secret to the last, vital ingredient. "And that's how we're going to beat him at his own game."

I took out the map of the Five Provinces and pointed out our position. "Listen, once we dock, we're less than half a day's journey to the aircaves. All we have to do is head north, obtain the milk, and come back. He's only got a day's head start. We just have to find a way to return to Vengekeep ahead of him. We surprise him and steal back the satchel with the ingredients. Then, well, we deal with the tapestry."

Callie's lip curled with skepticism. "'All we have to do is get the milk?'" she said. "That's always been the hardest part of this entire plan. It could take forever. Let's face it. We're finished."

I hated to admit it, but she was right. It all *sounded* simple, but it wouldn't be quick and easy. By the time we devised a plan to get the milk, Edilman could go to Vengekeep and waste the ingredients, trying to make the solvent himself. Without the ingredients, Vengekeep was doomed. For the first time since we started this trip, I believed we were finally defeated.

"Actually," Talian whispered, laying his finger on the aircaves as represented on the map, "I might be able to help you out there."

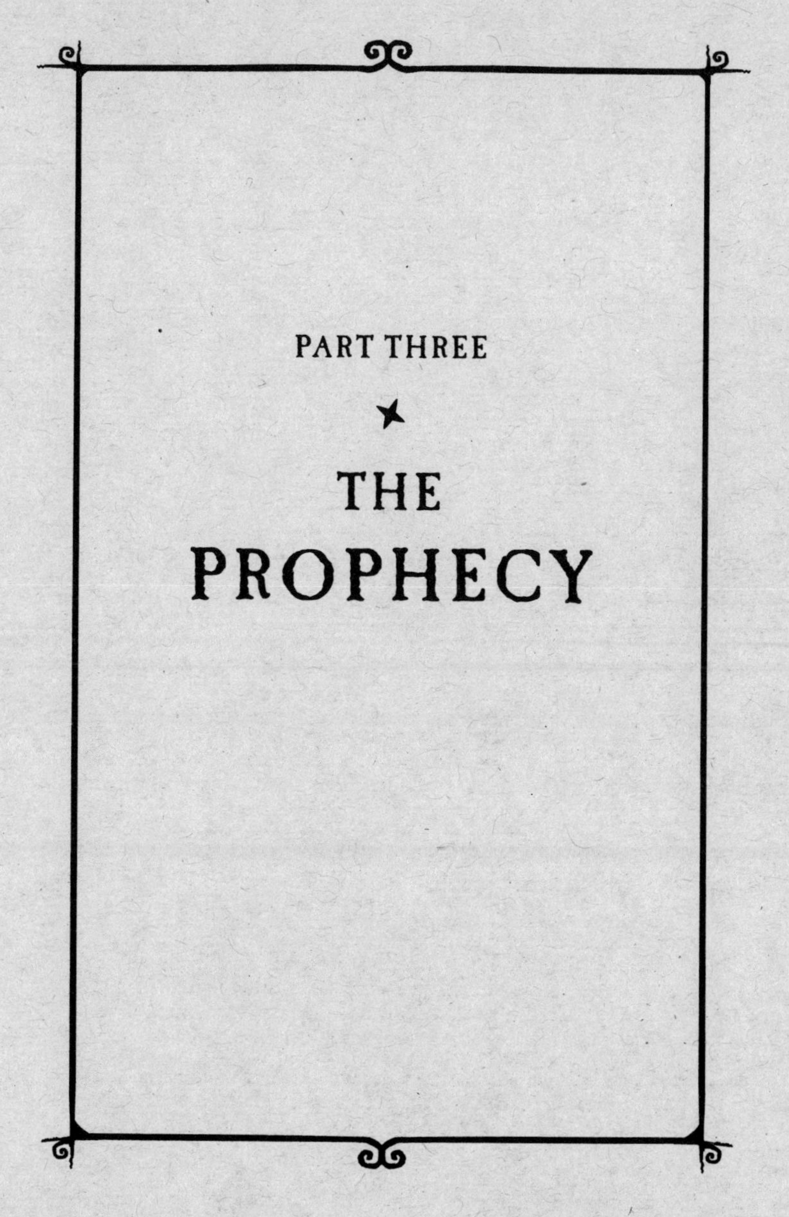

PART THREE

THE PROPHECY

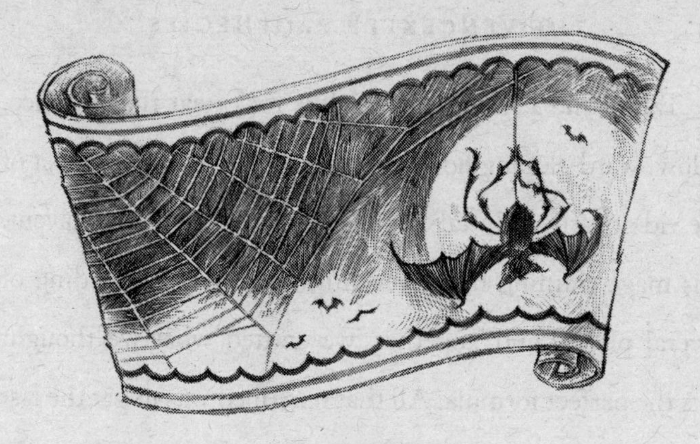

21

The Aircaves

"An alibi is worth its weight in copperbits, but a bag of silvernibs makes it worthless."

—*The Lymmaris Creed*

The aircaves were all that remained of a massive volcano that exploded thousands of years ago. The area where the mountain once stood was flat, made of smooth, glasslike obsidian. The aircaves got their name from the torrents of hot air rushing through the caves that had once fed magma to the volcano. Many people would visit the mouth of the caves just to see the beauty of the flawless obsidian cascades. But we were going one step farther: into the caves themselves.

Talian and I sat on a bubblelike rock near the entrance, a downward-sloping hole in the ground. We'd spent most of the ride on the ship talking over how to make the solvent. His mage training had given him a wide understanding of several plants, and, together, we crafted what we thought was the perfect formula. All that remained was to get the last ingredient, retrieve Callie's pack from Edilman, and destroy the tapestry.

Easy.

Ha.

Talian and I drank heavily from my water-filled flagon as Callie sat nearby, holding her stomach and looking very, very ill. Her face had gone a bit green and she tried very hard not to let her teeth chatter. I offered her water, but she shook her head.

"Are you going to be okay to do this?" I asked, afraid of what might come out if she opened her mouth.

She fixed me with a murderous glare. "Jaxter, here's something you should know about me. I don't like spiders. I don't like bats. Now . . . *guess how I feel about spiderbats*!"

I looked at Talian, who simply grinned, and I said to

Callie, "You knew we'd eventually come here."

She tossed up her arms. "Yes, but I've been hoping that when we arrived, *you'd* take care of this part." She pivoted to stare at her cousin. "I didn't realize that *I'd* be important to the plan."

Talian shrugged, setting his water aside. "The spiderbats live in a matriarchy. They'll respond better to a female."

In what little I'd read about spiderbats, none of the books mentioned one very important fact: spiderbats were intelligent. Thankfully, in addition to studying botany, apprentice mages spent years of intense study on magic-resistant creatures, and Talian knew a lot about how to interact with spiderbats. Although, when Callie wasn't listening, he'd quietly admitted to me that everything he knew was theory; he'd never had the chance to try any of it. We decided that Callie was better off not knowing that part.

Talian stood and walked carefully across the slick obsidian. "Everything will be fine." He held out his spellsphere. "Jaxter and I will be nearby. Just speak and the spellsphere will translate into the spiderbats' tongue. It'll appear as though the words are coming directly from you. They'll consider it a great honor that you speak their language."

Callie eyed the spellsphere dubiously. "It's that simple?"

Talian considered for a moment, then did something terrible. He chose to be honest. "Not exactly. Remember, the spiderbats are magic-resistant. Their webs cancel out magic. I'm relying on that to hide what I'm doing from the Sentinels, otherwise they'll just track us here and it's all over."

We had made it out of Cindervale before the Sentinels arrived. Now that they had a lead on Talian's location, it had become even more dangerous for him to use magic.

"Also," Talian continued, "the webs will dampen the spellsphere's effect. We'll need to be careful."

Talian nodded for me to join them and I slid across the obsidian, losing my balance and falling to the hard, rocky surface. Callie rolled her eyes and picked me up as Talian whispered to the spellsphere. The hot, white-blue glow returned to its core and Talian said, "Both of you. Touch the sphere."

Callie and I did as we were told. Although it looked hot, the sphere was ice-cold. I pulled back my finger and felt nothing but the lingering chill.

Right. Can you hear me?

The voice was Talian's, but his lips hadn't moved. I'd heard it in my head.

Callie nodded. "Yes."

No, Talian's voice said. *Think it. This is how we'll communicate once we're in the caves.*

Callie nodded again and then I heard her voice in my head. *Yes, I can hear you.*

Talian looked to me. *Jaxter?*

I smiled. *Present and accounted for.*

Talian's hand closed around the glowing sphere. "Excellent. Now listen, the spiderbats are all about formality and protocol. Starting a dialogue with them can be tricky, but I'll guide you. Just make sure you say *exactly* what I say, how I say it. Then let the spellsphere do the rest."

Callie looked unconvinced. To take her mind off it, I looked around and scooped up a small, perfectly round chunk of obsidian. "Here," I said, dropping it into her hand, "our souvenir from the aircaves."

Callie snorted and pocketed the black marble. "Right. Because I'll always want to remember this."

Talian nodded at the cave entrance. "Shall we?"

We gathered our supplies and made our way down into the caves. The moment we crossed the threshold, we were met with a burst of hot, humid air. With only my small lantern and Talian's spellsphere to light the way, we soon found ourselves in near total darkness. The rocks on the cave floor were jagged, a sharp contrast to the smooth rock at the entrance. As the hot air wove around us, it made a howling noise that echoed down the passage. Tunnels splintered off in various directions, but Callie and I kept our eyes on Talian, who led us directly forward.

Although the air was stifling and both Callie and I were sweating, Talian seemed to be feeling it far worse. Even in the dim light, I could see he'd grown pale and his face practically glowed with a sheen of sweat. "You okay?" I whispered to him.

He nodded. "When you spend a lot of time working with magical energies, they tend to linger in your body. This is how I know we're getting closer to the spiderbats. Mages don't fare so well in the presence of magic-resistant creatures."

The tunnel we followed curved to the right and opened up into a massive cavern that looked like the mouth of a cargabeast, with teeth of obsidian hanging from the roof and jutting up from the floor. Slung across the cavern ceiling was a gigantic, intricately woven web of clear, glistening silk. I spotted two spiderbats hanging from the thick strands of webbing, their underclaws gripping the silk tightly. They hadn't seen us yet.

Callie shuddered when she spotted the creatures and looked around. "I don't see very many."

I nodded. "I knew they were dying out, but I didn't realize their numbers were so sparse."

Talian, looking more nauseated than ever, leaned forward on a large pile of rocks. "Callie," he whispered, "Jaxter and I will wait here. Go make contact."

Callie swallowed and I gave her hand a squeeze. As she stepped around the rocks and walked slowly toward the center of the cavern, I crouched near Talian. The light from the spellsphere was finally drawing the spiderbats' attention. A few more took flight, their leathery wings snapping in the darkness as they hovered overhead. I counted six of them now and they all seemed to be giving Callie a wide berth.

Just then, Callie froze, her eyes locked on the ground. Peering through the dark, I tried to see what she was staring at. Strewn about on the cavern floor were the bodies of several very dead-looking spiderbats.

Talian closed his eyes and sent instructions to Callie in his thoughts. Callie paused, cleared her throat, and said, "I bring you greetings in the name of peace from the outside world. My name is Callie Strom and I humbly seek an audience with your queen."

She paused and listened to Talian's voice in her head. "I come here with open arms"—she held out her arms to show they were empty—"and the knowledge that I, as a mere human, do not deserve such an audience. So it is with greatest respect and admiration that I—"

A high-pitched chirping sound interrupted her address. A moment later, the spellsphere translated the sound.

"Go away!"

The voice was feminine and heavy with sorrow. More chirping and then, "We rrregrret the day we everrr saw humans!" the female voice cried out.

From somewhere in the shadows overhead, we heard a stirring. Then a spiderbat, a bit larger than the rest, swooped down, grazing the top of Callie's head, causing her to squeal. The large spiderbat landed on the cavern floor and crawled until it stopped at Callie's feet. It chirped.

"Humans hunt the spiderrrbats! Humans send beasts to capturrre the spiderrbats. We want nothing to do with humans. Nothing!"

I could see Callie's hands shaking nervously. But somehow, she summoned the courage to go down on one knee, look the spiderbat in the eyes, and say, "What's happened?"

Callie, I could hear Talian's distressed thoughts, *don't break protocol. That is the queen spiderbat. It's very important that you say only what I tell you and don't—*

But Callie waved her hand behind her back at us, telling Talian to hush. "What's happened?" she asked again.

The queen's wings fluttered softly as her legs thrashed about. "Two days ago, the beasts came. Sent by the mage."

At this, Talian's eyes narrowed and we shared the same thought. *What mage?*

"They took ourrr people," the queen said. "Stuffed them into grrreat bags, killing those who rrresisted them. We arrre all that rrremains." The chirping mixed with a gurgling sound and I realized that the queen was crying. "Ourrr husband! They took ourrr husband!"

Callie shook her head. "I'm so sorry, Your Majesty."

Talian growled to himself. *Callie, you can't just—*

The queen chirped loudly. "Yourrrr people did this!"

"It wasn't us!" Callie insisted. "We would never harm you. We came here because we need your help."

The queen paused, then emitted a short squeak. "Us?"

Just then, two spiderbats dropped quickly from the web on the ceiling, dangling from a self-made strand of silk, and landed on the rock near my head. They chirped excitedly at their queen.

"Please don't hurt them!" Callie pleaded. "They're my friends."

"Then why do the callow men hide in the darrrk?" the queen demanded as her two drones bared their sizable teeth at me and Talian.

Callie straightened her posture and said, "Because I

wanted to discuss this woman to woman." She then told the queen the story of Vengekeep and how we'd come all this way to get the spiderbat milk. She paused and said, "Maybe we can help each other."

The queen clicked and chirped, leaping up and flying directly in front of Callie. "How so?"

"We could help you . . . rescue your people. Your husband. Get them back from these beasts. Allow us to show you that not all of our kind are your enemies."

Callie, Talian moaned. The extremely close proximity of the spiderbats and their strands of web were taking their toll on him. He could barely move, and even his voice in my head sounded weak. *You are breaking all the rules of protocol. There's no way—*

"Ourrr people arrre being held in Splitscarrr Gorrrrge," the queen chirped. "If you get us what we rrrequirrre, then you shall have what you rrrequirre."

Callie stood and did her most elaborate curtsy. She backed away, then turned and joined us at the rocks. Together, we slung Talian's arms across our shoulders and made our way back toward the exit of the caves. Behind us, we could hear the flutter of wings as the remaining spiderbats assembled and followed at a distance.

"Bet you never learned *that* in your diplomatic lessons," Callie said, shooting her sickened cousin a self-satisfied grin.

22

Talian's Trials

"A patsy should thank you for shifting the blame to them and giving them the chance to hone their skills at speaking quickly."

—Ancient par-Goblin proverb

We spent the next three days walking northwest across some of the most desolate terrain in the Five Provinces. With no roads or paths to guide us, we knew where to go only by looking up, where the spider-bats flew high above, leading us to our destination. For the most part, we moved on in silence, stopping only once when we came across a patch of vegetation. We scrounged what little food we could find but, by the end of the second day, we were hungry and tired.

Callie, having faced two of her greatest fears, walked with her head high, proud of her accomplishment. Talian had grown quiet and lagged behind us. I kept my concerns to myself. Now wasn't the time to quarrel.

An hour before sundown, we stopped at a stream near the edge of Splitscar Gorge. As Callie and I filled our flagons, Talian peeled off his boots and waded ankle deep to soothe his feet.

"I don't get it," I said, dipping the neck of my flagon into the water. "You're a mage, right? Can't you just use your spellsphere to make us appear wherever the spiderbats are taking us? It would be a lot quicker."

Talian chuckled softly as he sat on a rock in the stream. "That would require a quickjump spell. And even if I had one in the spellsphere, which I don't, quickjump doesn't work that way. I can use it only to go places I've been, a place I can visualize in my mind. I have no idea where we're going."

We rested a while longer in silence until, finally, Callie burst out, "Just spit it out, Jaxter."

I looked up innocently. "What?"

She pointed at my hands. "You always rub your thumb and forefinger together when you're trying not to say what's on your mind."

I immediately stopped exactly what she said I was doing and slid my flagon into the holster around my waist. "It's just . . . the longer it takes, the farther ahead Edilman gets. He's probably in Vengekeep by now. We're going far out of our way here to help out the spiderbats. Don't get me wrong. What happened to them is terrible, but what's happening in Vengekeep is terrible too."

Callie planted her fists on her hips. "You think I don't know that? What was I supposed to say to the queen? 'Real sorry to hear about your husband and all. Mind if I snatch a bit of milk while I'm here?' You heard what she said. They hate people. She wouldn't have given us the milk any other way."

Talian scoffed, his back to us. "If you'd just done what I'd told you—"

"*At least I did something!*" Callie whirled on her cousin, her voice filled with fire.

Talian wouldn't look at her. "What's that supposed to mean?"

"You know what I mean," she said. Then she looked at me. "Jaxter, did I ever tell you why I moved to Vengekeep? Just before the new year, there was a fire at the lower school in Ankhart, where I'm from. Children were trapped in their classroom. While the village stood by gawking, waiting for the fire brigade to arrive, my parents ran into the building and rescued everyone inside. No one asked them to do it. They did it because they had to. But it was too much for them. They died of their injuries. They might still be alive if the people of Ankhart had helped them."

She walked right up to Talian and looked him in the eye. "That's why I can't stomach cowards. So tell us, Talian, why are you still here? You had your spellsphere with you in gaol. You could have escaped anytime. Why didn't you? Why come with us? We wouldn't want to keep you from hiding from your duties."

Talian's shoulders straightened. When he stood, he did so slowly and deliberately. He fixed Callie with a hard stare that matched the one she was shooting at him.

"Do you know what the Trials are, Callie?" he asked in a soft, dangerous voice. Before she could respond, he continued, "Most people assume the Trials are spent casting spells, mixing potions, and proving how adept you are at wielding magic. But that's just one very, very small component. You know how you spend most of your time in the Trials? Thinking."

He stepped from the stream and slid his boots back on, all the while keeping his eyes on Callie. "Not just thinking. Brooding. From the instant you wake until you drop from exhaustion at night, you're locked in a tiny room and forced to contemplate your responsibilities as a mage.

"Because that's what it's all about. Responsibility. Hour after hour thinking about what it *really means* to wield magic. When you're a mage, you're held to a higher standard than council members, Castellans, even the High Laird. You have a responsibility to use your power wisely, to help the greater good. And after months of sitting in the darkness, the reality of that responsibility sinking in deeper and deeper with every passing day, the weight of it all threatens to crush you.

"When I was twelve, everyone my age wanted to be Lotha's apprentice. Everyone had dreams of casting spells and possessing that much power. We all thought it would be fun. Well, there's nothing fun about it. Every time you cast a spell, you take a risk. Something could go wrong; someone could get hurt. And when I was riding home to Vengekeep, I couldn't bear the thought of looking into everyone's eyes as I arrived. They'd be expecting me to save them. To get out my spellsphere and take responsibility. And that scared me. So I ran."

He stood and walked right up to Callie, looking down at her. "Why am I still here? I'm still here *because* of you. Both of you. You shamed me. I ran to Cindervale because I didn't want the responsibility. I never thought that two kids would charge out into the world, not even thinking about what they'd taken on. Only knowing that Vengekeep was doomed if they didn't do something.

"I didn't use my spellsphere to escape the jail in Cindervale because I'd accepted my fate. No matter where I hid, the Sentinels would find me. I'd decided to just let the Palatinate do whatever it wanted with me. But then you two arrived. You showed me that fate can change. I ran because I figured a better mage than me would save Vengekeep. But I can't run anymore. Because after months of having the immense responsibility of my position pounded into my head by the Lordcourt, I'm sickened that it took the two of you to really make me learn the lesson."

Without saying another word, he turned and walked toward Splitscar Gorge. We watched him walk away. Callie sat dumbstruck. I nudged her and we gathered our things. Loaded up, we sprinted to catch up with Talian.

The tan stone walls of Splitscar Gorge rose on either side of us. The sun had started sinking on the horizon, painting the gorge with dark, foreboding shadows. High ahead, the spiderbats flew, guiding us forward among the twisting, rocky footpaths. We squeezed through a slim opening between two enormous rocks and found ourselves in a crescent-shaped canyon filled with boulders and weatherworn mesas.

Without warning, the spiderbats dropped from the sky and surrounded us. The queen perched herself on Callie's shoulder. Callie went pale and I thought she was going to faint. The queen chirped and a moment later, the spellsphere translated.

"Therrre," she said. "Ourrr people arrre therrre."

We stared directly ahead into the canyon but saw nothing other than stones. No spiderbats, no mages, nothing.

"I don't see anything," Callie said tentatively.

"Therre! Therre!" the queen's chirps insisted.

Talian nodded, a grave look in his eyes. "She's right. There's something there, but we can't see it. An illusion is hiding whatever's in the canyon."

I squinted but saw only the canyon. It finally occurred to me that the spiderbats, being resistant to magic, could see past the illusion. But until *we* could see where her people were, we wouldn't be much help to the queen.

"Can you break the illusion?" Callie asked Talian.

He closed his eyes, his brow furrowing. "I don't know. It's pretty powerful. I might—"

Just then, the spiderbats leaped into the air, flittering about and squawking agitatedly. Before the spellsphere could translate their warning, we were attacked.

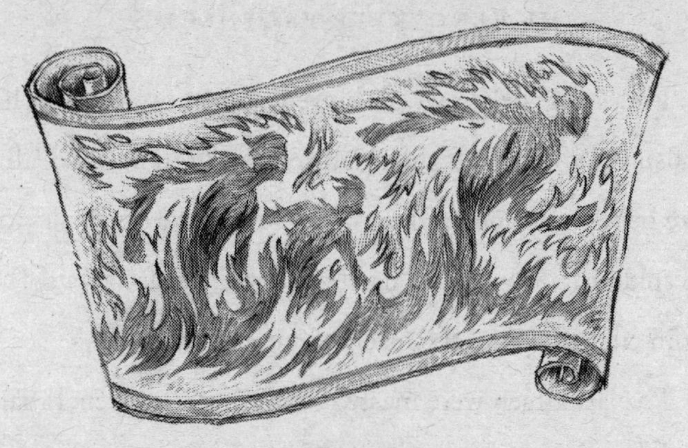

23

Xerrus

"Evidence is the debris of a careless mind."

—*The Lymmaris Creed*

I remember a flash of dark gray fur as my legs flew out from under me. My head struck a rock when I hit the ground. I winced as powerful hands pinned my arms and legs. As my eyes focused, I saw what looked to be a jackal crouched over me. But, although it had the head and body of a jackal, its thin legs and paws had been replaced with what looked to be human arms, hands, legs, and feet, all covered in the same gray fur. Dangling from its neck on a chain was a round, gold medallion with black sigils etched on the front.

Thrashing helplessly, I prayed Talian would use his spellsphere to fight off the creatures. But both he and Callie were being restrained as I was. I looked to the sky, believing the spiderbats would save us. They remained far above, flying in circles beyond the reach of our captors.

The jackalmen were massive, towering over even Talian, the tallest of all three of us. The creatures growled and grunted, staring down at us with their dark yellow eyes. My heart raced; I was certain we'd come all this way and now we were dinner. But instead, the jackalmen bent over and slung us over their shoulders. From out of nowhere, three more jackalmen joined the procession.

The jackalmen gave a howl and, as one, the pack took us closer to the center of the canyon. Callie looked over at Talian. "Can't you do something?"

Talian grunted, the shoulder of the jackalman below him digging into his stomach. "I could. Let's just see where we're headed."

"Not to question your superior mage mind," I said, wincing as the jackalman carrying me squeezed harder, "but I *don't* want to see where we're headed."

"Remember what the spiderbat queen said?" Talian asked. "She said 'beasts were sent by the mage.' These aren't just wild animals. They work for someone. If they wanted to kill us, we'd be dead."

I studied the medallions around the necks of the three jackalmen who brought up the rear. Every so often, a sparkle of light raced across the decorative etchings. Because they were made of gold, I assumed they were magical. And only mages were permitted by law to possess gold. It seemed Talian was right. A mage was responsible for this.

I looked to Talian, who grimaced. "Brace yourselves," he whispered to us. "We're about to pass through the illusion barrier. It's . . . unpleasant."

Just then, the air around us roiled and the landscape shimmered. I felt dizzy and sick to my stomach, so I squeezed my eyes shut until the feeling passed. When I opened them again, I found we were still in the canyon, but there, in the center where only a small mesa had once been, was a gigantic crystalline spire. Twisting up out of the ground, it looked like a jagged streak of black lightning. My stomach fell when I realized that this ominous structure was our destination.

The jackalmen took us through a set of double doors near the base of the spire. Torches with green-blue fire lit the circular room just inside. Once the doors were shut, the jackalmen threw us to the floor and surrounded us. They growled softly, a clear message that any attempt at escape would end badly.

"What is this place?" Callie asked, looking around.

"I think," Talian said, eyeing the room, "this might be an Onyx Fortress."

Callie gasped for both of us. I stared past the jackalmen at a rickety wooden staircase leading up to a doorway in the wall: the only other way out of this room that I could see. "I thought they'd all been destroyed after the Great Uprisings," I said.

Talian nodded. "Supposedly. But every now and then, some relic from those dark days shows up. Onyx is used by mages to store magical energy. This fortress must be packed with it. It would take an incredible amount of power to keep up the illusion that hides this. Otherwise the Palatinate would have found it years ago and put it out of commission."

"But who's behind all this?" Callie asked.

Right on cue, we got our answer. The wooden stairs creaked as a tall, lean man descended to the chamber where we lay on the floor. Green-blue light shone off his bald head. A thin strip of black hair dropped from the bottom of his lip, following the cleft of his chin. The burgundy and black mage robes hanging limply from his body had seen much better days, patches covering holes of various sizes. A medallion, slightly larger than the ones worn by the jackalmen, hung from his neck on a sparkling gold chain.

As he approached, the circle of jackalmen around us bowed low, and they each emitted a high, soft whimper.

"Lord Xerrus, we have the intruders," one of the jackalmen said. Its voice was harsh and slurred, a cross between a bark and a child learning to speak.

When the jackalman addressed the mage, I caught a flash of recognition in Talian's eyes, which he quickly hid by looking down. The jackalmen parted as Xerrus stepped forward and loomed over the three of us.

"There are stories," Xerrus rasped, his voice like the sound of two rocks grinding together, "of the dangers that inhabit Splitscar Gorge. Every child knows them from an early age. It's a shame you didn't pay them more heed."

He addressed this veiled threat to Callie and me, then turned to Talian, raising his eyebrow. "You. I can feel magic pulsing through your veins. You're a mage."

Talian swallowed, then looked up at Xerrus and met his gaze. "Yes, Lord Xerrus. I've come to Splitscar Gorge looking for you."

With Xerrus's back to her, Callie shot Talian a questioning glance, but he ignored her, his eyes never leaving the tall mage.

Xerrus took in a sharp, short breath that rattled in his lungs. "And you have found me. Although, I doubt you will find that discovery to be fortunate." Xerrus held his palm up and whispered something. A ball of green fire appeared just above his hand, twisting and churning. "Who are you?"

Callie moved to protest, but I held on to her shoulder firmly, hoping that Talian had a plan.

"My name is Talian Strom," he said, lowering his head respectfully. "And I've come to serve you."

Ice spread through my chest. Talian had been acting strangely since we left the aircaves, and it was just a little too convenient that he knew our captor and was now offering to work for him. I began to suspect that maybe Callie and I had been fooled . . . again.

On hearing Talian's name, Xerrus laughed and clenched his fist, extinguishing the fireball. "Talian Strom!" he cried so loudly that the jackalmen cowered and whimpered. "I've heard of you, Talian Strom. You're wanted by the Palatinate. You went rogue. Why would you do such a dangerous thing?"

Talian took a deep breath. "I might ask you the same, Lord Xerrus."

As he said this, Talian dared a quick look at me and Callie and I understood. He was trying to tell us that Xerrus was a rogue mage, himself hiding from the wrath of the Palatinate. Although, I should have been able to piece that together myself. Only a rogue mage would dare hide out in an old Onyx Fortress.

Xerrus motioned his hand upward, signaling Talian to rise. As Talian stood, Xerrus moved to the nearest jackalman and gave it a scratch behind the ear. "There is some knowledge," he croaked, "that one can only attain alone, without the interference of rules and laws." The mage spun around and pointed at Callie and me. "And what of these two?"

Talian nodded at us. "They're under my thrall and do my bidding. I brought them as a gift. They'll serve you as willingly as I."

Out of the corner of my eye, I saw Callie ready to speak up, but I stopped her by saying, "I live to serve Master Talian." I allowed my eyes to glaze over as I said this. A bit cheesy, really. But I hoped it was convincing.

Callie caught on and her face went blank. "Command us, Master Talian."

"This is Lord Xerrus," Talian said, looking us squarely in the eye, "a very *powerful* mage. You are to *watch him* and *listen to him* very carefully. Do as you're told. Do you understand?"

Very clever, Talian was. Telling us to keep our eyes and ears open and making it sound as though he was telling us to do as Xerrus told us. Callie and I nodded.

Xerrus smiled, his eyes lighting up as he folded his hands together. "Excellent!" He turned to the jackalmen. "Escort our guests to my sanctum. I'll be along shortly."

Talian bowed, then Callie and I followed his lead. The six jackalmen—three at the front, three at the back—led us up the creaky staircase, down a short hall, then to a massive stone staircase that wound up along the interior of the spire. As we started trudging up the long parade of stairs, I saw Talian's hand slip into the pocket where he kept his spellsphere.

Callie? Jaxter? Can you hear me? Talian's voice rang in my head.

Yes, Callie and I said at the same time.

We don't have a lot of time. Listen, Xerrus is a very dangerous man. The Palatinate has been trying to find him for two years. It's amazing he's been able to evade them for so long. The Palatinate Sentinels exist solely to track down rogue mages and they're usually much more efficient.

Callie glanced around and thought, *Is it the Fortress? Is that why they can't find him?*

Talian nodded. *Probably. There's a reason these were destroyed after the Uprisings. They're brimming with power.*

I always heard they were full of dark magic, Callie said.

There's no such thing as dark magic, Talian replied. *Magic is energy. It's the use to which it's put that is good or bad. Just our luck: Xerrus is as bad as they come.*

I casually took a swig of water from my flagon, eyeing the jackalmen as they huffed and slobbered with every step. *What are these things, Talian? These creatures. I've never seen anything like them.*

Me either, Talian said. *That's what worries me. If half the rumors I've heard about Xerrus are true, we need to get out of here as quickly as possible. But for now, we just play along and hope we get the chance to escape soon. Stay close and remember that you're under a thrall. As long as he thinks we're all willing servants, we should be safe.*

Just when I thought my legs would collapse from all the climbing, we came to a doorway. Once through, we found a massive circular chamber. Near the entry, we passed a large stone podium atop which sat a thick, open book with jaundiced pages. I caught a glimpse of the writing: magical sigils. It was Xerrus's spellbook. I looked to see if Talian had seen it, but his attention was elsewhere.

The jackalmen herded us toward the center of the room. Light poured in from the north, where a large portion of the wall was a giant window. Near the window sat an antiquated desk and chair from which you could see a spectacular view of the gorge. I guessed we were at the very top of the spire. To the left sat a series of tables holding a collection of glass jars and tubes and small cauldrons over fires.

The overpowering smell of animal fur and sulfur made me cringe. I followed Talian's gaze to the right, where I saw a collection of cages. A different animal occupied each cage, but I didn't recognize a single one of them. They all seemed to be odd combinations of familiar animals.

In the cage closest to me, there was something sporting the feathers and head of a hemmon and the burly, furry body of a panna. Next to that, a miserable-looking creature with the bulbous shape of a junfrog and the spike-covered face of a sardigan croaked mournfully. Each of the beasts was lethargic; some looked to be in pain. Talian nudged me to look at the largest cage to the far left: the queen's spiderbats had been crammed in so tightly they couldn't move. My hands went cold. I had to turn away.

And that's when I saw the skeletons.

Everyone had heard of the balanx: gigantic creatures who'd roamed the Five Provinces before there even were Five Provinces. Many people guessed they'd died out thousands of years before recorded history. Their skeletons, unearthed every so often, served as the only evidence that they even existed. Scholars believed they were reptilian in nature, walking upright with colossal wings on their back. Fully assembled, a complete skeleton stood as tall as the clock tower back in Vengekeep. In the exact center of Xerrus's sanctum, a dozen fully assembled skeletons stood motionless. And when I squinted, I could see a small bit of gold embedded in their foreheads. It looked similar to the medallions worn by the jackalmen.

I stared at the balanx skeletons. I'd only ever seen them in books. Standing near them, I couldn't shake the feeling there was something else familiar about them. I didn't have a chance to put my finger on it because Xerrus joined us a moment later.

"Welcome to my bestiary. What do you think?" he asked, sweeping into the room.

Callie and I wiped the looks of amazement from our faces as Talian gazed around with respectful awe. "It's quite amazing, my lord," Talian said, his eyes landing on the cages. "Very peculiar specimens. Am I to believe you've been researching ways to use magic to combine two different animals into one?"

Xerrus raised an eyebrow, seemingly impressed. "You're very clever, Master Strom. I've not only been researching . . . I've been succeeding. And I've made some extraordinary discoveries."

Xerrus moved to the table full of jars and stood next to a small cauldron, the liquid inside bubbling from a fire below. Xerrus pointed to the junfrog-sardigan mix. "Take that, for example. The result of combining a junfrog and sardigan never lives more than a few days after the transformation. It spends its entire life vomiting up a most interesting substance." He indicated the thick liquid in the cauldron next to him. Taking a two-handled quaich from the table, he dipped the cup down into the boiling juice. But instead of pulling out a sample of the liquid, the quaich had dissolved, leaving a single, scorched metal handle. "A most powerful acid. It's no wonder the new hybrid creature doesn't survive."

Xerrus turned to look at the pack of jackalmen to the side. "Some of my experiments have been highly successful, yielding creatures of intelligence and usefulness."

"Brilliant," Talian said. "I can see why you left the Palatinate. They wouldn't condone illegal experiments such as these. I assume you control the creatures through that amulet." Talian indicated the medallion around Xerrus's neck. As Xerrus regarded his own amulet, Talian gave Callie and me a quick look. I instantly knew what he was telling us: the key to escape was getting the medallion away from Xerrus.

Once more, Xerrus seemed to eat up the compliments. "Correct again, Master Strom. You were taught well. Yes, the amulet allows me to exert my will on anyone wearing a complementary talisman."

Talian leaned in, carefully studying the etchings on Xerrus's medallion. "That must be exhausting. Magic use can be draining."

Another clue from Talian. He was telling us that Xerrus was probably exhausted from controlling the jackalmen. Indeed, when I looked at the older mage closely, I could see signs of fatigue.

Xerrus waved his hand. "It can be quite taxing, but I'm

close to developing a way to control vast armies with hardly any effort at all."

While Xerrus went on about his experiments, I began to drift toward him slowly, my eyes never leaving the control medallion around his neck. If I could just get close enough . . .

Xerrus clapped his hands together. "Your arrival was fortuitously timed. I believe I'm ready for my greatest experiment yet." He turned to address Callie and me. I froze in place. "I have the perfect use for you both. I've wanted to try mixing a person with a gexa. Having a servant who can run as fast as a gexa would be very useful."

Out of the corner of my eye, I saw Talian slip his hand to touch the spellsphere. Then I heard in my mind, *Don't react. You're supposed to be under a thrall. Just play along for a mite more. I'll figure something out.*

Aloud, Talian said, "Of course, Lord Xerrus. These two would be excellent subjects. How may I assist you?"

Xerrus turned to Talian slowly. "I'm afraid you don't understand. I'll be using *all* of you as part of my work. I can't run the risk that you're a spy for the High Laird. *You* intrigue me most of all, Master Strom. I'm quite eager to see what happens when I combine a mage, infused with magical energies, with a sanguibeast. I'm sure the results will be most fascinating. . . ."

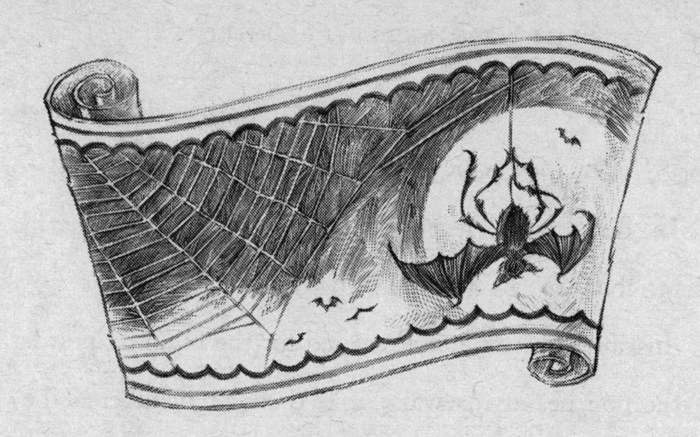

24

Battle at the Bestiary

"If marks were legal tender,
we would all be rich indeed."

—*Zepherax Grimjinx, Castellan of Blackfalchion*

Everything happened so quickly. Talian pulled the spell-sphere from his pocket, glowing and ready for a fight. I made a move for the medallion. But I stumbled and fell into Xerrus instead. In the blink of an eye, the older mage threw his arm around my neck, closing off my air supply. A second later, I felt the sharp point of a dagger against my temple.

"Make any sound," Xerrus rasped at Talian, "and I will kill the boy."

Talian's eyes darted from me to Xerrus. He remained poised, glowing spellsphere at arm's length, prepared to strike. But the hesitation on his face told everyone that he wasn't about to risk Xerrus killing me.

Instinctively, my hand reached for the blinding powder in the pouches at my waist, and then I remembered they were back in Cindervale. And empty besides. I kept still, feeling as helpless as I had back in Vengekeep when the fake prophecies began coming true.

Xerrus's head snapped around to Callie. "You, girl! Take his spellsphere."

Talian cursed under his breath as Callie moved reluctantly toward him. Relaxing his defensive stance, he held out the spellsphere, its inner glow dying. Callie drew her hand from her pocket and took the spellsphere from Talian. She looked to Xerrus for more instructions.

"Over here," Xerrus ordered, nodding to the cauldron filled with boiling acid. "Drop it in there."

Callie walked to the cauldron and held her hand over the bubbling liquid. When she hesitated, Xerrus jabbed me with the dagger and I cried out. Closing her eyes, Callie dropped the spellsphere into the acid, where it disappeared with a hiss.

Growling, Xerrus shoved me toward Callie as Talian went to her side. Touching his medallion, Xerrus uttered a magical command. The air filled with a high-pitched whine as the companion amulets around the necks of the jackal-men sparkled. Their ears perked up and, hands raised, they advanced on the three of us.

We backed up to the giant window overlooking the gorge. Talian and Callie searched for an escape route. Me, I was more concerned with what I saw out the window. A distant black cloud told me that all was not lost yet. I just needed to distract Xerrus.

As if reading my mind, Callie provided the distraction. She stepped forward, met Xerrus's eye, and said, "Can I talk you into letting us go?"

Keeping an eye on the black cloud beyond the window, I tried to read Callie's face. Why was she so calm?

Xerrus sneered. "Nothing you can say would make me do that."

"Oh, really?" Callie asked. "How about this?" She held

out her arm, opened her clenched fist, and revealed Talian's spellsphere. "Ta-da."

She tossed the sphere to Talian. Before Xerrus could react, I shouted, "Duck!" Talian and Callie hit the floor as I picked up the nearby chair and sent it through the huge window.

The sound of shattering glass filled the room. Xerrus cursed and ordered the jackalmen to attack. But as the beasts moved to pounce, the black cloud—a swarm of spiderbats—flew in and attacked our would-be captors. The jackalmen howled, swatting at the spiderbats, who fought back with impressive fangs and the occasional claw.

Callie and I dove under the desk as Talian ran for the far side of the room.

"You switched the spellsphere with your souvenir," I said, recalling the obsidian stone I'd given her. "If we make it out of here, you're definitely an honorary Grimjinx."

As the sound of fighting grew louder, I peered out. Talian was weaving through the melee, trying to get to Xerrus's spellbook. But the older mage spotted Talian and moved to intercept.

Before Xerrus reached his spellbook, Talian shouted a command and a burst of light from his spellsphere blew the door off the cage holding the spiderbats. The rest of the queen's subjects poured out of the cramped quarters, creating a barrier that kept Xerrus from getting to the podium.

"You know," I said to Callie over the sounds of spider-bat chatter and jackalmen howls, "for a couple of heroes, we spend a lot of time hiding."

Just then, the spiderbat queen landed on the floor next to us, surprising Callie and making her squeak. The spider-bat chirped and even though the spellsphere was across the room, we heard the translation.

"You have held up yourrr end of the barrrrgain," she said directly to Callie. "Now I will honorrr mine. Come with me." The queen flew through the only doorway leading from the room.

Callie gave me a queasy look that said *She wants to do this now?* Shrugging, I passed her the empty glass vials from my pack. She hunched over and followed the queen. Hoping to help Talian, I scurried out and hid under the nearby tables, waiting for a chance to strike.

Backing away from the spiderbats, Xerrus roared and closed his fist around the amulet, chanting and spitting at the same time. The high-pitched whine returned to the air and I turned to see what the jackalmen would do next. But Xerrus's magical command had done nothing to the jackalmen, who continued to fend off the aerial attacks of the spiderbats. Instead, I heard a faint rattling sound that quickly grew louder.

As I looked around, my blood froze. The balanx skeletons were *moving*. Their massive bone wings spread out as the creatures stood upright, flexing their skeletal legs and claw-like arms. The bones flapped as if the balanx were trying to fly. Without any membrane between the bones, I thought this would be impossible. But as the gold medallions in their skulls glittered, the balanx rose up into the sky, sustained solely through magic. The largest of the skeletons threw its head back and dropped its jawbone, emitting a terrible, earsplitting screech that was echoed by its brethren. Soon all twelve skeletons were flying near the roof of the sanctum.

At a word from Xerrus, they dove, clawing down with their bony talons, aiming for the spiderbats and Talian.

Caught off guard at their agility, Talian spun as a sharp bone toe sliced across his face, leaving a deep gash. He fell to the ground, dropping his spellsphere, which rolled over near the cages. The animals within were going wild, squawking and bleating as if cheering us on.

Xerrus ran toward the tables. I crouched near his feet where he couldn't see me. He took an empty glass jar and began filling it from the cauldron of acid. I jumped out from under the table, pulled the amulet from around his neck, and dropped it into the cauldron. A plume of black smoke and fire rose up as the amulet blistered and dissolved.

I retreated from Xerrus's reach as the horrified mage realized what I'd done. He whirled, raising the jar of acid to throw at me. But before it could leave his hands, a thick jet of something wet and white hit him squarely in the face. More sticky strands descended, forcing him to drop the glass to the floor. I looked up to find a group of spiderbats, squirting Xerrus with webbing. Its magic-resistant qualities had an immediate effect. Xerrus doubled over weakly as the spiderbats continued to subdue him, gluing him to the spot to ensure he couldn't escape.

Callie reentered, bearing the vials filled to the brim with a viscous, pink liquid.

"You got it!" I cried. "You know the answer: How *do* you milk a spiderbat?"

"Sorry, Jaxter," she said with a smirk, carefully depositing the sealed vials in my backpack. "That's between us girls."

The sounds of battle faded. With the amulet destroyed, the jackalmen had stopped fighting. They dropped to all fours and cocked their heads, as if listening for something that was no longer there. Most whimpered and cowered, unsure what to do now that they were no longer under Xerrus's control. When the fight left the jackalmen, the swarm of spiderbats had turned their attention to the balanx skeletons in the air near the ceiling.

But the skeletons were also feeling the effects of the medallion's destruction. Their attacks ceased as they hovered above the sanctum, great bony wings rattling with every flap. The largest balanx turned its head to scan the room, as if determining its next target. But the eyeless sockets of the skull came upon the shattered window and lingered there. The jawbone dropped and it let out another eerie squawk.

The creature turned and dove toward the floor, pulling up just in time to fly out the window, bearing due south.

I watched as one by one, the other skeletons did the same, screaming before escaping out the open window. And as each one did, numbness drained the feeling in my arms and legs. I knew where I'd seen them before. These were the creatures on the tapestry, the ones that were destined to attack Vengekeep. The scariest of all the prophecies was about to come true . . . and it was all my fault.

"Zoc!"

Talian's curse snapped me out of my horror. He'd snatched his spellsphere from under the cages and was now racing through the pages of Xerrus's spellbook. Callie and I ran to join him.

"The balanx!" Callie cried, pointing out the window.

"I saw! I saw!" Talian grunted. He held one hand to his face where the balanx had sliced open his cheek. The bleeding had nearly stopped, but the wound looked deep and painful. "I'll give you one guess where they're headed."

"We could get some mangs," I said. "The balanx don't have real wings. They can't fly that fast. If we rode mangs, we could beat them back to Vengekeep—"

Talian shook his head. "Look at the jackals!" The jackals had all lain down like docile dogs, and some had dozed off. "Destroying the medallion broke the magical hold on the jackals. It should have done the same with the balanx. They should have just collapsed. Something else is keeping the skeletons alive."

I couldn't bear to look at either of them. "The tapestry. It's my fault." I suddenly understood how Ma felt when all the trouble started in Vengekeep. It was her tapestry that brought the problems to town. It was my stupidity that had sent the worst of those prophecies charging to Vengekeep's door.

"Don't waste time laying blame," Talian said. His rummaging through the spellbook slowed and he studied each page carefully. "It would take us days by mang to get to Vengekeep. With the tapestry's power, the balanx will be there in hours."

"No!" I said, pulling out the calendar I'd carried since we left Vengekeep. "Mooncrux isn't for three days."

Talian looked up from the spellbook and studied the

calendar. "Jaxter," he said quietly, "that's last year's calendar. This is a quellyear."

Quellyears occurred on our calendar every five years. During a quellyear, the third month lost three days. Mooncrux was *tonight*.

Talian thumped the spellbook as he found what he was looking for. Taking out his glowing spellsphere, he held it to the book and ran the sphere over the hastily scribbled spell he'd located. As he did, the strange words on the page began to squirm and twist. Then they shot across the surface of the parchment and disappeared into the spellsphere. A moment later, the entire page was blank.

"The quickjump spell," Talian said, holding his spellsphere triumphantly. "We can still beat the balanx to Vengekeep."

He stared into the glowing orb and whispered a few hurried words. At first nothing happened. Talian closed his eyes and chanted again. Still nothing.

Opening his eyes, he stared upward. "It's the spiderbats. Their presence is making it harder to cast the spell."

I'd forgotten about the spiderbats. With the jackalmen

subdued and the balanx gone, most of the spiderbats had taken to hanging from the ceiling while others scaled the walls. A few flittered over Xerrus, now standing frozen, covered from shoulder to foot in thick webbing. He appeared to be unconscious. Talian looked rather pale and I remembered how ill he'd gotten in the aircaves.

Callie looked up and around, waving to the spiderbat queen. The queen broke from her formation above and swooped down next to Callie.

"Your Majesty," Callie said, bowing humbly, "you've done us a great honor today by assisting us in our time of need and providing us with . . . that which we came for. We've no wish to keep you here any longer. You should attend to your people."

The queen chirped. "You honorrr us with yourrr thanks, Callie Strrrom. Should ourrr paths crrross again, you will be welcome in ourrr caves." The queen emitted a string of high-pitched bleats. The rest of the spiderbats responded, swarming around their queen, then flying out the broken window into the approaching night.

"Thank you," Talian whispered to Callie, and closed his

eyes to attempt the spell again. This time, the spellsphere responded. Slowly, a ring of green light flew up and out of the sphere. It rose into the air, widening as it did. The ring floated over to a bare spot of floor and dipped down, coming to rest just above the stone. As Talian continued whispering, the ring of light sizzled with energy and turned blue. I peered down into it. Instead of seeing the sanctum floor underneath, I saw what looked to be thatched roofs and cobblestoned streets as viewed from directly above. The scene within the ring had a dark blue hue, as if twilight was near.

"That's Vengekeep!" Callie noted, pointing into the ring.

Talian traced the pulsating circle with his finger. "Once you step into the ring, you'll find yourself back there."

"Bangers!" I said.

"What do you mean 'once *you* step into the ring'?" Callie asked, eyeing her cousin suspiciously. "You're coming too, right?"

Talian glanced over at Xerrus, immobilized by the spiderbat webbing. "I can't tell you how many Palatinate strictures Xerrus has broken here. I know that Vengekeep's in trouble, but my first duty as a mage is to see that those strictures are enforced. The Palatinate has to be notified about what Xerrus has been doing here. They'll do something to help these poor creatures." He pointed to Xerrus's caged mutations.

When Callie looked unconvinced, Talian said, "You don't need me. You need to warn Vengekeep and destroy the tapestry. Jaxter's got a terrific plan and now you've got the final ingredient. You just have to find that Edilman character and get back everything else you need for the solvent. Callie, I have to do this."

"C'mon, Cal," I said, putting my arm around her shoulders. "We'll see him again soon."

Callie nodded. She gave Talian a hug and I shook his hand. "Hurry," he said. "Who knows how long it'll take you to find Edilman and make the solvent. Warn Vengekeep."

Callie and I stood at the edge of the glowing ring. I felt her hand slip into mine and squeeze tightly. The burns on my hands had mostly healed so I screamed only a little.

"Think this will make it into the Grimjinx family album?" she whispered, a smile in her voice.

I squeezed her hand. "Better be in huge block letters."

Together, we jumped into the ring.

It turned out that the picture we saw in the ring—of the streets of Vengekeep from above—was quite literal. I closed my eyes, expecting to feel disoriented, like when we passed through the illusion barrier. But I didn't feel the slightest tingle leaping into the quickjump ring. We instantly found ourselves in Vengekeep. Or, more accurately, we found ourselves falling down from quite high up onto the hard, stone streets of Vengekeep.

Of course, falling was nothing unusual to me. I'd seen the ground coming up to meet me more times than anyone should. Even from that height, I knew how to prepare for impact, roll, and walk away harm free. Which is what I did. Callie wasn't so lucky.

As I hit the ground and rolled, I heard Callie collide with the street, and a crack rang out with her scream. I jumped to my feet and went to her side. She held her left arm to her chest, her face racked with pain.

“You okay?” I asked, helping her up.

“I think it’s broken,” she said, wincing through gritted teeth.

“Let’s get you to the healers—”

“No,” she insisted. “Talian’s right. We have to warn everyone about the balanx. I’ll be fine. Let’s go to the Castellan and—”

“There’ll be plenty of time to see the Castellan later.”

We both froze on hearing the rough voice from behind. We turned and there stood Maloch, sword drawn, flanked by three members of the stateguard.

“But first,” he said with a smirk, “you’ll be paying a visit to gaol.”

I looked up to the night sky. Both moons hung directly overhead, moving slowly toward one another, minutes away from crossing. . . .

25

Mooncrux

"A man with one eye on his coffers and the other on his purse is blind to the theft caused by a lie."

—*The Lymmaris Creed*

"You're making a mistake, Maloch," I protested as my former friend and three stateguards with spears marched me down the steps leading to the dungeon under Vengekeep's gaol. The dungeon had gone unused for a century. For them to lock me up down there meant serious, serious trouble.

"The prisoner will be silent," Maloch barked.

That was all he'd said since the arrest. Repeatedly. Callie

and I had been taken to Aronas's office. Despite our attempts to warn of the coming danger, we were ignored and separated. Aronas, seeing he could score points with a member of the town-state council, turned Callie over to her uncle for punishment. Aronas gave his apprentice the pleasure of seeing me locked away.

"You remember those flying beasts?" I asked over my shoulder. "The ones in the tapestry? Well, they're on their way to Vengekeep now. They'll be here any minute. You've got to let me go to my family so I can—"

"We're taking you to your rotten family," Maloch said.

As we reached the bottom of the stairs, the moldy aroma of the dank dungeon air filled my nostrils. My feet slid on the mildew-coated floor as Maloch shoved me forward roughly.

"Jaxter!"

I looked ahead, where my entire family sat in a cell. Ma clutched the bars as Da, his arm in a sling, rose from a wooden stool. Nanni threw a handful of what I guessed was the gaol's excuse for food at the stateguards who opened the cell doors. The guards thrust me through into Ma's waiting arms. I held her for a moment, then turned as Maloch was about to disappear up the stairs.

"Maloch!" I yelled. "I won't be able to warn you again." But he never turned around.

Before I could say a word, Aubrin pulled me into a hug. Then she stepped back and showed me the black book I'd given her before leaving. "I did just as you said," she whispered. "I wrote down everything that happened while you were gone." She thumbed through the book, revealing pages and pages of writing. "And then some."

"Bangers, Aubrin," I said with a smile. I turned to my parents. "What the zoc is going on here?"

Ma ignored my cursing. "The last day has been crazy. Yesterday, some old geezer approached the Provincial Guards surrounding Vengekeep, claiming to be a cursebreaker from beyond the Five Provinces. Apparently, word of Vengekeep's problems has spread across the seas and he came to offer his services."

Da picked up the story. "The whole town-state's been on edge and of course Jorn, eager for any solution, let him in. This 'cursebreaker' took one look at the tapestry and announced that the scholars had misinterpreted what it meant. It didn't say 'The star-marked family alone shall be the salvation of Vengekeep.' He claimed it said, 'The star-marked family alone shall be the *sal'viton* of Vengekeep.'"

I groaned. *Sal'viton* was par-Goblin for "mortal enemy."

Da continued. "And that's all Jorn needed to hear. He had us arrested and locked up. So that leaves us with a curse-breaker trying to break a nonexistent curse. He probably doesn't even realize that the tapestry is the source of all the problems!"

I nodded grimly. "Oh, he realizes. He's not a curse-breaker. It's your old friend Edilman."

I reported everything that had happened to me and Callie. My parents were genuinely alarmed to hear that their old partner in crime was somehow involved in this mess. I finished by telling them how he'd stolen the solvent ingredients and was intending to destroy the tapestry to earn the High Laird's pardon.

"A death sentence?" Ma scoffed. "We warned him about dealing in illegal materials. That's why we went our separate ways in the first place."

"Maybe we should just let Edilman do what he plans,"

Da said. "If he destroys the tapestry and saves Vengekeep, the High Laird will pardon him and they won't have any reason to hold us."

Nanni wasn't convinced. "If he destroys the tapestry," she said, "he'll have to explain why he did it. He'll tell everyone it was fateskein. Since we're the only ones who feature in a positive light in the tapestry, it won't take them long to figure out who wove it in the first place."

"I bet he's already tried to make the solvent himself and failed," I said. "Nanni's right. If he'd succeeded already, you'd be on trial for fateskein possession by now. But he never knew about the spiderbat's milk. That's why his solvent isn't working."

"So what do we do?" Da asked. "That fool Edilman's going to use up all the ingredients trying to get the mixture right and then we'll be stuck where we were before."

"It's worse than that," I said. "The winged creatures are on their way to Vengekeep."

Everyone exchanged looks. Aubrin's eyes were wide. "You mean, you've seen them?"

I grinned at her and Ma tousled her hair. "She's been

chirping like a bird since you left. We can hardly get a word in."

I nodded to Aubrin. "They're going to tear the town-state to shreds if we don't destroy that tapestry."

Our discussion was interrupted by the clatter of metallic boots. Aronas descended the stairs, opened the door to our cell, and pointed at me. "You! You're wanted."

"Why?" I asked defiantly.

"The cursebreaker heard of your return to Vengekeep and thinks you may be important. He wishes to interrogate you himself. Come!"

I looked to Ma and Da gravely. "Don't worry about me. The 'cursebreaker' and I need to talk."

Two members of the stateguard thrust me into the Viewing Room. The first thing I noticed was the small pool of yellow liquid that had formed beneath the tapestry, which continued to drip. A tall man in green robes, holding a staff, stood in front of the tapestry. Long silver hair spilled down his back to the base of his spine. A thick beard did likewise down his front. A sprybird with gray feathers around its eyes sat perched on his shoulder.

“Hello, Edilman,” I said.

Edilman chuckled. “Oya, Jaxter. Glad to hear you made it to the party.”

Nearby, I saw Callie’s pack and a large wooden bucket. Water had spilled all over the floor and bits of chopped plants were strewn everywhere. One of the wraithweed pods, now desiccated, lay discarded in the corner.

Edilman went over and gave the pack a light kick. “Fat lot of good it did me, taking all this. I should have known it wouldn’t be that easy to make the solvent on my own. Maybe it was my pride. I figured if a snot-nosed kid could do it, how hard could it be? So I tried making my own version.”

He held up his right hand. The skin was red and blistered. “I forgot the wraithweed was acidic. I’m sure you know that my solvent did nothing to the tapestry. So I figured that either I wasn’t mixing it properly . . . or you hadn’t told me about all the ingredients. Which is it?”

I folded my hands behind my back. “Little of each, actually. I hope you didn’t use up everything we collected.

Otherwise, I'll never be able to make the solvent."

Edilman charged across the floor at me. "Wrong. *I'm* going to make the solvent. Oh, you'll be there to provide guidance but if anyone is going to be thanked by the High Laird for saving Vengekeep, it's me."

I glared right back at him. "If you had just told us about your plan to get the High Laird's pardon, Callie and I would have figured out a way to make it work. You didn't have to steal the ingredients. You could have trusted us."

Edilman snarled, throwing his staff to the floor. "I *trusted* your parents! Years ago, the stateguard caught me dealing in muskmoss and were hunting me down. I went to your parents, asking them to hide me until the heat died down. They refused and cast me out into the street. The stateguard captured me and I spent six years in prison! So you'll have to forgive me if *trust* isn't high on my list of priorities."

I remembered what Callie had suggested at the Dowager's. "Did you . . . did you sell Ma the fateskein?"

For a moment, Edilman looked confused. Then a slow, dangerous smile slid across his lips as he laughed. "No," he said, "I got caught dealing fateskein in Tarana Province. But wouldn't it have been poetic if I *had* sold it to dear old Allia?"

"So you're angry at my parents and you're willing to let Vengekeep—"

"This has nothing to do with your parents!" he spat. "It's not like I've been wandering the Provinces dreaming of revenge. I don't care about your parents." He breathed heavily for a moment and then calmed down. When he spoke again, his voice was measured and more like the reasonable Edilman I remembered. "We both want the same thing, Jaxter. We want that tapestry destroyed. I just want the credit for doing it. All you have to do is help me."

I glanced over at Callie's pack. I had no idea how much of the ingredients he'd already used. Based on the formula Talian and I had devised, what remained might not be enough. But I had to try.

"On one condition," I said slowly. "You can't mention the fateskein to anyone. Once you get your pardon, you can't say anything that can incriminate my family."

"I can't make that promise, Jaxter. The High Laird is more likely to commute one death sentence if he thinks he can enforce another."

I swallowed. "Then there's no deal."

Edilman reached out, gripping my tunic in both his fists. Perrin shot into the air with a squawk. I struggled, but his grip was unbreakable. "Give me the last ingredient!" he screamed.

His threats cut off at the sound of smashing glass. Looking up, we both only just managed to dive out of the way in time as huge shards of the skylight above rained down and broke into millions of pieces on the floor. Two great skeletal talons reached down into the Viewing Room. I heard the balanx's unearthly shrieks. The hole in the roof was too small for the beast to get in but that didn't stop it from feeling around, trying to grab us.

Edilman and Perrin bolted for the door and I snatched Callie's pack. The beast's talon thrashed around, accidentally wrapping itself around the cables that suspended the tapestry and its copper frame. Realizing it couldn't reach us, the beast suddenly lurched upward. The cables holding the tapestry snapped and the beast flew off . . . taking the cable, frame, and tapestry with it from the Viewing Room. The sky beyond the open window darkened as the balanx hordes descended on Vengekeep.

26

The Siege of Vengekeep

"Accusations are merely the envy of the unenlightened given form."

—*Ancient par-Goblin proverb*

Memories of the magma men and firestorm came flooding back as the balanx began their attack. Screams filled the streets as, everywhere I looked, people ran for cover. But no place appeared to be safe. Hugging Callie's pack to my chest, I charged through the streets and watched as one of the skeletal beasts wrapped itself around the clock tower and tore it to shreds, leaving a pile of dusty bricks and twisted clockwork. I dodged debris as one by one, the balanx laid waste to homes and businesses alike.

Passing near the perimeter wall, I saw members of the stateguard scurrying around, loading small catapults and hurling stones at the flying beasts. Occasionally, a stone would connect, severing a balanx's arm from its body. But a moment later, the fallen bones would leap back up into the air and reattach themselves, good as new.

I kept my head down, trying to stay focused on the task at hand. "Make the solvent, find the tapestry," I repeated over and over to myself. "Make the solvent, find the tapestry . . ." Then, for good measure, I threw in, "And try not to die doing either."

Thick dust clotted the air. I covered my mouth with my hand and made the turn down the street toward the Strom house. Arriving outside, I pounded on the door. A moment later, Callie answered. Her broken arm hung in a leather sling.

"Good evening, madam," I said, tipping a hat I didn't have. "I don't suppose you know anything about tapestry solvents—?"

She saw her pack in my hands and, with her good arm, yanked me into the house. I immediately went to the fireplace in the living room and began stacking wood inside. "I need a size-four kettle," I said, setting aside the solvent ingredients. "And fill it with water."

"Uncle Masteron!" Callie cried, running to the kitchen. "I need your help!"

Mr. Strom emerged from a broom closet, shaking. He looked around nervously. "C-callie," he whispered, "I think we need to stay where it's safe—"

"Zoc that," she said, pointing to the space on the wall where they hung their kettles. "I need that kettle. Filled with water."

Like everyone who'd ever met her, the Keeper of the Catacombs knew better than to cross Callie. Mr. Strom obeyed promptly, taking down the cauldron and filling it from a cistern in an alcove.

We all ducked when we heard a mighty crash outside. Glancing out the window, I saw the house next door reduced to rubble, smashed by a catapult most likely dropped there by a flying balanx. I struck the flint and started the fire roaring. A moment later, Mr. Strom carried the water-filled kettle to the fireplace and positioned it over the fire.

Callie joined me. "What do you want me to do?"

I handed her the recipe that Talian and I had concocted. "Once the water's boiling, read this off to me. Be sure to tell me the amounts."

As bubbles rose to the surface of the kettle, it finally sank in how the odds were against us. The tapestry was missing. The recipe Talian and I had created was nothing more than a guess. And Edilman had used nearly all the ingredients, making a second chance at mixing the correct formula unthinkable. I felt queasy. The only sure thing was that we had exactly one shot.

With the water boiling, Callie started calling out ingredients, when she wasn't complaining about my penmanship. I added the necessary roots and herbs to the cauldron. Soon, an earthy aroma filled the Strom house. With all the ingredients in place, I slowly poured the prized spiderbat milk into the cauldron.

"We have a small problem," I said, and then I explained about my encounter with Edilman and how a balanx had accidentally taken off with the tapestry. "It could be anywhere by now."

"It has to be near the town-state hall," Callie reasoned. "I can't imagine the balanx letting it dangle from its leg for long."

Once Mr. Strom had fetched us a bucket, we dipped it into the kettle and filled it to the brim. The solvent had the pungent smell of ernum tree sap.

"You stay here," I instructed Callie. "You're hurt. You can't—"

"Not in a million years, Jaxter Grimjinx," she said fearlessly. "You need two sets of eyes to find that tapestry and I'm not—"

With a bang, the front door swung open, coming off one of its hinges. Standing there, dagger in hand, was Edilman. He'd shed his cursebreaker disguise, and without his old man wig and beard, he looked crazed and dangerous.

"Oh, Jaxter," he tsked. "I'm embarrassed that we share the same name. You didn't even try to shake me when you came here. You must have known I'd follow you."

"No," I said, glaring at him. "I just assumed you'd run away like the frightened maldok that you are."

His eyes narrowed. "Give me the solvent. I'll destroy the

tapestry and put an end to all this. Give it to me now or I'll kill Callie."

Mr. Strom, meek as he was, steeled his shoulders and stepped between Edilman and his niece. "You won't touch her."

"Wanna bet?" Growling, Edilman advanced with his blade. Then, a purple flash of light behind him froze Edilman in his tracks. He looked down and found that he was slowly rising into the air. Thrashing about, he gazed around, perplexed. Suddenly, he shot straight up, his head smacking into a beam in the ceiling. Then he flew across the room, hitting the far wall before falling into a battered lump in the corner.

We turned to find Talian standing in the doorway, his spellsphere glowing. "Sure," he said to Edilman's sleeping form, "I'll take that bet."

Leaving Mr. Strom to return to the safety of his broom closet, Talian, Callie, and I charged into the ravaged streets of Vengekeep with the solvent.

"After I sent word to the Palatinate, I waited at the Onyx Fortress for them to take Xerrus into custody," Talian explained. "I told them that I was prepared to deal with the charges of desertion but first I had to help Vengekeep."

"What did they say?" Callie asked.

"Didn't really give them a chance to respond," he admitted. "I used the quickjump spell before they could argue."

"Glad you could join us, Talian," I said, "because we've got a new problem."

Callie and I told him about the missing tapestry. Talian took out his spellsphere and whispered to it. A moment later, it glowed a dark, deep red.

"If there's fateskein in Vengekeep," he said, "this will find it."

The spellsphere lifted gently from Talian's palm and then flew off down the streets. We ran to keep up with the flying ball. The deeper into the town-state we got, the harder it became to follow. The streets were littered with the remains of buildings, forcing us to climb over and around to continue our pursuit. We came across throngs of injured people, stumbling about blindly amid the ruins. *You can't help them until you destroy the tapestry,* I reminded myself as we continued on.

The spellsphere took us to the heart of Vengekeep and, as Callie had predicted, not far from the town-state hall. There, dangling from the edge of a pub's roof, hung the discarded tapestry, blowing in the wind. A momentary peace prevailed in this part of town, the balanx having turned their attention to the stateguard mounted along the perimeter walls.

"So what do we do?" Callie asked. "Do we have to say any spells or anything?"

I shook my head. "The solvent's not magic, remember? Let's lay the tapestry on the street so I can pour the solvent over it. And at that point, if you'd like to say a little prayer, I think that would be okay."

Talian agreed. "Callie, climb on my shoulders."

He bent over and Callie did as she was told. I waited with the solvent as Talian stood to his full height and Callie reached up for the tapestry. It hung just beyond her grasp. She stretched with her good arm, grunting with effort.

As her fingers grazed the edge of the tapestry, something happened. Every balanx stopped. As one, their jaws dropped and their terrible screech rang through every city street. Suddenly, they all turned and flew directly toward us. Within moments, they were all swooping down, swiping at us with skeletal talons and claws.

Talian stumbled, sending him and Callie to the ground. I covered my head with one hand and lugged the bucket of solvent behind the rubble that was once a cheesemonger's shop. "Over here!"

Talian and Callie scrambled across the street, avoiding the onslaught of balanx who hovered over the pub where the tapestry hung.

"What's going on?" Callie asked, holding her sore arm.

Talian shook his head. "It's the fateskein. I think it knows what we're up to. It's protecting itself." He put his hand on my shoulder. "We've got one chance, Jaxter. Callie and I will draw them away. You go for the tapestry." He turned to his cousin, whose eyes had grown dark when she realized what he was saying. "Ready?"

She nodded. As one, they bolted from where we hid, each running in a different direction. The ploy had the desired effect. The balanx, confused for a moment, divided, half chasing Talian, the other half pursuing Callie. I eyed the pub. If I climbed the drainpipe on the side of the building, I could pull the tapestry down. It just meant fending off my clumsiness for one, shining moment.

I took a deep breath and jumped out. But I'd gone only two steps before I fell face-first onto the street. I knew on the way down, though, it wasn't my fault. A leg had swept out of nowhere and tripped me. My glasses flew from my face, landing beyond my reach. I looked up, half-blind, and saw Edilman's blurry form charge across the street. Before I could stand, he'd shimmied up the drainpipe and snagged the tapestry.

I retrieved the bucket of solvent and ran at him, but he held the tapestry away from me. "This ends now, Jaxter," he warned. "Give me the solvent."

I couldn't see Callie and Talian or the balanx that pursued them. But the second Edilman grabbed the tapestry, the creatures appeared above to protect it. The skeletons shot up into the air, screeching, and dove down toward us. Edilman didn't even see them; his eyes never left the bucket of solvent.

He was right. I had to end this now. I glared at the tapestry in Edilman's fist and, raising the pail, I took aim and tossed the solvent.

In a panic, Edilman attempted to shield the tapestry and both got doused. The boiling liquid hissed as it made contact with fateskein and flesh. Edilman dropped the tapestry and clutched his face, screaming as the wraithweed acid burned away at his skin. He ran blindly to a nearby watering trough and threw himself in to wash away the solvent.

The tapestry smoked as red and blue sparks shot out. The brown fabric quickly dissolved, great chunks falling away, eating themselves and turning to small piles of ash. The prophecies burned as the fateskein crackled, its power vanishing.

High overhead, the balanx gave a final cry of agony. I looked up to see the skeletons, their necks arched backward as they screeched. Then, as one, the balanx collapsed, showering Vengekeep with their brittle bones. The air still stank of smoke and dust. People still cried and screamed. But it was over.

27

Doing What You Have to Do

"Innocence is a multicolored cloak."

—*Ancient par-Goblin proverb*

A week later, with Vengekeep still struggling to rebuild, the Grimjinxes were cordially invited to an assembly in the town-state council chambers. The sort of cordial invitation we'd become accustomed to: enforced by an armed escort.

My family, Callie, and Talian all sat on one side of the massive wooden table that split the chamber in two. On the other side sat the Castellan, the High Laird's Chancellor, Captain Aronas, and a woman we were introduced to as

Neryn Hordrin, the head of the town-state council. You'd never guess they'd all been saved from disaster, the way they were scowling.

Standing behind them were three mages—two women and a man—in skullcaps and burgundy robes with golden embroidery. The clear jewels sewn on their robed shoulders like rank insignias identified them as members of the Palatinate's Lordcourt. While the Castellan and the other Vengekeep officials stared at me and my family, the Lord Mages watched Talian intently as he offered his version of events.

"So you see," Talian said, decked out in his emerald mage robes and matching skullcap, "it occurred to me on my journey from the Palatinate to Vengekeep that while a curse couldn't possibly have been placed on the entire town-state, there was a very real possibility that a curse had been placed on the *tapestry*. In the five centuries that Vengekeep has heeded the tapestries of the Twins, never once have they predicted such horrible events. It seemed logical to conclude that a curse to create these terrible events had been placed on the tapestry years ago. Quite possibly just as it was first sealed into its glass tube."

The Castellan threw a cautious look over his shoulder to the Lord Mages, who frowned as one. For a long time, they said nothing. Then one of the Lord Mages cleared her throat. She'd introduced herself at the start of the proceedings as Nalia. She looked slightly younger than Ma, with shiny black hair that stopped near her chin. In her right eye, she held an elegant, gold-rimmed monocle. Officially, no single member of the Lordcourt outranked another. But I got the idea the other two mages deferred to her.

"Our investigation has concluded," said Nalia, "that the source of Vengekeep's problems has indeed been eliminated." I found my eyes going to her often. Her raven-colored hair reminded me of Ma, but there was nothing gentle in her stony face. And from time to time, I caught her stealing glances at me.

As one, the Castellan and Aronas exhaled. It had taken a week of pleading to convince the Chancellor and the Lordcourt to enter the city gates in order to verify that the "curse" had been lifted.

"Although," Nalia continued, raising an eyebrow at

Talian, "we are curious about reports that you had disappeared, Master Talian. You had been branded a deserter."

Talian nodded. "An unfortunate misunderstanding. As I contemplated Vengekeep's woes on the trip back, it occurred to me that spiderbat milk might counteract the curse. I was travelling through Cindervale, on my way to the aircaves, when I was mistakenly arrested."

This was the riskiest part of Talian's story. It wouldn't take much to verify that Talian had been living in Cindervale for weeks, not just passing through. But if anyone suspected he was lying, no one said a word.

"I realize now that my haste to save Vengekeep prevented me from sending word of my plan to the Palatinate. I can understand why they would believe I'd gone rogue, and their actions were just. I only regret that my thoughtlessness caused such confusion."

Under the table, I felt Callie squeeze my knee with her good arm and I gave a secret nod. We'd all spent the better part of this last week crafting an airtight story that cast Talian in the role of hero and kept my family as far removed from this as possible. Now, reciting with absolute conviction this slightly skewed version of events, Talian could teach my family a thing or two about believable lies.

Captain Aronas narrowed his eyes at Vengekeep's new town mage. "And you had nothing to do with this . . . cursebreaker?"

Talian shook his head. "No. In fact, I don't believe he was a cursebreaker of any kind. When I arrived to destroy the tapestry, he attempted to stop me. In our struggle, I noticed a brand on his forearm. I believe him to be an escaped criminal under death sentence." At this, Talian turned to the Chancellor. "You might check with the Provincial Guard to see if they have any records of someone matching the man's description. He disappeared after the tapestry was destroyed."

My mind flashed to Edilman. I wondered if there ever really was a ship that could take him from the Provinces and his death sentence. Was he headed there now? Or was the ship just another lie and had he already moved on to his next con?

"A curse on the tapestry makes sense," Jorn said thoughtfully. "It could explain why the Grimjinxes were so cruelly thrust into the middle of all this."

He wasn't fooling anyone. What he really meant was *A curse is the only thing that would ever make the Grimjinxes out to be heroes.* But Jorn was smart to hide his contempt.

Talian shrugged. "Perhaps. As it is, I do need to thank Jaxter Grimjinx. He proved invaluable by assisting me in the tapestry's destruction. That part of the prophecy played out correctly: a Grimjinx *did* contribute to the salvation of Vengekeep."

I blinked. This hadn't been part of the story we'd rehearsed. But Talian had found a way to acknowledge my role without casting suspicion on my family. I did my best to smile modestly at the panel of magistrates. But, and I'm just being honest, Grimjinxes are terrible at modesty.

Nalia raised an eyebrow. "Indeed. How fortunate young Jaxter was there to help." My eyes met hers again and I was certain she was looking through me.

The Castellan folded his hands and leaned forward. "It's a shame the curse tainted the tapestry's true message. Apparently, we'll have to rely on our own mettle and deal with what comes the rest of the year without any guidance."

He never took his eyes off Ma and Da, who smiled innocently back at him. I got the idea that he still wasn't convinced of Talian's story, but at this point, I think he was so happy that the quarantine had been lifted and the disasters were over that he'd decided not to push the issue.

The other female Lord Mage—Lorina—held out a piece of parchment. "With the question of your 'desertion' put to rest," she said to Talian, in a far kinder tone than Nalia's, "I am to offer you a commendation for your role in the capture of the renegade, Xerrus."

Talian nodded humbly. "Thank you. It was shocking to learn of the existence of an Onyx Fortress. I hope it will be destroyed as the others were."

I sensed tension between Talian and the Lord Mages. If I hadn't known better, I'd have thought there was a tone of accusation in Talian's voice. If the Lord Mages were offended by the mild challenge, they gave no sign. Nalia smiled a distant, ingenuous smile and said, "The matter is being dealt with as we speak."

The male Lord Mage, whose name I'd missed, nodded. "It seems Vengekeep will be busy rebuilding. As we're no longer needed, we'll be returning to the Palatinate."

Talian rose and bowed to the Lord Mages, who returned the gesture. He followed them out of the room with the High Laird's Chancellor in tow. As the rest of us stood, Neryn, the head of the town-state council, said, "Just a moment."

We all froze. The Castellan and Aronas looked at each other and scowled. But as Neryn turned to address my parents, she smiled widely. "Mr. Grimjinx, the town-state council met recently to discuss your role in recent events."

We Grimjinxes all looked to one another, each of our brains readying an alibi to protect us from whatever she said next.

"You showed a great deal of courage and leadership during the crises," Neryn continued. "You assisted the Castellan with a plan to save the town-state from flooding, you and your family provided disaster relief during the firestorm, and you consistently came to Vengekeep's aid throughout these trying times." She paused, tilting her head just slightly. "Not quite what we've come to expect from the Grimjinxes, to be sure."

"Oh, we're full of surprises," Nanni said.

Neryn concurred. "The town-state council asked me to convey their deepest *regrets*"—she hit the last word, casting a glare at the Castellan and Aronas—"at your arrest and treatment when the alleged cursebreaker arrived. This was not a fitting response to someone who had spent the preceding months defending Vengekeep. To acknowledge the contribution you've made and to demonstrate the trust you have earned, we would like to offer you the post of Protectorate, a seat on the town-state council."

My jaw dropped as Callie elbowed me in the ribs. Everyone in my family looked at one another in shock. Neryn was, in short, asking Da to be head of Vengekeep's law enforcement. He would be Aronas's boss and work closely with the Castellan on the security and safety of the town-state.

Ma's tapestry had certainly never predicted that.

Da stammered for quite some time, but in the end he stunned us all by accepting. Even the Castellan and Aronas could hardly believe Da was saying yes. As Neryn shook Da's hand, the Castellan banged his gavel to put an end to the session before skulking angrily from the council chambers.

Back at the house, Callie joined us for a celebratory dinner. Outside, work crews sifting through the damage and rebuilding Vengekeep had become a common and welcome sound. With the threat of the remaining prophecies extinguished, life in our little town-state looked to be headed back to normal.

"So," Callie said wistfully, "that's it then. The Grimjinxes are going straight."

"I don't know about that," Da said, a gleam in his eyes. "I would think that serving as Protectorate might make it easier for me to cover up some of the family's more nefarious exploits."

It was Ma, of course, who remained practical. "However, in light of recent events, I think it's safe to say we'll be cutting back on our . . . other activities quite a bit. Now we have *two* legitimate sources of income. It could be fun to see how the other half lives for a while."

Aside from my father's new post as Protectorate, the second source of income to which Ma referred was the phydollotry shop. While we were gone, Nanni and Aubrin had rallied to get Ma out of her depression. The three of them took over the phydollotry shop and made it into something real: a doll-making shop! They'd been in business since the second week after Callie and I left Vengekeep. They'd even managed to make a bit of money doing it.

"How's your arm, Callie?" Aubrin asked.

Callie smiled. "I'll be using it again in no time. I need two good arms to assist Talian."

A couple days earlier, Talian had asked Callie to be his apprentice. He'd admired how she'd handled herself with the spiderbat queen, saying her poise reflected all the qualities necessary in a mage. Callie still needed to go through several interviews with the Palatinate, who had become notorious of late for accepting fewer apprentice candidates. But once she got their approval, they could begin formal training.

While everyone enjoyed Da's burnwillow crumble, I pulled Aubrin aside. "So, Jinxface," I said quietly, "are you going to tell me why it took you so long to speak?"

She brushed her hair from her eyes and gave me the oddest, saddest smile. "When it matters, you'll know."

Bangers. I'd always hoped Aubrin would start speaking.

I never dreamed she'd be so cryptic. "At least show me everything you wrote," I said, reaching for the black book in her hand.

She snatched it away and shook her finger. "It's not time."

Nanni, who'd disappeared to her room after we returned home, came downstairs and joined the family at the kitchen table. She looked at me and smiled, cradling the family album.

"As keeper of the family album detailing all significant events in Grimjinx history," she said, "I've noticed that our records have become terribly outdated. It's time to correct this."

Nanni took a seat and laid the book on the table. Da passed her a quill and a pot of ink. Nanni nudged Callie. "You too. You're one of us, you know."

Callie beamed and slid her chair closer to mine. Quill in hand, Nanni wrote swiftly as Callie and I spent the next hour recounting our adventure. Graywillow Market, Edilman, the Dowager, Xerrus . . . When we were finished, the family applauded and Nanni closed the book carefully.

"Not bad," she said. "Although, I think it's the first time

a Grimjinx story didn't end with 'And then we were rich beyond belief.'"

Dinner continued. But for all the jokes and stories, I couldn't take my eyes off the family album. I was in there. Now and forever.

So why did it feel wrong?

As evening fell, I walked Callie home. People smiled at both of us as they passed in the streets. It seemed unlikely I'd ever get used to people not hiding their moneypurses when I walked by.

"Feels good, doesn't it?" she asked. "To be able to just stroll quietly without being chased down by crazed peddlers or living statues or jackal creatures."

"I dunno," I said, not very convincingly, "I was just getting adjusted to life as a night bandit."

Callie laughed. "So does that mean you're off to find your fortune as a master thief in training?"

"Um, no. If I've learned anything from this, it's that I don't have what it takes to make it as a thief, master or otherwise."

I'm not exactly sure when that realization had hit. In the gaol at Cindervale? Trekking to Splitscar Gorge? I loved my family dearly and I loved the skills and knowledge they had given me. But my interests definitely lay elsewhere. I just wasn't quite sure how to tell them that. It helped that, for the most part, the Grimjinxes would be lying low with our illicit activities. But if I feared disappointing them because I was an incapable thief, I was even more afraid of telling them that I couldn't be one at all.

Callie must have read my mind. "So what are you going to tell your parents?"

"I'm going to tell them," I said plainly, "there's something I don't *want* to do, but it's something I *have* to do."

28

The New Apprentice

"Fate is a lazy man's excuse for avoiding curiosity."

—Sirilias Grimjinx, liaison to the par-Goblin Rogue Triumvirate

"Let me go!" I cried, as the pair of brutish Provincial Guards threw me forward. I tripped on the transparent grass and landed with my face just inches from an empty space that once was home to walking, talking mushrooms. I wondered where they were.

The thunderous *chug-chug-chug* of the Dowager's steam-powered machines rang throughout the foyer. Nearby, the magical rain cloud that watered the plants rumbled, as if even it was angry to see me again. Oxric, the majordomo, stared down at me with his yellow eyes narrowed to mere slits.

"It's not what you think!" I shouted. "This is all a mistake!"

"Oxric, what is the commotion?"

The Dowager appeared at the top of the stairs, decked out in her leather uniform. As she pulled the goggles from her face, she gasped to look down and see me on all fours.

"These guards arrested the boy, ma'am," Oxric announced, as the Dowager descended the staircase.

The first guard, looking menacing with a battle-ax in one hand, bowed to the Dowager. "Your Majesty." He spoke loudly to be heard behind the visor of his helmet. "We found the boy in Vengekeep."

The second guard, wearing a similar helmet, stepped forward and presented the chest of jewels that had been found among the "cursebreaker's" abandoned possessions. "We saw Your Majesty's seal on the box and knew this belonged to you," she said. "We believe he was trying to sell these. He claims he was going to return them to you."

"I was!" I said quickly, looking up at the Dowager

with baleful eyes. "They nabbed me while I was leaving Vengekeep. I was on my way to bring them back."

The Dowager looked down coldly and I could feel her disappointment burn into my skull. "You've done well, Guards. I assume the boy will be disciplined?"

"Oh, yes, ma'am," the male guard said with a grunt. "Very stiff penalties for this sort of thing in Vengekeep. First, he'll be covered in sparkleeches—"

"What?" Neither the Dowager nor Oxric could contain their shock.

"Sparkleeches, ma'am," the female guard said, wriggling her finger like a sparkleech. "All over his body. Then the meanest children of the town-state get to come spit on him and pull the leeches off."

"That's barbaric!" the Dowager cried, clutching her throat.

"That's justice!" the male guard declared proudly.

"Dowager, please," I begged. "I was going to return—"

"And after the sparkleeches," the female guard said, "he'll be taken to the Vengekeep gaol and tied to the rack. He's a mite small, isn't he? Well, he won't be, after a good stretchin'."

I cringed and whimpered as the guards took turns describing more of the horrific and grisly punishments that awaited me back in Vengekeep. When she first arrived, the Dowager looked ready to enforce any punishment herself. But as the guards continued—in very vivid detail—I could see her opinion on my fate change.

"You're treating him like a common thief," the Dowager said in disgust. "Which . . . I suppose in many ways he is. But this boy has *potential.* You can't just take him and—"

"Castellan Jorn has already signed the papers," the male guard said, shrugging. "He believes that if the thieves of Vengekeep are too dumb—"

"This is not a dumb boy," the Dowager said. "He has a brain."

"Oh, sorry, ma'am," the female guard said, bowing her head. "We understand now. If you'd like to pop around and collect his brain from what's left when we're done with him—"

"Enough!" the Dowager shouted, tossing her goggles to the ground. She snapped her fingers and Oxric helped me to my feet. "You will not harm a hair on this boy's head.

Because . . . this boy . . . is my apprentice!"

The ice that had filled my chest since my return to Redvalor Castle shattered when I heard her say this. I did my best to look stunned instead of happy. Which was easy because I was a little of both.

The Dowager took the box of jewels from the female guard. "Yes. My apprentice. As a member of the royal family, I am invoking my privilege to . . . to . . . not let you hack my apprentice to pieces. I asked the boy to sell the jewels . . . as part of an experiment. And . . . it worked. Very well. You're both to be commended for your duty. Wait here."

The Dowager turned on her heel and strode from the room, Oxric close at her side. The second she was gone, I exhaled long and loud. "Well, that was easier than I thought."

The first guard lifted his visor, revealing Da's smiling face. "You're just lucky she didn't agree to let us do all those nasty things to you. Mighty big risk you took there, Son."

I looked to where the Dowager had exited and shook my head. "Not a chance she'd let that happen. We're too much alike."

Ma poked her face out of the other visor. "You're sure

this is what you want?"

The knots in my stomach twisted harder than when I first went to Ma and Da to tell them that being a thief just wasn't in my future. "Are *you* sure you're okay with it?" I asked in return.

Da set down his battle-ax and laid his gloved hand on my shoulder. "Jaxter, your ma and me knew from the time you were five, and you got your finger stuck in a lock you were trying to pick, that a life of thievery might not be right for you."

"We've just been waiting for *you* to figure it out too," Ma said, pulling me tight.

Holding Ma, I closed my eyes. Even now, tricking the Dowager into taking me back, it seemed like thievery would always be a part of me. Why couldn't it be a bigger part? "I just feel . . . like I'm doing something wrong. I keep thinking about the family album. All those Grimjinxes—"

"All those Grimjinxes were demonstrating exactly what they do best," Ma said, lifting my chin. "Being a Grimjinx has never been about thievery, Jaxter. It's about doing what you love."

"It's purely coincidence that, for most of us, it's stealing," Da said with a sniff.

I wiped at the tears that had somehow accidentally fallen down my cheeks. "Thieving is all I know."

"Now, Son," Da said, "you wouldn't be half as remarkable as you are if that was true."

The Dowager and Oxric returned to the foyer. Ma and Da hastily lowered their visors and bowed as the High Laird's sister approached. She handed them each a small drawstring purse that jingled with coins.

"You have served your sovereign well," she said. "Return to your duties. I will deal with the boy."

The "guards" bowed again, shook their fists at me—I almost burst out laughing—and allowed Oxric to show them out. Now that we were alone, I straightened my shoulders to face the Dowager, meeting her eye with something I'd never had to muster before: true humility. It felt . . . strange.

Just as when she entered, her face grew dark and for just a moment, I wondered if she was actually considering that bizarre sparkleech punishment Ma and Da had made up.

She circled me slowly, looking me up and down. I found myself wishing she would start yelling at me. The silence hurt twice as bad as any insult she might hurl.

When she finally stopped pacing, she pointed a finger at me. "You blew a hole in my wall."

I swallowed. "Maybe I could fix it." I didn't sound very confident. Destroyer of enchanted tapestries, yes. Stonemason, no.

"Don't think for a minute that all is forgiven," she snapped. "I seriously considered letting them take you back to Vengekeep and doing all those horrible things."

"Did you really?" I asked.

She rolled her eyes. "Of course I didn't. But I considered considering it."

I was confused.

The Dowager took in a long breath. "You have a wall to fix. I'd be willing to bet that some jewels are missing from that box. They must be repaid. And there is trust that must be regained. I invoked royal privilege to spare you. That is not a debt to be taken lightly."

I nodded. "I understand, Dowager. It took me a long,

long time to figure it out . . . but I understand. We can make this work."

The creases near her eyes smoothed out and that child-like twinkle returned to her expression. "Make no mistake," she said, a bit softer, "that this will be hard work."

The very idea made me shudder involuntarily. But I bowed my head in agreement.

The Dowager sighed. "Very well. You'll start immediately. I've asked Oxric to prepare your room." She laid a finger to the side of her face. "Perhaps we should have asked your parents to send your belongings before they left."

I waved the idea away. "I'm sure when they get back to Vengekeep, they'll—"

Wait. What?

I looked up to find the Dowager squinting, a devilish gleam replacing the innocent sparkle that normally stared back. She was far too happy with herself.

"How did you—? But they—? My parents—?" My tongue fought to find the words to express my shock. It failed miserably.

The Dowager pulled a folded piece of parchment from a

pocket on the front of her uniform. She opened it to reveal a copy of the WANTED poster that Callie and I had seen in the Aviard nestvillage. I found a badly drawn picture of myself staring back. Big ears and all.

"This was sent by special courier from the Provincial Guard two days after you and your friends arrived," she said. She glanced at the poster. "Imagine my surprise to find I had a member of the infamous Grimjinx clan under my roof."

My head whirled. After years of playing the con artist, I'd finally been conned. "So . . . you were on to us from the beginning?"

"Not immediately," she said, pocketing the poster. "When I figured out you were here under false pretenses, it was quite disappointing."

I thought back to the night I'd found her brooding alone in the ballroom. I didn't understand then what had made her so suddenly depressed. Now I knew. She'd learned who I really was and was giving me a chance to come clean.

"You could have had us arrested at any time," I said. "Why didn't you?"

The Dowager put an arm across my shoulders and led

me up the stairs. “Surely you don’t think that you and your friends were the first to try to swindle me? I can spot a fake intellect in a heartbeat. It took longer with you because . . . well, you weren’t pretending, were you, Jaxter?”

I thought back to all the deep discussions we’d had, how we lost ourselves in research to the point where I forgot about Callie and Edilman. No. There was no way to fake that.

“I kept telling myself, ‘They’re here to rob you, Annestra.’ But deep down, I knew you didn’t really have your heart in thievery.”

I don’t know how she could have known when it was only something I’d just figured out. Then I realized: I was much better at fooling myself than I was at fooling everyone else. “How could you have known I’d come back?”

“I didn’t *think* you’d come back,” she said, as we reached the second floor landing. “But I’ll admit I was *hoping* I’d see you again. There’s no way someone who’s read *The Kolohendriseenax Formulary*, who can sit and listen to me prattle on about constellations and magic-resistant plants, who can—”

“Finish your sentences before you?” I said with a grin.

She laughed. "There's no way someone like that can stay away. I know better."

What she meant was what I'd already said: we're too much alike.

The Dowager lifted her long, regal arm and pointed down the corridor. "I believe you know where your room is. And, Jaxter, one more thing: if I suspect for even a moment that you've returned to your thieving ways while living under my roof, I will send you back to your parents by the fastest means possible. Catapult, if necessary!"

I clenched my teeth and looked away. The Dowager nodded primly and said, "I'll expect to see you for breakfast first thing in the morning."

I bowed at the waist. "Maybe we can find a way to change the mushrooms back into humans."

The Dowager grimaced. "I already tried. I suppose the braincube would work better if I were a mage. I wish the Palatinate had given me instructions on its use. In any event, the servants aren't mushrooms anymore. Now they're cats." Then her eyes glazed over with glee. "But, yes, let's work on that, shall we?"

As I lay in bed that night, I thought about giving up my life as a thief. Even if I wasn't very good, it would be hard turning my back on my upbringing completely. Devoting my life to research *seemed* ideal, but I had no guarantee I wouldn't fail. But then, some learning has failure built in; like failing to pick the Castellan's pockets. I might not succeed, but I'll come out the other end smarter . . . if not always richer.

While a Grimjinx might fear arrest, prosecution, and the occasional doomsday prophecy, one thing we didn't fear was a challenge. There was so much to learn, now that I wasn't fated to be a master thief. Of course, after everything that happened with the tapestry, I figured fate was *highly* overrated. Besides, as my grandfather, Sirilias Grimjinx, always said, "Fate is a lazy man's excuse for avoiding curiosity."

I couldn't agree more.

"One thing you didn't do—if you valued your life—was ignore a summons from the Shadowhands."

Turn the page for a sneak peek at

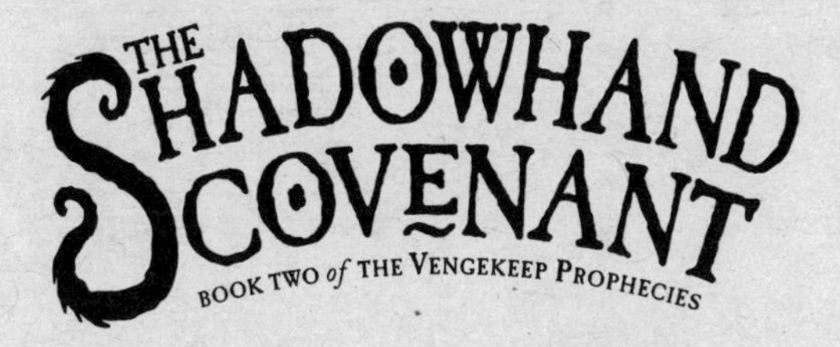

1

Good-Bye to Nanni

"Whenever things seem to be exactly as they should,
lay down money that they're not."

—*Ancient par-Goblin proverb*

It was exactly the funeral Nanni always wanted.

The morning sun glistened off the fresh sheen of snow across the hillside. The nip in the winter air, crisp and clean, chilled without being too cold. Huddled together for warmth, the crowd of mourners stood around the freshly dug grave in the cemetery just outside Vengekeep as a hemmon chirped in the nearby trees.

I brushed snow from the lenses of my silver-framed glasses and gave my sister Aubrin's gloved hand a squeeze.

She looked up, eyes swollen with tears, and returned a fragile smile. To my right stood Da, wearing the traditional burgundy shawl of mourning, staring down at his feet as though looking at the grave would be too much. Ma's arm reached around his shoulders from the other side, comforting the bereaved son.

While we were never what you might call religious, we still thought it proper to hire a vicarman to say a few words about my grandmother, whom we called Nanni. He stood near the casket, talking about all the lives she'd touched and how much she meant to us, the Grimjinx family. When he spoke of how much Nanni loved making singemeat stew, Da released a loud, heaving sob. I put my free hand on his forearm as Ma whispered loudly, "Be brave, love."

Talian Strom, Vengekeep's town-state mage, uttered a single word. His spellsphere sparkled, and the heavy casket descended into the frozen earth. Nearby, the widow Bellatin tugged on the strings of an oxina and played a plaintive song. Da stepped forward, scooped up a handful of dirt, and said in staggered breaths, "Ma . . . Nanni . . . you'll be missed. Always." He tossed the soil into the grave, then returned to Ma's waiting arms, where he broke down crying.

The mourners—dozens and dozens of our neighbors in Vengekeep—waited in line to pay their respects. We hardly knew them. Many were among the wealthiest people in the town-state, no doubt hoping to impress Da—the town Protectorate—by simply showing up.

We stood at the edge of the cemetery, receiving the well-wishers one by one. Aubrin was the bravest of all. She looked everyone in the eye and thanked them sincerely for coming. Ma spoke for Da, who eventually had to withdraw when his sobbing overtook him. He murmured excuses, then walked back toward the town-state gates and home.

I shook hands and accepted condolences with a stoic face. As the line of mourners thinned, I found my best friend, Callie Strom, in a modest crimson dress. Teary-eyed, she pulled me into a tight hug.

"She was a lovely woman, Jaxter," she said, her voice broken. "I can't believe she's gone. I keep thinking we'll see her again."

I coughed and gave Callie a look. She lifted a handkerchief to her eyes and moved on to Ma. Once the receiving line was finished, Aubrin tugged at my sleeve.

"Can we go home yet? Everyone here looks so grave."

I groaned. She hadn't spoken a word for the first ten years of her life, and now that she was talking, she couldn't stop making bad jokes. "Why don't you head back to the house and help Da? Ma can finish up here."

Aubrin raised an eyebrow. "What about you?"

I looked up toward the rim of the valley that surrounded Vengekeep. "I have a quick stop to make and then I'll be along."

I hugged Aubrin, then trudged up the valley slope through the snow. I glanced back at Vengekeep. I hadn't seen my hometown for nearly six months. I couldn't have guessed the reason that had finally brought me back.

At the top of the hill, a large, gray, copper-trimmed carriage drawn by four silver-maned mang waited near the edge of the forest. On my approach, the footman, who'd been hugging himself to stay warm, leaped off his perch.

"Oya, Tren," I said to him with a wink. Tren winked back. I stood beside the carriage and took a deep breath. More than a little nervous, I nodded at Tren, who opened the carriage door. I climbed inside.

Red velvet lined the carriage's interior. I sank down in the rounded bench at the fore, my back to the mang out front.

Sitting across from me, the Dowager Annestra Soranna, wrapped in a thick fur serape, inspected an unruly stack of parchments on her lap. She leafed through the pages, frowning at what she saw and clicking her tongue with disapproval.

I studied her quietly. Silence between us had been the norm recently. Right now, I couldn't tell if she was still upset with me or just busy. In training me to be a thief, my parents had taught me how to read people's thoughts and emotions based solely on their body language. But when the Dowager worked on official state business, she was inscrutable.

"How did it go?" she asked absently, absorbed in her reading.

"A beautiful service from start to finish," I reported. "Callie sang a lovely dirge. Something about ladygills blossoming in the spring. Or was it autumn? Not sure. Wasn't really paying attention. Anyway, there was quite a turnout. I wish Nanni could have seen it. She'd have loved it."

The Dowager nodded, but I wasn't sure she'd heard me. Shortly before we'd left Redvalor Castle three days ago, she'd received an urgent message. A herald from her brother, the High Laird who ruled all the Five Provinces, had arrived and delivered the parcel of parchment now before her. The entire trip, the Dowager had pored over the papers and grown increasingly distressed with what she read.

I said, "Don't tell me. The High Laird has decided to give up his post for a life as a novelist."

The Dowager snorted. When she looked up, I finally saw the warmhearted woman to whom I'd been apprenticed these last six months. She had a slight, odd smile on her lips, eyes that flittered about, and a gentle sway to her head. Even with the tension between us, it felt good to make her laugh.

"Not exactly," she said. "Although maybe I'll recommend it to him. Honestly, Jaxter, I moved into Redvalor Castle so I wouldn't have to deal with things like this. Missing artifacts, suspicious thefts . . . And he's got no one to blame but himself. If he'd listened to my advice . . ."

Her voice trailed off as she turned another page of the High Laird's report. Since moving to Redvalor Castle to do research with the Dowager, I'd learned that frenzied missives from her brother seeking advice were commonplace. She, not he, had been groomed by their father to be High Laird. Sometimes it showed in her brother's hasty decisions. He spent a lot of time consulting her, often *after* he'd made terrible mistakes.

The Dowager set her papers aside. "You do understand why I couldn't join you at the service, don't you, Jaxter?" she asked delicately.

"Of course," I said. "It's for the best that you stayed away. Everyone understands. Besides, it's all over now."

The Dowager gazed out the window at Vengekeep. Last night's snow had painted the walls surrounding the town-state, making them hard to see against the blanket of white that covered the valley. "That must have been very difficult for you."

I shook my head and grinned. "Nah. Not really. I'm starved. You ready to eat?"

When the Dowager and I arrived at Ma and Da's house, we found Da dancing jubilantly around the kitchen, making a show of dropping chopped vegetables into a boiling kettle and singing a silly jingle about par-Goblins. Ma knelt near the fireplace to check on the two plump gekbeaks roasting on the spit. Aubrin sat curled up in a large, plush chair in the corner, scribbling furiously into her black leather journal.

My sister had turned eleven last month and had taken a

sudden interest in writing. Now, whenever I saw her, she was holding a small leather-bound book, scribbling away. As I walked past, I snatched playfully at her journal. She pulled it to her chest with a smile and wagged a finger at me.

"It's not time," she said. That's what she always said when someone tried to read her journal. No one knew why.

Ma swept across the room to take the Dowager's fur. "Dowager Soranna," Ma cooed, bowing respectfully, "we are honored to have you in our home."

"Please," the Dowager said, her head lilting side to side, "call me Annestra. I think it's a perfectly lovely name. The problem with having a lovely name and being a member of the royal family is that no one ever uses your lovely name."

"Annestra it is," Ma said as Da stepped forward to shake the Dowager's hand and show her to the dinner table.

I answered a knock at the door and nearly fell over as Callie burst into the house, threw her arms around me, and wailed, "Oh, Jaxter! The pain! The loss! However will you get by?"

"Be respectful," I warned, pushing her gently away. "This is a house of mourning."

Callie giggled. She'd changed from her funeral dress

back into the gray robes she was required to wear as Talian's apprentice mage. She gave me a mock curtsy. "I thought my performance was brilliant."

"This morning, yes," I said. "But you were a bit over the top just now."

Ma pulled the gekbeaks from the fire just as Aubrin brought bowls full of boiled vegetables to the table. Once we all took our seats, Da poured ashwine for the adults, while Aubrin, Callie, and I helped ourselves to glasses of mang-milk. Ma struck her glass with a fork and stood, raising her arm in a toast.

"To Nanni!" she said. "May she rest in peace!"

We all raised our glasses and repeated, "To Nanni!"

Just then, we heard a creak as the back door in the kitchen opened. Turning, we watched a hooded figure carrying a large cloth sack waddle in. The sack dropped with a metallic crash as the figure pulled back the hood to reveal Nanni, grinning widely.

"You didn't start without me, did you?"